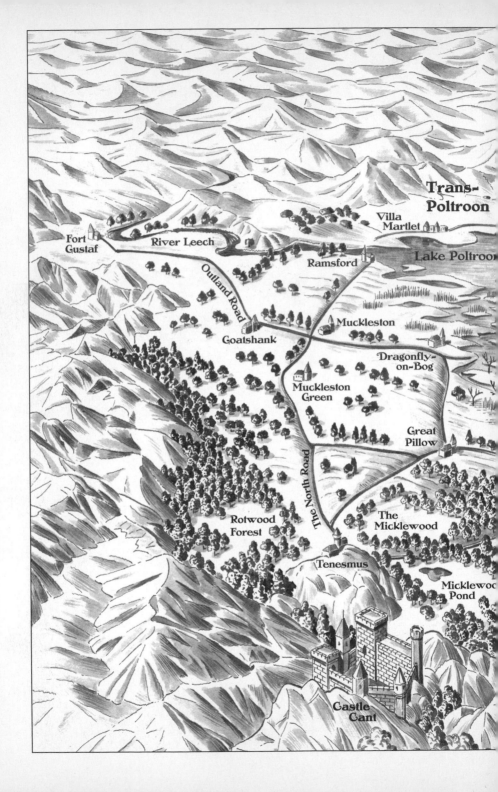

K. P. Bath

with artistic embellishments by
Leah Palmer Preiss

LITTLE, BROWN AND COMPANY

New York ~ Boston

Text copyright © 2006 by K. P. Bath
Illustrations by Leah Preiss Palmer

All rights reserved.

First Edition: September 2006

Little, Brown and Company

Hachette Book Group USA
1271 Avenue of the Americas, New York, NY 10020
Visit our Web site at www.lb-kids.com

Library of Congress Cataloging-in-Publication Data

Bath, K. P. (Kevin P.)
Escape from Castle Cant / K. P. Bath. — 1st ed.
p.   cm.
Summary: Having escaped from Castle Cant during the Chewing Gum Rebellion,
Lucy and Pauline try to elude their pursuers and one of the girls discovers
a surprising truth about her parentage.
ISBN-13: 978-0-316-10857-7 (hardcover)
ISBN-10: 0-316-10857-X (hardcover)
[1. Identity — Fiction.   2. Fantasy.]   I. Title.
PZ7.B3225Esc 2006
[FIC] — dc22
2006001174

10 9 8 7 6 5 4 3 2 1

Q-FF

Printed in the United States of America

Map illustrated by Rodica Prato

The text was set in Centaur, and the display type is Swank.

In memory of Herbert "Lanky" Snyder

A Note from the Author

*I*n this modern age of computers and juice boxes, I admit I hesitated to publish the history of the Chewing Gum Rebellion. Few readers had even heard of the Barony of Cant when I took up my pen to write *The Secret of Castle Cant,* and cynics predicted that no one would buy a book about that realm, where iron plows are but a recent innovation, where pogo sticks and televisions are scorned as travelers' tales.

The cynics, happily, were proved wrong. The book found a grateful audience, and since its appearance my readers have clamored to learn more of Lucy Wickwright, the humble servant who, to save one she loved, rejected the opportunity to rule.

Her story was in some respects grim, certainly. Lucy was still playing with dolls when a villain plotted the murder of her family. Taken to the castle to serve Lord Cant's daughter — the Adored & Honorable Pauline — Lucy endured the relentless teasing of the older maids, and then became an unwitting pawn of the rebel cause.

The Loyalist faction swore allegiance to Lord Cant and Pauline, and its followers claimed that Lucy aided the Causists in hope of personal gain. It was chiefly to correct this fiction that I told her story, for Lucy had no more ambition than a blade of grass. It was simply as a helpful and obedient servant that she carried money to Arden Gutz, the Cause's imprisoned leader, and it was only after he convinced her that Pauline's life was at risk that she agreed to become his spy. Yet the secret she uncovered shook the Barony to its foundation, and within a fortnight the Chewing Gum Rebellion had begun.

Now I take my readers to war. Gum gave the conflict its name, but at stake was the very rulership of the Barony. For Lucy had discovered she was the firstborn child of Lord Cant, abandoned as an infant on the Wickwrights' doorstep. After the Baron's death the rebels hailed Lucy as their Baroness, and Arden Gutz claimed the title of August Provisional Regent. Lucy would serve as his puppet, and he would rule in her name.

So a new dynasty might have begun, had not Lucy been a girl both brave and true. With the help of a defector from the Cause — the astronomer Luigi Lemonjello — Lucy rescued Pauline out of the dungeon where Gutz had imprisoned her, and together the girls fled the men who would divide them. For Pauline, too, had her would-be regent. Vladimir Orloff claimed that office on the Loyalist side, who as Commissioner of Posts to Pauline's father had introduced gum chewing to the Barony. Readers of my earlier history will know his bitter role in Lucy's life. Pauline was soon to learn his ghastly part in hers.

The lines were drawn, and the battle joined. If I were to write the full history of the Chewing Gum Rebellion my tale would run to many volumes, but my ambition is not so grand. The Battle of Muckleston Green I leave to other scribes. The Slapping Contest of Twee, while gripping, is not within my scope. And though the Siege of the Seven Seamstresses was crucial from the tactician's point of view, I cannot claim to be a military historian.

A single thread of the tapestry will suffice for my small talent. I have given readers the tale of Lucy Wickwright, a humble girl who rose to lofty heights. But what of the other great figure of those tumultuous days? Born to greatness, heiress of unthinkable wealth, Pauline von Cant saw her future burst like a bubble of gum. As war wages in the land she might have ruled, she finds herself beset on every side by danger. She is hungry, homeless, and wearing uncomfortable boots. With her my tale begins.

K. P. Bath

I offer my readers the following list of characters as an aid to memory (and an incentive not to scribble in the book). While the Chewing Gum Rebellion sprang from a fertile bed of grievances — chief among them the burdensome tithes paid by common folk to support a luxury of the nobles — it is enough to remember that the Causist rebels denounced gum chewing and swore allegiance to Lucy Wickwright, Lord Cant's child born out of wedlock. The Loyalist side, by contrast, upheld the noble privilege of gum chewing and believed that Pauline von Cant should rule the Barony. Sensibly rejecting the wishes of grown-ups, the girls held fast only to each other.

K.P.B.

The Characters

Adolphus, Lord Cant (*deceased*): father to Pauline von Cant and natural father to Lucy Wickwright. The Exalted & Merciful Protector of His People, the twelfth Baron Cant.

Pauline Esmeralda Simone-Thierry von Cant: Lord Cant's child by his marriage to Lady Esmeralda. Held by the Loyalist faction to be the rightful Baroness of Cant.

Lucy Wickwright: Pauline's former maidservant, and daughter to Adolphus by his tickling of a chambermaid. Proclaimed by the Causist rebels to be the rightful Baroness of Cant.

Arden Gutz: leader of the rebel Cause. Self-proclaimed regent to Lucy Wickwright.

Vladimir Orloff: Postal Commissioner of the Barony, author of the gum trade, and self-appointed regent to Pauline von Cant. A Loyalist.

Sir Henry Wallow: leader of the rebel forces under Arden Gutz. A Causist.

Sir Tybold Retsch: Captain of the Guard to Lord Cant, and now in league with Vladimir Orloff. A Loyalist.

Sir Gaspard Simone-Thierry: grandfather to Pauline von Cant. A Loyalist.

Luigi Lemonjello: Chief Astronomer of Cant. Imprisoned by Arden Gutz for aiding Lucy's rescue of Pauline from the dungeon. A defector from the Cause.

Blaise Delagraisse: under-footman at Castle Cant.

Hippolyte Swanson: guardsman at Château Simone-Thierry.

Lillian Lungwich: a tinker.

Harriet Holstein-Quack: an herbalist.

Primo Furstival: a merchant of Boondock.

Apryl Poke: Deputy Director of the American Mission at Tenesmus. An outlander.

The Reverend Mr. Pius Frodd: Director of the American Mission. An outlander.

Dr. Fatima Azziz: Baronial Librarian and friend to Lucy Wickwright.

Dr. Horst-Wilhelm Sauersop: Master Herald of Cant and friend to Lucy Wickwright.

Mr. Cheswick Splint: personal physician to Lord Cant (*deceased*).

Chapter 1

The Fugitives

With a groan Pauline von Cant pulled on her riding boots. The dew had come up and soaked her clothes in the night, leaving her cold and stiff. As she rubbed sleep from her eyes a star fell beyond the northern hills, and the clouds there flickered red.

"That's queer," she murmured.

She stepped gingerly over Lucy Wickwright, who dozed on the grass beside her, and then loosened the knapsack's drawstring and opened its mouth. Pauline had been mistress of Castle Cant before the death of her father, Lord Cant, and she was used to having a sweet at breakfast. She was not, strictly speaking, *stealing*. The food in their pack belonged to both of them. She was simply taking her share.

She pushed aside their bread and medical tin, thrusting her arm to its elbow down the knapsack's throat. Lucy had buried the prize well. *There!* Under the wrinkled mourning dress, her fist closed on a tablet of chocolate. When she had tied up the pack she scurried away and greedily tore off the silver wrapper.

Another star fell, glowing so brightly that it shone on the cast-off foil. How *very* queer! Pauline thought, licking chocolate from her lips. Had Luigi Lemonjello foreseen this rain of fire? Her father's astronomer had lately come down from his observatory to help Lucy rescue Pauline out of the dungeon, where she had been imprisoned by the Causist rebels. He remained there now as their captive.

Again flames lit up the sky, and with a cry Pauline leapt to her feet. It was a curious star indeed that rose from the earth before falling! She peered at the horizon, where missiles now flew thick and fast. The belly of the clouds glowed orange, and she heard a distant thunder of hooves.

"What is it?" asked a sleepy voice.

"Lucy! Come and see!"

Her sister put on her glasses and stumbled through the grass, warming her hands in the pocket of her jumper (called a "sweatshirt" by Miss Poke of the American Mission, where Lucy had found it in the charity box). The fiery missiles traced arcs on the lenses of her glasses.

"Is it a dragon?" Pauline breathlessly asked.

"Don't be dramatic, Pauline," said Lucy, yawning. "There are no dragons in Cant."

"Aren't there?" Pauline demanded, pointing to the flames.

Lucy squinted. Even with her glasses she did not see well at a distance.

"Well, I don't think there are dragons *now*," she answered (for all Cantlings knew the legend of Baron Gustaf, "the Fey," who had killed a dragon with only a sling and a darning egg as weapons).

"We'll never find out standing here," Pauline said. "Come, let's go and see!"

"Pauline, if there *are* dragons I think we should go the *other* way."

"Don't be frightened, Lucy," said Pauline. "I'll get the pack!"

She raced back to their camping place. Only lately had they learned that Lucy, too, was a daughter to Lord Cant — indeed, his firstborn child, got on a chambermaid before his marriage to Pauline's mother — and since their escape from the castle Pauline had realized that Lucy was far from ready to rule the Barony. It stood to reason. An orphaned maid would hardly show the qualities of a prince, having been so long humble and obedient. So Pauline — by pouting and whining and never taking no for an answer — had been teaching Lucy the noble ways. And nothing could be more noble, in Pauline's view, than facing down a dragon.

She flung the knapsack over her shoulder but, as she hurried back, a look from her sister stopped her cold. Lucy held the chocolate wrapper. Pauline uneasily licked the corners of her mouth.

"What is this?" demanded Lucy.

"Lucy, the land is swarming with dragons. We haven't the time to —"

"You *agreed* that we should save the chocolate, Pauline!"

Pauline blinked at the silver foil. "Is that a chocolate wrapper?"

"Oh, you're impossible!" Lucy moaned. "Do you understand how many days' marching we face? We have no gold or silver and already we've gone through most of the food. What do you propose to eat when the chocolate is gone?"

"Cake?" suggested Pauline. Lucy did not smile.

"We'll be reduced to eating mud if you — what is that?" Lucy spun around. The sky now glowed like an uncanny dawn over the hills, and above the clamor of hoofbeats rose a woman's anguished cry.

"A damsel in distress!" cried Pauline. "Come!"

She ran off with Lucy at her heels. They were making for La Provence, at the far reaches of the Barony, where Pauline might shelter from the rebel threat with her grandfather, Gaspard Simone-Thierry. But Pauline saw no reason why they should not have adventures along the way. She climbed a bluff overlooking the high road from Tenesmus to Great Pillow, and watched there until Lucy caught up and pulled her down into the tall grass.

"Don't let them see you!" Lucy said.

Two wagons roared and crackled under clouds of whirling ashes. They had been fired upon by flaming arrows, and now the bowmen galloped around the burning wrecks, the flanks of their horses glistening with sweat. One of the carters struggled to loose her mule from the shafts, her cap tilted to shield her face from the flames.

"Highwaymen!" Lucy whispered.

Pauline gazed intently at the scene. "Those are no highwaymen," she said.

"How can you tell?"

"Look at their bows. A robber can't go about the realm of Cant with a longbow dangling from his arm — not if the sheriffs are doing their work. Those weapons came out of the armories, Lucy. They're guardsmen's bows!"

Lucy squinted at the horsemen. The Causist rebels now held the armories of Castle Cant.

"Are they Gutz's men?" she asked.

"I can't tell from here," said Pauline. "We must get closer!"

"Pauline, no!" cried Lucy, but already Pauline was gone. The road curved around a hill not far away, and there Pauline crossed it, pushing through a hedgerow that ran along the other side.

Lucy raced after her. Hidden by the greenery, they ran to where the horsemen stood asking questions of the carters. As Pauline pushed aside the leaves one of the flaming wagons fell to its axles.

"This is sheer lawlessness!" the younger carter protested. She held the bridle of her skittish mule, whose smoldering tail showed how close the flames had come. Lucy knelt panting behind Pauline, who held a *shush*-ing finger to her lips.

"I might ask what lawful business you're about before the sun is yet come up," said the horsemen's captain. Sir Henry Wallow, commander of the rebel forces under Arden Gutz, wore a soldier's tunic, and had stuck a fancy yellow feather in his cap. "Or perhaps your cargo wants the cover of night, eh? Boy! What have you found?"

"It's as you thought, sir!" cried a lad. He had thrust a pike into one of the burning wagons, and now he came forward and showed the weapon to his captain. From its head hung long gooey tendrils blackened with ash.

"Chewing gum," said Wallow.

"Aye, it's gum," said the elder carter. "Polly and me has been hauling it these five years and more — oft times for Lord Cant himself, may he rest in peace. Had you not set fire first and asked questions later, you might have seen the postal seals, granting me leave to carry it!"

"You shall haul gum no more, Mr. Carter. Give me the order, Prillington."

One of his men opened a purse and handed Wallow a sheet of foolscap. The nobleman cleared his throat importantly before reading the document aloud.

"Harumph! *By order of Mr. Arden Gutz, by right and common consent the August Provisional Regent to Lucy, Lady Wickwright, be it hereby known that all permissions, grants, and licenses pertaining to the import, transfer, and purchase of chewing gum, also known as 'gum,' are forthwith revoked, annulled, and voided! —*"

"I don't understand a word of it!" said Polly Carter.

"*To the bearer is given authority to seize, confiscate, or destroy any shipments, cargoes, or ladings* — Blast! Must he repeat everything three times? The point is," Wallow said, "chewing gum has been outlawed in the Barony of Cant."

"You're a lot of Causists!" cried Polly. "You're blooming rebels!"

"Nonsense," said Wallow. "You're only a rebel until you win. After that you're the government." He pressed the order into the old man's hand. "You can keep that," he added.

"And who'll pay for our wagons?"

"That's incidental damage. No one pays."

"You'll pay with your heads if Lord Cant's men catch you!" said Polly.

"Lord Cant's men!" scoffed Wallow. "They may as well join the Baron in his tomb. The house of Cant is fallen, woman, and the Loyalists have scattered like chaff before the wind."

To hear such a saying from that feathered fop of a rebel — and scarcely a fortnight after her father's death — was more than Pauline could bear. "Treason!" she blurted. Too late, Lucy clapped a hand over Pauline's mouth.

"Hark!" said Wallow. "What was that?"

"I think it came from the hedgerow," Polly Carter said.

Don't give us away, you cluck! thought Pauline.

"Men!" Wallow barked. "See what you may find!"

Two rebels jumped the ditch at the road's edge. Lucy dashed off, but as Pauline raced to follow her a young girl flew out of the hedge. She, too, had been spying on the scene. Pauline bowled the girl down, and then stumbled over a smaller boy who ran beside her. The girl glared at Pauline through a furious tangle of hair.

"Can't you keep still, you dumb bunny!" the girl hissed.

Pauline picked up the knapsack, which had fallen from her shoulders. "*Hwee!*" she piped. She meant to say "I'm sorry!" but the collision had got her wind.

"Halt!" a voice cried.

Wallow's men tore through the hedge. Pauline had been ready to face down dragons, but now her chocolate courage melted. She sprinted away from the children, following Lucy's path through the dewy grass. The girl screamed behind her, and one of the rebels cried out as the boy bit his hand. Lucy waited anxiously beyond the bend in the road.

"I could track you like a hound!" Pauline gasped.

Lucy looked behind her. Their trail was as clear as a line on a map. "We'll have to take the road," she said. "Come!"

Lucy broke through the hedgerow and together they ran away from the burning wagons. Scarcely had they reached the next bend, however, when a second troop of horsemen appeared. One of the forward riders gave a shout and, standing in his stirrups, loosed an arrow at the fugitives.

"Run!" cried Lucy, but Pauline could not outpace the arrow. It whistled into her knapsack and she tumbled headlong into the ditch. With a cry Lucy leapt after her and, grabbing her sister's arm, pulled her through the hedge. With Lucy's help Pauline struggled to her feet and together they hobbled to a thicket not far away, where they flung themselves down.

Seconds later a rider spurred his horse towards the breach in the hedge. But now his comrades had spied Wallow's men ahead, and at a word of command he galloped with them towards the burning wagons. When the last horse had passed, Lucy lifted the knapsack from Pauline's shoulders and plucked out the arrow.

"Who were they?" Pauline gasped.

"We shall soon find out," said Lucy. "Look!"

A broadside had been tied around the arrow's shaft. Lucy unknotted the string and spread out the paper, from which a familiar face gazed back. It was the official portrait of Pauline, taken on her last birthday.

MISSING! [the broadside exclaimed]

The Adored & Honorable **PAULINE VON CANT**, only daughter and heir to our late beloved Adolphus, Lord Cant. Last seen on the 6th June and believed **KIDNAPPED** by a Causist rebel, by name **LUCY WICKWRIGHT**. A reward of **FIVE GOLD PIECES** shall be given for the safe return of Miss Cant, or the capture (or head) of the rebel, **WICKWRIGHT**.

Chapter 2

Thieves in the Night

"*K*idnapped!" cried Lucy.

Below Pauline's portrait a description was given of her abductor, "a girl of perhaps six stone, dark of hair and not yet come to full height." The reader was advised to look out for her "outlandish clothes and spectacles" and warned that, by devious wiles, the rebel had won over Miss Cant to her lying claims.

"You can't possibly weigh six stone," Pauline wheezed. "That's a lie, at least."

"This is awful! Did you take any hurt from the arrow?"

Pauline showed her back to Lucy. "Did it draw blood?" she asked.

"No, thank goodness."

"It missed the chocolate, anyway, so no harm was done,"

said Pauline, glancing into the knapsack. She took the broad-side from Lucy and read it over again. "But what can it mean? I'd thought the fighting was all at the castle."

"I've a dreadful suspicion," said Lucy. "Come, we must find out."

She helped Pauline up and they crept back to the burning wagons. The second troop of horsemen had drawn up perhaps a score of yards from Wallow's men, and the latter gazed warily at the newcomers. Among the new arrivals Lucy saw Tybold Retsch, who had been Captain of the Guard to Lord Cant. He spurred forward his horse and gazed scornfully at the rebel troops.

"What manner of mischief is this, Sir Henry?" he demanded. Wallow's bowmen had remounted their horses and taken a position behind the smoking wagons. With the carters and their mules stood the children Pauline had run over in the hedge.

"It is you who ought to state your business, Retsch," Wallow answered. "Gum chewers and their lickspittles have no leave to ride armed on the roads of this Barony. But lay down your weapons, and I may urge clemency on your behalf from the August Provisional Regent."

This was idle talk, Lucy saw. Behind Tybold Retsch waited a mounted force twice the size of Wallow's. The girl Pauline had trampled gazed at this army, and evidently did not like her chances with the rebels. She broke away suddenly from the carters and, leaping a ditch, sprinted through the tall grass on the far side of the road.

"Seize her!" Retsch ordered. At once a horseman whipped his mount and galloped off in pursuit of the girl, who was perhaps eight years old, and not a fast runner. He caught her dress in his fist and charged triumphantly back to his commander.

"I got 'er, Captain!" he cried. "I caught the rebel girl!"

"Marci!" the boy yelled, running from behind Polly Carter's skirt. One of Wallow's men leapt from his horse and dragged him back, and the boy helplessly stretched out his arms. "Let go o' my sis!" he pleaded.

"That's the girl who tripped me," whispered Pauline. "They think she's you!"

"They won't for long, I'm afraid," said Lucy. As maidservant to Pauline she had more than once run afoul Tybold Retsch, who knew her face well. As though to confirm her fears a harsh voice rose at the back of Retsch's troops.

"Let go the girl!" it commanded.

So grating was that voice, so steeped in threat and malice, that an uneasy hush fell over Retsch's horsemen. Even Wallow's troops fell silent. The mounts of the Loyalists snorted and shied as a rider came forward through their ranks, his hair gray and his face etched by time and bitterness. From a white bandage around his throat stuck out the barbed shaft of an arrow; the feathered end of it projected gruesomely at the back of his neck.

"Let her go!" he repeated. The horseman dropped his prize, and Marci ran back to her brother. The sky had lowered and cold rain began to fall, the drops hissing as they struck the smoldering wagons.

"Vladimir Orloff," said Henry Wallow. "I had thought that arrow would teach you the foolishness of opposing our Cause, but it seems you are a slow pupil. Begone, lest I tutor you with this!" he said, drawing his sword.

The Loyalist forces stirred in their saddles, but Orloff held up a hand to still them. He spoke a word to Tybold Retsch and his captain handed him a broadside. Orloff then spurred forward his horse until he came abreast of the smoldering wagons. Had he glanced sideways he might have seen Pauline and Lucy watching from the hedge.

"Oh, this is awful!" whispered Lucy.

Vlad Orloff had served as Commissioner of Posts to Lord Cant, but his ambition had far exceeded that modest office. He had introduced chewing gum to the Barony, and as Postal Commissioner he had grown rich by the sale of gum stamps. Now the great prize was within his grasp. With Lord Cant dead a regent must rule until his heiress came of age, and Orloff had claimed that privilege on the Loyalist side. All he needed was to find Pauline von Cant.

"We are seeking Lord Cant's daughter, who has been kidnapped by a rebel," Orloff said, showing Pauline's portrait to the old carter. "Help us, and you will have a rich reward when Miss Cant assumes the baronial cap."

"Miss Cant kidnapped!" said Polly Carter.

"I've not seen her," her father said. "But who's a-going to pay for these wagons, and a cargo of gum these blackguards have burnt up? That's what I want to know!"

Orloff ignored this outburst and looked at Marci, who stood clutching her brother.

"Girl! Have you seen Pauline von Cant?" Orloff demanded.

"I have, mister!" said her brother, breaking free. "I seen her!"

"Sammy!" Marci cried.

"Come here, boy," said Orloff. Sammy ran to him, and Orloff

held down the broadside. "Are you certain this is the girl you saw?"

"That's the girl, mister. She was right over there!" He pointed to the hedge not far from where Lucy and Pauline crouched. "She ran away just a-fore you got here. I'll show you!"

"Good lad," said Orloff. He let the broadside fall to the mud, then lifted up the boy by his arm, setting him astride the horse's neck.

"I think we should leave!" Pauline whispered.

"No!" said Lucy, holding her back. "We'll surely be caught if we run!"

"Then have you a plan?" Pauline urgently asked.

Lucy's nose dripped, as it always did when trouble loomed. She looked about frantically, and her eye fell on a stone the size of a pigeon's egg. She grabbed it and pressed it into Pauline's hand.

"Here!" Lucy whispered.

Pauline gaped at her. "What am I to do with *that*?"

"Throw it!"

At first Pauline stared blankly at her, but then understanding dawned on her face. In her long career of tantrums she had developed a strong arm, and a frightful aim with a teacup. Lucy only hoped the arrow had not hurt her throwing shoulder.

Wallow's men had fitted arrows to their bowstrings, but such was Orloff's resolve that no one opposed him as he rode to the ditch. Pauline stood and weighed the stone in her palm. When Orloff came up to the gap in the hedgerow, she let the missile fly.

Gustaf the Fey, with his sling and darning egg, could not have made a deadlier shot. "Whoa, Hellion!" cried Orloff, but the stone had stung his horse's flank and the beast charged madly into the crowd of rebel bowmen. Tybold Retsch yelled to the Loyalist troops, and with a roaring of hooves they charged down the road, sending the rebels into panic. Polly Carter saw her chance, and after first helping her father on to a mule she jumped on her own and raced after him over the hills.

Such was the Battle of Great Pillow Road. It lasted hardly longer than a line in a history book, but to Lucy it seemed an eternity. The soldiers' eyes shone with fear and violence. Rain poured down their faces, and they seemed to weep as they attacked one another with curses and steel. Seeing his force outmanned, Wallow quickly called a retreat, and his rebel horsemen galloped away with the Loyalists in close pursuit.

When the hoofbeats had faded only Marci was left on the field of battle. She stood ankle deep in mud and trembled with sobs. Lucy pushed through the hedge and timidly approached her. Pauline followed with the knapsack.

"Are you all right, little girl?" Lucy asked.

Marci looked up, and when she saw Pauline she lunged at her.

"It's your fault!" she said, raindrops flying from her fists. "You gave us away with your squealing, you dumb nob!* Where'd that man take Sammy? Huh?"

"I meant you no harm!" said Pauline. "Stop *hitting* me!"

She swatted Marci's hand but that only maddened the girl, who answered with a blow to Pauline's belly. Pauline doubled

---

*Nob: a noble person

over, and Lucy ran to pin Marci's arms. Even then the girl did not relent, landing a few more punches with her bare feet before Lucy dragged her away.

"Where'd he take Sammy!" she screamed.

"Please, don't *hit*," begged Lucy. "Tell her you're sorry, Pauline. Go on!"

"That *hurt!*" Pauline gasped.

"*Please*, Pauline!"

"Yes, yes, forgive me!" Pauline groaned.

"There!" said Lucy. "Now we can be friends."

"*No!*" Marci squealed.

Lucy struggled to hold her. She had no experience of dealing with children (unless one counted Pauline), and not knowing how else to tame the girl she resorted to bribery.

"I'll give you a sweet if you promise not to hit!" she said.

Marci went limp in her arms. "What kind of sweet?" she asked, rubbing rain from her eyes.

"Give her a chocolate, Pauline," said Lucy.

Pauline gaped at her. "But you said we ought to save —"

"*Pauline!*"

"Oh, very well!" Pauline answered, opening the knapsack. She tore the wrapper from a tablet of chocolate and gave it to the girl, who gobbled it down as though she had not eaten in days. The rain slackened, and Lucy put back the hood of her jumper. When Marci had finished eating she pointed accusingly at Lucy.

"You're the rebel girl," she said.

"What!" said Lucy.

"You are. That fellow thought I was her, and I got dark hair like you."

"I'm nothing of the sort," Lucy insisted. "Pauline von Cant wouldn't stand here willingly with her kidnapper, would she? I . . . I'm Miss Cant's maidservant. I'm helping her to escape."

"Why?" Marci asked.

"Why?" said Lucy. "Well, because Vladimir Orloff is after her. He's a bad man."

"That fellow with the arrow through him?"

Lucy nodded. She had last seen the Postal Commissioner at Lord Cant's funeral, when a rebel bowman, seeing Orloff about to strike her, had loosed the arrow that Orloff now carried in his neck. She had hoped never to see him again.

"Yes, that's him," she said.

"Well, now he's got Sammy, thanks to you two!" said Marci, again bursting into tears.

Lucy awkwardly consoled the girl, petting her tangled hair.

"We'll help you find Sammy," she promised.

"If you don't I'm in big trouble!" the girl sobbed. "I was lookin' after him!"

"Where are your parents?"

"Up at Great Pillow, for the shearing," Marci said. "Granny sent me and Sammy out to look for strays. She said, 'Any sheep a-wandering loose at shearing time must be looking for a tinker's cookpot, Marci Frelock!' But we didn't find none yesterday, so we laid down to sleep in the hedgerow."

Lucy might have guessed the girl was a tinker. It was rare for Cantlings to talk against the nobles, and only a tinker would have dared to call Lord Cant's daughter a "nob." The tribe had no settled homes but wandered Cant in colorful wagons, mending pots and shoes, shearing sheep, or offering cures for warts. Lucy cast a downhearted glance at Pauline.

"Come, Marci," she said. "We'll take you back to Great Pillow. Very likely we'll find Sammy on the way."

It proved a long and wet day's hiking, and by the end of it even Lucy's patience wore thin. Marci complained they walked too fast, and several times sat in protest till they promised to slow down. She squabbled with Pauline, and begged endlessly for sweets from the knapsack. If Sammy is anything like her, Lucy thought, I hope we never find him!

But her hope was dashed as darkness began to fall. The fugitives were obliged to leave the road whenever they saw a traveler, for with Orloff scattering broadsides they dared not be seen. They were crouched behind a bush to let a woman go by with her donkey when Marci jumped as though stung by a wasp.

"Sammy!" she cried, pointing down the road.

Indeed it was her brother, looking none the worse for his adventure. Marci raced out to him with Lucy and Pauline at her heels. The boy refused to talk until he was given something to eat, so Lucy was forced to part with another tablet of the chocolate.

"That man with the arrow in his neck is looking for you," Sammy told Pauline, having gobbled the sweet as quickly as his sister before him. "He said he'd give me five shillings if I found you!"

"Five shillings!" said Pauline. "Why, that's insulting!"

"What did you say to him?" Lucy asked.

"I asked how I was supposed to find *him* again, if I found *her*. He said all of Cant was a-lookin' for her, and I was to tell a constable if I scared her up. He called *you* a lot of bad names," he told Lucy. "He said you was a no-good rebel and kidnapped the Baron's daughter!"

"I knew you was the rebel!" cried Marci.

"Shh!" said Lucy, for an oxcart was coming down the road. "Let's get off the highway and find somewhere to camp. We'll not reach Great Pillow before dark."

She led the party across country, skirting small farmsteads and drovers' huts, until they found a copse of oaks where they might shelter for the night. The tinkers proved themselves old hands at gathering wood. When they had built a campfire, Lucy appealed to their better natures. As she had no money it was the only appeal she could make.

"Please don't tell on us," she begged. "Mr. Orloff — that man with the arrow — is an awful villain and a liar. It's true I spied for the rebels, but I've renounced them. And I've not kidnapped you, have I, Pauline?"

"It would take more than one girl to kidnap me!"

"You should give us five shillings *not* to tell on you," Marci reasoned.

"We haven't any money," admitted Lucy.

"That other fellow does," said Sammy.

"We've given you chocolate!" said Pauline. "Why, that must be worth a bucket of shillings! Papa complained it cost him a fortune, as it had to be brought from the outlands."

"Is there more?" Sammy asked.

"You mustn't eat sweets at bedtime," said Lucy. "But if you

promise not to tell on us, we'll give you both another chocolate in the morning. That's more than fair, don't you think?"

"But! —" began Pauline.

"Are we agreed?" Lucy asked.

Sammy looked at Marci, who nodded. Lucy sighed in relief and shared out two pieces of bread from the knapsack. They were running perilously low on food, but the chocolate would be a small price to buy the tinkers' silence.

When the campfire had burned down they huddled round it to sleep. Lucy tossed through the night, troubled by some foreboding, and woke well before the dawn. Rain dripped dismally from the trees. The night was black as a dungeon, and only when the sun rose behind the clouds did she see the knapsack lying open-mouthed before her. She started up in a temper. Pauline had done it again!

She turned to scold her sister but found her sleeping soundly by the ashes of the fire, her face as innocent as new-made soap. Marci and Sammy, on the other hand, were nowhere to be seen. Lucy searched the knapsack but found neither bread nor chocolate. The tinkers had robbed them blind.

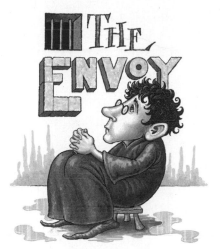

Chapter 3

The dungeon was no place for a man who loved the stars. A gray pall of clouds covered the sky, so that even from the high, barred window of his cell the Chief Astronomer saw nothing to lighten his heart. Rain seeped through the stone walls and puddled on the floor. It was spring in the Barony of Cant.

In the eighth year of Lord Cant's reign Luigi Lemonjello had famously predicted the arrival of a comet, which many took as a Sign foretelling the Baron's marriage to Esmeralda Simone-Thierry. But he had seen nothing in the stars to warn him of Lord Cant's death, or the uprising that followed it. No omens had foretold his imprisonment for helping Pauline von Cant escape the rebels. Those Signs had come from below, when Miss Cant came to look through his telescope with her maidservant, Lucy Wickwright.

Since then the Barony had turned upside down. Rebels held the castle, and those loyal to the house of Cant had fled or been imprisoned in the dungeon. Lemonjello shared his cell with a fervent Loyalist, Sir D'Arcy Trimmingcrust, who, with his chewing gum seized by the rebels, had become a wreck of a man. He paced the cell from morning to night, and left off gnawing his fingers only to pour out scorn on Lucy Wickwright.

"Lord Cant would hardly leave his firstborn child on a chandler's doorstep!" Trimmingcrust argued. "The girl is more likely some tinker's brat than a daughter to Lord Cant."

Lemonjello hated being drawn into a fight, but he could not keep silent while an innocent girl was abused.

"The t-tinkers are a plain-toed folk," he reminded Trimmingcrust. "Lucy has six toes to each foot, as did Lord Cant before her, so she can hardly be a tinker's child. You may say what you like about Arden Gutz, but don't slander poor Lucy. She would never have spied for his Cause if that scoundrel hadn't deceived her."

"I have no doubt she was deceived," said Trimmingcrust. "And you, sir, may wish to make cause with deception, but I for one shall stand with the old-fashioned virtue of honesty, which reigned in this Barony until your Arden Gutz seized power!"

"But Lucy was deceived *by* Gutz. *She* d-didn't deceive —"

"Oh, I give up!" said Trimmingcrust, throwing up his hands. "I can't argue with a man who won't see logic. Guard! Guard! I demand to be removed to a cell where the prisoners can see common sense!"

As it happened, there was no need to call for the guard. A jangling of keys announced his arrival at the door, which presently swung open with a sour squealing of hinges. Their gaoler wore the flat helmet of Lord Cant's Baronial Guard, but his boots and rough tunic marked him as a soldier of the Causist rebellion. A man in physician's robes waited in the corridor behind him.

"My good fellow," said Trimmingcrust, "for pity's sake I beg you to return my purse to me. I simply want my gum. You may keep whatever else takes your fancy as a reward for your trouble."

"Back off, you blighted cow," growled the guard. "I've not trudged all the way from Haslet March to run errands for gum chewers. Anyway, the gum's all gone. Our men've been through the castle with hounds and sniffed out every last piece of it."

The nobleman's face fell.

"That's thievery!" he whimpered. "Sheer thievery!"

"Shut it," said the guard, "or you'll get a lash for every word. Understand? Right, then. The doctor here is worried what kind of poxes may be festering in the cells, so he's come to have a look at your tongues. And that's the *only* thing I want coming out of your mouths. Come in, guv'nor."

He stepped aside and the doctor entered the cell.

"Splint!" hissed Trimmingcrust. "Don't tell me you've gone over to the rebels?"

"My place in time of war is with the sick and wounded," said Mr. Cheswick Splint. "I will give to the vilest rebel the same care I gave Lord Cant himself. Please to show me your tongue."

The tongue, according to the natural philosophy of Cant, enjoyed a nervous connection to the liver, spleen, and other vital organs. After examining Trimmingcrust's with a wooden paddle, Mr. Splint pronounced him to be suffering from moral exhaustion, turgid bile, and peevishness.

"Such afflictions are common to gum chewers who've been deprived of their cud," he said. "A diet of hard crusts and plain water is the best remedy. Deep knee bends provide some relief."

"Look here," Trimmingcrust whispered, with a sidelong glance at the guard, "a single tablet of gum would put me right straightaway. If you'll but fetch me one piece, Splint, I shall reward you handsomely when these ruffians have been defeated!"

"You'll be a better man without it," said Splint. He turned to Lemonjello. "Now, let's have a look at you, sir."

Lemonjello showed his tongue. The two men had never met, but the astronomer knew that Splint was a friend to Lucy Wickwright. The physician poked and prodded with his paddle.

"I see you're a man of science," he murmured, glancing at the astronomer's robe.

"Luigi Lemonjello at your service. Ch-chief Astronomer to his late Lordship."

Splint nodded meaningly. He put away the tongue paddle and turned to the guard.

"This prisoner must be removed at once," he said. "He shows early signs of rabbit fever, dropsy, and Draperer's Lament. If he's left in this dungeon you'll soon have an epidemic on your hands."

Trimmingcrust gasped. He backed away from the astronomer.

"Oy!" said the guard, covering his mouth. "Is it catching?"

"You'll want to wash your hands."

"And what of me?" said Trimmingcrust. "The wretch has breathed all over me!"

"I'll return in three days," Splint assured him. "If by then you're not dead, you may assume the contagion has missed you. See that no other prisoners are allowed into this cell," he instructed the guard. "Mr. Lemonjello, please to come with me."

The astronomer followed Splint up through the gatehouse and into the ward, where a troop of rebel soldiers drilled in the falling mist.

"I c-cannot thank you enough," said Lemonjello, "for daring —"

"*Shh!*" said Splint. He led the astronomer to the north flanking tower and down its steps to the cellars, where a torch burned in an iron bracket. Splint took up the brand and strode down a stone passage to a cheese cellar, where he took a bundle from his bag and ordered his patient to undress. Lemonjello — who had taken off his spectacles to wipe rain from the lenses — blinked nearsightedly at this command.

"Er . . . what? I'm not really sick, you know."

"You dare not show yourself at liberty in this castle," said Splint. "Arden Gutz will not soon forget your helping Miss Cant to escape. I had the foresight to bring a disguise. Be quick!"

The bundle held the tunic, stockings, and cape of a wandering peddler. When Lemonjello had put them on, Splint took a burnt cork from his bag and drew heavy eyebrows and moustaches on the astronomer's face, examining his handiwork by the guttering flare of the torch.

"It's not pretty, but it will serve," he said. "Come, our friends are waiting!"

Lemonjello hurried after him. They passed through a labyrinth of rusted armories and ratty crypts to the castle keep, and then up flight upon flight of stairs to the Baronial Library. The boards of the reading room echoed hollowly under their feet. The scholars all had fled, their pens no match for rebel swords. In dark taverns they waited for the dust of war to settle, that they might write its history.

Splint extinguished his torch in a bucket of sand and rapped sharply on the door to the librarian's chambers. It was answered by Horst-Wilhelm Sauersop, the Master Herald of Cant. He stood aside and, after listening a moment at the threshold, bolted the door behind the newcomers. Dr. Fatima Azziz waited within. The four now gathered in her chambers had taken it in turns to hide Lucy after she denounced Arden Gutz and the rebel Cause, and with her they had plotted the rescue of Pauline. Dr. Sauersop took Lemonjello's hand.

"Here we are at last," he said, "and our dear friend safe and sound! Come, sit by the fire. You have paid a great price, Luigi, but your sacrifice was not in vain. Lucy and Miss Cant have escaped. But I must say, those eyebrows are ridiculous," he added, squinting at the astronomer's disguise.

"Ah . . . well, you s-see, Mr. Splint —"

"Those will lift off with cold cream," said Dr. Azziz. The librarian wheeled her chair to Lemonjello and handed him a cup of tea. "The moustaches, however, become you. You must consider growing real ones. I fear you'll not be safe in Cant as long as Arden Gutz is in power."

Lemonjello gratefully sipped the tea.

"What n-news have you heard of Lucy and Miss Cant?" he asked.

The librarian glanced at Sauersop.

"Silence is the best we may hope for," she said. "Vladimir Orloff is offering five gold pieces for Lucy's head, and you may be sure he will not lack for customers if the girls are seen. As long as we hear nothing we may assume they are still on their way to La Provence."

"I h-hope you are right."

"What concerns us now is how Lucy will be welcomed there," said Sauersop, whose monocle glinted in the firelight. "Gaspard has waited many years to see his granddaughter in the baronial cap, and I fear he will not easily accept her demotion — in favor of her maidservant, no less! The man is proud — and still ambitious, for all his years."

"And there is another concern," said Splint. "While you languished in the dungeon the Loyalists made their stand in the south wing. Now the rebels have driven them out, and we fear that Orloff may himself travel to La Provence and try to turn Gaspard against Lucy. He was once in Gaspard's service. Indeed, as Gaspard's man he arranged Lord Cant's marriage to Esmeralda."

Sauersop nodded. "We've discussed the matter at length, Luigi, and concluded that an envoy should be sent to La Provence," he said. "He must advise Gaspard against acting rashly, and above all our envoy must ensure that Lucy is treated fairly. He must vouch that Lucy has always acted with Miss Cant's welfare at heart. We propose to send someone who knows the dangers Lucy faced to free Miss Cant from the dungeon."

"It is an excellent p-plan. I wholly concur."

Sauersop smiled. Dr. Azziz wheeled her chair nearer to the astronomer.

"We knew we could count on you," she said. "The girls have a head start, of course, but they are on foot, so you should have no trouble arriving ahead of them. I shall lend you my own mount."

"But — but — but —"

"I've prepared a pack with food for your journey," said Splint, "and I've put in a burnt cork as well. It may be best to maintain your disguise until you're well away from the castle."

The astronomer sprang up.

"But I'm n-no envoy!" he said.

"You'll do splendidly!" said Sauersop, standing up. "The chief thing is that you care for Lucy and Miss Cant. I know you are fond of the girls, Luigi."

"Of c-course I am! But — but — ah — perhaps you hadn't noticed, but I have rather a c-catch in my speech. You d-don't want a stammamamering astronomer going before a g-great lord like Gaspard!"

"Luigi," said Sauersop, "there is no one else for the task. I am far too old to undertake such a journey. Dr. Azziz has not the use of her legs. Mr. Splint's duty is with those injured in the recent fighting. Who else in the castle may be trusted?"

"But I'm n-no horseman!" said the astronomer. He had a morbid fear of low places, and having escaped the dungeon his only wish was to climb up to the peace and solitude of his tower.

"Mr. Lemonjello," Splint said abruptly. "Lucy Wickwright stands between Orloff and power. He sought to destroy her when she was but a suckling babe, and he succeeded in murdering her family. We must not let him influence Gaspard. The girl's life may be at stake."

The astronomer let out a long, defeated sigh. He was not a cowardly man, but he was a slight and timid one. He had chosen the scientist's life in part to escape the rough and tumble of human affairs, the bruising contact with bigger men. In his tower he had charted the courses of planets, and ignored the ways of the world. Then he had joined the fight against chewing gum. He had taken his eyes off the stars, and now he must wallow in the mud.

"I'll d-do it," he said. He swallowed his tea at a gulp. He could not think of his own comfort while two girls wandered alone in the wilds of Cant.

"Splendid," said Dr. Azziz. She took the cup and saucer from him and wheeled over to a low sideboard, where she put them down. "I've ordered Guinevere to be saddled. You'll find her ready in the stables."

Lemonjello sputtered. His tea had gone down the wrong pipe. "What!" he cried. "I'm to leave *now?*"

"I believe we agreed the matter was urgent?" said Splint.

"I agreed to n-no such thing!" Lemonjello said.

"Nevertheless, you must leave," said Sauersop. "I'll come with you to the stables."

He barely allowed the astronomer time to thank the librarian for his tea. Sauersop may have been too old for a journey to La Provence, but he moved spryly enough in the halls of Castle Cant. Lemonjello was hard-pressed to keep up.

"I c-can't believe I'm the best man for this mission," he complained as they went down the steps of the northeast tower.

Sauersop turned around. His monocle swung on its silver chain.

"You are the *only* man for the job, Luigi. You'll have to become the best as you go."

He turned and walked briskly down the stairs.

The stables leaned against the south wall near the gatehouse. They were old, thatched, ramshackle affairs and looked for all the world as though the wind had blown them there. The astronomer took heart in the bracing smells of dung and hay. The journey would at least improve his skills in the saddle. But when the groom led out his mount, he doubted he should make it as far as the drawbridge.

"I'm t-to ride to La Provence on *that*?" he cried.

"Guinevere's a good girl," the groom assured him. "Not much to look at."

She was *too* much to look at, thought Lemonjello. The librarian's mule was a riotous patchwork of ill-matched colors, and long tufts of hair sprouted from her ears, which were of differing lengths. She squinted sadly at the scientist, as though harboring doubts of her own.

"She looks like t-two clowns in an old blanket!" blurted Lemonjello.

"I shouldn't talk if I had eyebrows like those," muttered the groom.

Lemonjello had forgotten his disguise.

"At least put a proper saddle on the beast!" he begged.

"It can't be done," said Sauersop. "She's used to carrying Dr. Azziz, you see. You'll simply have to go upon sidesaddle. You'll be teased by young boys and pelted with sticks and such, but it can't be helped. Don't let them provoke you. Remember, you're the grown-up."

"Oh, help me up, then."

The groom brought a stool and with his help Lemonjello mounted the animal. He had never been a talented horseman and he felt even less one on a sidesaddle, but a few turns around the Stone of Justice gave him some confidence with the reins. Sauersop came from the stables to see him off.

"Go with all haste!" he counseled. "It's vital that you speak to Gaspard before Vlad Orloff has had the chance to deceive him."

"And what if I'm too late?" Lemonjello asked.

Sauersop hesitated. "You'll find a purse in your provisions with some coppers and pieces of silver," he said. "If all else fails, you may need to buy a sword and rescue Lucy by main force. Fare well, my dear Lemonjello! Off you go!"

He slapped the mule's rump, and before Lemonjello could stammer a protest Guinevere galloped across the ward and over the booming drawbridge. Black clouds had massed overhead. When the rain came Guinevere slowed to a walk and, bleating glumly, carried the envoy down to the plain of Tenesmus.

Chapter 4

The Tale of the Bogwife

$\mathcal{T}$he lands south of the Great Bog presented an almost impossible challenge. The ground was everywhere scribbled by streams or pushed up by knuckles of rock. Often Lucy had to climb to some height, consult her compass, and peer ahead to find a path that would end, after a furlong or two, in yet another impasse. March by frustrating march she led them forward.

Pauline, meanwhile, looked back. From the time they skirted Great Pillow she had heard whispers and rustlings behind them, and often she spun around, hoping to catch a glimpse of their pursuers. Lucy insisted she heard only the wind or the creatures of the wild, but Pauline trusted her ears. She marched with the hairs of her neck on end.

When at last they crossed into Haslet March the fugitives stopped by a stream so Pauline might try her hand at fishing.

They had neither hook, line, nor spear in their pack, so she waded downstream with her hands held over the water, ready to pounce like a bear. The sun had come out hot, and the water felt wonderful to her sore feet. Lucy lay on the ground and read from that invaluable guidebook, *Flora & Fauna of Cant.*

"I don't believe fish *live* in this abominable ditch," Pauline complained. In the two days since their bread was stolen they had "borrowed" food from gardens and kitchens, leaving notes that promised payment from the Baronial Exchequer. But the last cottage was far behind them and the last pie eaten. Pauline's belly ached awfully.

"Fish live everywhere, Pauline."

"I saw a frog. Are you fond of frogs' legs?"

"I'm sure a fish will swim by if you're patient," Lucy said, flipping the pages of the guidebook. *"The lands south of the Great Bog abound in game animals and edible plants,"* she read aloud. *"The huntsman will find deer, wild boar, and other quarry, while the waters teem with fishes."*

"They're not teeming here!" said Pauline.

"Nor will the woodsman want for a hearty repast," Lucy went on. *"His spadework will uncover roots such as the Witch's Knuckle, Autumn Onion, and Pig's Carrot, while cane berries, rhubarb, and succulent leaves are his for the plucking.* Here's a drawing of the Pig's Carrot. I believe I saw one not half an hour ago. So we shan't starve."

"Pig's Carrot?" wailed Pauline. "Can't we go to an inn, just once? We could disguise ourselves as tinker girls — we're already dirty enough. I fancy I should look quite charming as a tinker girl."

"And how would we pay?" Lucy asked.

"Why, we'll leave a note and run away, just as always."

Lucy turned a page in the guidebook.

"Honestly, Pauline, you know very little of the world if you think an innkeeper's going to feed two little tinker girls on credit. Why, my Uncle Hock made sure he saw their coppers first when tinkers came to the Perch & Pillow. Besides, no one would mistake us for tinkers in these clothes."

Lucy wore castoffs from the American Mission, and Pauline looked almost as outlandish to Cantling eyes in a riding outfit of jodhpurs and woolen shirt. She waded hopefully upstream, but still she saw no fish.

"I suppose it's Pig's Carrot, then," she moaned. "Where do we find them?"

Lucy looked at the book and frowned.

"I'm afraid they're not in season. In fact, it seems we're too early for most of the plants. But it does say, *The springtime of upper Haslet March provides a bounty of succulent leaves.*"

"*Succulent leaves?*" cried Pauline. "Do I look like a rabbit? Have I a furry little tail?"

She splashed out of the stream. One would think Lucy might show some pity towards her, who had been brought up in idleness and luxury and sumptuous feasts. Instead, Lucy seemed to believe that Pauline wanted toughening. You know very little of the world, indeed!

"I wish you *were* a rabbit," said Lucy. "Then I might have a good meal."

"I should like that very much. I'd eat my own leg if only I had some mint sauce."

"Oh, Pauline!" Lucy cried.

"Well, I should cook it first, of course."

"No, look!"

Pauline followed Lucy's gaze to her feet, where dozens of

leeches were feasting on the sores opened by her boots. With a scream that surely carried half a league, she fell to her back and tried to shake off the greedy parasites.

"Get them off! Get them off!" she begged, landing such a kick on Lucy that her sister fell over. Startled leeches flew through the air, not knowing their heads from their tails. Finally Lucy caught hold of Pauline's legs and began to peel away the bloodsuckers.

"Do be still, Pauline!" she begged.

"I'm going to be ill!"

"It's not as bad as that! Here, I've nearly got them."

Pauline groaned as Lucy plucked the disappointed worms. When Lucy had finished she looked closely at Pauline's feet. They were rubbed raw in places and had blisters on their soles.

"Why, your feet are wearing away!" she exclaimed.

Pauline peeked through her fingers.

"They are beastly little things," she said. "In another minute I'm sure they would have eaten me alive. Thank you, Lucy."

"Leeches didn't do that, Pauline. Your boots are too small!"

Pauline pulled her feet away.

"They did rather shrink in the rain," she admitted. "It's a pity. They were new."

"Why didn't you tell me?"

"It's nothing, I'm sure."

"But it must hurt like anything!"

Pauline looked away. At the castle she had worn silks and lace while Lucy dressed in castoffs from the Mission. She did not like to admit that such hardships had made Lucy a tougher girl than the exalted daughter of Lord Cant.

"I'm sure I can bear a little blister on my feet," she muttered.

"Little blister!" Lucy cried. "Why, they're falling apart like boiled fish! You must take my stockings."

Pauline gazed longingly at Lucy's outlandish "socks." They were ankle high, with stretchy tops that held them up without garters. Their stripes were red and black, the colors of the house of Cant.

"Nonsense," she said, swallowing hard. "I'm not as soft as you think I am, Lucy Wickwright."

"No one said you were soft," said Lucy, untying her shoes.

Pauline's lip trembled.

"I'm soft and spoilt. You needn't deny it."

"Very well, you're soft and spoilt. But if you wear down your feet to stumps I shall have to carry you all the way to La Provence. Your grandfather will be very cross if I bring you to him without feet."

Pauline sniffled. Her feet really did hurt dreadfully. "Perhaps I might borrow them for a day or two."

"I'll just rinse them out in the water. They'll dry quickly in this sun," said Lucy. "We'll have a good rest and then carry on hiking until dark. Perhaps the rhubarb is up early this year and we'll have a good supper as well."

While the socks dried, Pauline studied *Flora & Fauna of Cant*. She discovered that any number of ground-nesting birds dwelt in upper Haslet March, so they might gather eggs. A plant called Blacksmith's Beard produced edible shoots this time of year. Among the plants growing in or near the Great Bog itself were pussy willow, bulrush, sedge, cattail, and —

Pauline sat up with a gasp.

"Lucy!" she cried. Lucy started. She had dozed off in the grass.

"Mf? What is it?"

"Lucy, it says in *Flora & Fauna of Cant* that marshmallows grow in the Great Bog!"

Lucy rubbed her eye.

"Yes, the bog is simply a great marsh. One would find marshmallow there."

"Is it far? Can we go? Don't you *adore* marshmallows?"

"We weren't given them in the servants' hall," Lucy said. "I understand they're delicious, but even supposing we find marshmallows, how do you propose to cook them?"

"I'm perfectly content to eat them raw," said Pauline.

Lucy rolled her eyes. "Do you suppose you pick marshmallows off trees, like cherries?" she asked.

Pauline glanced at *Flora & Fauna of Cant.* "Is it a vine, then?"

"No, it's not a vine! Marshmallows come from the root of the marshmallow plant. You have to peel the root, and cut it up into pieces, and boil the pieces in sugar syrup. Then they have to cool on waxed parchment, with a kitchen maid standing ready to shoo away flies."

"Oh!" Pauline said, looking gloomily towards the bog. A cloud rose above it. She was used to having marshmallows brought her on a little plate, and had never suspected there was so much work involved.

"You're more likely to end as a meal than find one in the Great Bog," Lucy said. She took the guidebook from Pauline and read aloud. "*The Great Bog is treacherous and best avoided, except in the company of a seasoned guide. Pigs, cattle, and Cantlings of all classes are* regularly lost there, and grief has befallen many a mother whose babe chased after the Bogwife's Lantern."

Pauline shivered. Her father had told her the story of the Bogwife. Indeed, it was the only bedtime story she had ever heard from him, for Lord Cant had been a great, busy man and rarely had time even to kiss her goodnight. Perhaps he had chosen the tale because it took less than a page in that beloved treasury, *Folk & Faerie Tales of Cant:*

The Tale of the Bogwife

Once upon a time there lived a Cantling lass who sadly had a great wart at the end of her nose. The girl was promised to a cobbler of her village, but he would not marry her because of this wart, which sprouted ugly hairs as she grew. The years passed, and the village children laughed at her and called her old maid — especially the children of the man she had loved.

Now, one day the youngest child of the cobbler wandered off to gather cattails in the bog. Night came, and he did not return. So the villagers took up torches and candles and went to look for him, and the ugly maid went too, and took her lantern.

She searched long into the night and at last she found the boy. "Come, and I will lead you home," she said, and he gladly followed her lantern. Now those were days of a great famine in the land, and the old maid was hungry, for she had no man to help her. She led the plump lad deep into the bog, and where no one could hear his cries she ate him.

So she wanders with her lantern still, and woe betide the Cantling child who follows.

Pauline gazed at the mists hanging over the bog, which stirred as though something moved within. Who had gathered marshmallows there, she wondered, that she might have sweets brought her on a dainty plate in Castle Cant?

"Do you believe in the Bogwife, Lucy?" she asked.

Lucy, deep in *Flora & Fauna of Cant*, looked up.

"Dr. Azziz says the Bogwife's Lantern is simply a vapor," she said.

"A *vapor*? What utter nonsense."

"It is not. Dr. Azziz says that when an animal rots it gives off a vapor that glows in the dark. She said the Bogwife is a tale of the unlettered and superstitious."

"But the Bogwife leads you on with her lantern," said Pauline. "You believe she's leading you home, but you only get loster and loster. With all respect to Dr. Azziz, I believe she has peculiar notions. Remember when she told us that in the outlands one could see around the world through a glass box?"

"Yes, the television. Arden Gutz saw them, too."

"O, bosh! You should never believe travelers' tales, Lucy. People will spin any old yarn to draw attention to themselves." She gazed again at the mists swirling over the bog. "I have heard — and from *reliable* sources — that fishers on Lake Poltroon often find bones in their nets, where the bog drains into the lake. The Bogwife sucks the marrow right out of them, and when the wind blows through the hollow bones you can hear the lost children crying for their parents."

"Well, if you think you can carry on without marshmallows we shall avoid the bog altogether," Lucy said. "Now have a good look at this drawing of the Blacksmith's Beard. I believe I saw —"

"You stay where you are, little lass," a rasping voice warned.

Pauline gasped, and the words died in Lucy's mouth. The speaker, a swineherd, had crept from rock to rock and caught them unawares. He wore pigskin boots and a woolen tunic girt with rope. His legs were brown, and he clutched the long spear that herdsmen used to fend off wolves and thieves.

"You're the rebel girl," he said, aiming the spear at Lucy. "You're called Wickwright, ain't ye?"

"I'm afraid you're mistaken," Lucy answered. After the encounter with Marci Frelock she and Pauline had adopted traveling names. "My name is Rosie Tooey."

The herdsman snorted.

"No it ain't," he said. "Ye've got spectacles and dark hair and outlandish britches, just like he said." He looked at Pauline. "And you're the little Baroness, what was kidnapped. I was sorry to hear about his Lordship's passing, miss. Adolphus was a good 'un, as far as Barons go."

Pauline very nearly said "Thank you" — which would have been foolish, if polite — but thanks to Lucy she remembered their story.

"You're mistaken again," she said. "I am Clementine Violetta de Gama Ortiz, though my friends call me 'Pooter.' Rosie and I were just gathering Blacksmith's Beard. Have you seen any, by chance?"

"You're them runaway girls," the man insisted. "Dressed up like outlanders, one of you skinny and dark and the other one plump and fair, just like he said. So come along nice," he told Lucy, "if you don't want this spear poking out between your shoulder bones."

Pauline put her hands on her hips.

"See here, we stole these clothes!" she said. "We're a couple o' common tinker girls, we are . . . and . . . and . . . we done left home, 'cause our pa used to beat us something awful. Now you leave us alone!"

The swineherd roared. Pauline's attempt at talking like a tinker was so wide of the mark that he could barely hold on to his spear. What Cantling girl would talk that way to a grown-up, unless she was born to cushions and jewels? He wiped tears of laughter from his cheeks.

"He told me as ye'd be under her spell, Miss Cant," he said. "The rebels are fond of the outlanders, he says, so I reckon it's no wonder she's got you dressed up in britches, too. Now, come along," he said, leveling the spear at Lucy.

"We ain't goin' nowhere with the like o' you!" insisted Pauline.

"You ain't got to come with me, Miss Cant," said the swineherd. "It's this lass I was a-lookin' for, and it's her I mean to take to him. You may come along or go as you please. He told me if I brought the rebel girl, you'd follow."

"Who is *he*?" Lucy demanded.

"Why, the chap what's giving me five gold pieces for you, Lucy Wickwright. He's a-waitin' back at my hut. Mr. Vladimir Orloff is the name, and he's all eager to get his hands on *you*, that he is. So come along, now. I hate to spear a little girl if I ain't got to."

$\mathcal{A}$rden Gutz frowned at the burnt muffin before him. Despite their poverty, many of the castle's staff had been loyal to the house of Cant, and when the soldiers of the Cause overtook its stronghold they had fled back to their native villages. There was hardly a decent cook left in the kitchens. He sighed and cut off the blackened crust. At least there was plenty of butter.

"I hope you'll forgive the food," he said to his two guests. The outlanders joined him nearly every day for breakfast, but always he felt compelled to apologize for the fare. "One can't expect fine things with a war on, I'm afraid."

"A soldier's grub is good enough for me," said the Reverend Mr. Pius Frodd. "An army marches on its stomach, as we say back in the States." He had tucked a large white napkin into his clerical collar. On his plate were bacon, ham, fried eggs, and sautéed mushrooms. His spoon rested in a half-eaten bowl of porridge.

"'An army marches on its stomach,'" repeated Gutz, his mouth full of muffin. "I say, that's well put. May I use that?"

"Of course you can, Arden," said Miss Apryl Poke, stirring honey into her tea. "It's a common saying. A cliché, really."

"I daresay we need some new clichés," said Gutz, jotting down the expression in his notebook. "Cant has been stuck in the past for far too long. When I mention televisions or tinned peaches, these people look at me as though I'm mad."

"Progress," said Frodd firmly. "You can't get anywhere without progress. If it weren't for progress, we'd be right where you Cantlings are, poking along on horses instead of putting a man on the moon."

"'You can't get anywhere without progress,'" muttered Gutz, writing that down, too.

They sat in what Arden Gutz called the "command room." Here he spent his days from dawn till dusk, leaving only to review his troops or inspect the castle's defenses. On one wall a map had been drawn of the Barony. When a village "turned" to the Causist side its red outline was wiped off with a damp rag and the area sketched in green. Day by day the rebellion spread. Already much of metropolitan Cant was solidly green, with only a few Loyalist strongholds here and there, like drops of blood on the felt of a gaming table.*

"Don't get me wrong," Frodd added, stabbing an egg yolk

---

*Metropolitan Cant *extended from the castle to the River Leech. The less populated regions of the Barony — collectively called the "the provinces" — included Haslet March, Trans-Poltroon, and La Provence.*

with a spear of bacon, "it's a fine country you've got here in Cant. Low wages, excellent fishing, lots of good old-fashioned morals. You don't hear kids mouthing off to their parents, like back home. Not even the orphans."

Orphans were Frodd's passion. He had established the American Mission in Tenesmus some years ago, arriving in Cant with his comely assistant, Miss Poke, at about the time Arden Gutz left the Barony to study at Oxford. There had been grumbling when the missioners came, for Cantlings did not care much for outlanders or their ways. In those days, they had never even heard of chewing gum.

But when Arden returned from abroad he found the orphanage flowering, while gum had been taken up with gusto by the noble classes. The latter development troubled him. He was all for bringing Cant into the modern age, but he had learned radical ideas at school. He did not like to see the workers' tithes paying for that noblemen's luxury.

Indeed, Arden Gutz's bowels burned against the rich. At Oxford his threadbare clothes and rustic accent had made him the laughingstock of his college, but when he returned to Cant he expected his schooling would earn him a position at court. Far from it! He went from ministry to ministry, his cap in his hand. There simply was not enough money to take on a new man, he was told time and again.

The final insult came at the Commission of Posts. Vladimir Orloff had scarcely looked at his diploma, and he had dared to offer Arden a postmaster's berth in a village of Trans-Poltroon. Trans-Poltroon! The name fairly reeked of the dirty feet of yokels. What place was that for an Oxford man?

Arden left the office in a rage. He earned a few shillings by copying documents for his Uncle Costive and other officials who did not merit secretaries, and by night he haunted the less wholesome taverns of Tenesmus. There, bold with ale, he cursed the gum-chewing nobles and gathered around him those malcontents who became the first recruits to the Cause.

And now look! The gum chewers were all but crushed, and Arden sat in a grand hall of the castle as August Provisional Regent, with his ladylove at hand. He smiled at Apryl, whose eyes twinkled over her teacup. She had harbored him in the first days of the rebellion, and while he hid at the Mission he had found a trusted advisor in the Reverend Mr. Frodd.

"But you can't make progress without trade," Frodd went on, wiping his mouth. "Let me give you an example, Arden. You always serve me a cup of tea for breakfast. Well, that's fine and dandy, but it's not progress. The rest of the world drinks coffee for breakfast. The man who brings the coffee trade to Cant will make a barrel of money, and benefit everyone else, as well. A rising tide lifts all boats."

Arden hesitated, unsure whether he should jot down the saying.

"A rising tide? I'm not sure I follow you, Pius."

"Trade is good for everyone, is what I'm saying," Frodd explained. "If Cant imported coffee, for instance . . . well, a farmer could have tea or coffee for breakfast, just as it pleased him. Think of it! A common, dirt-poor Cantling farmer, sipping a cup of coffee for breakfast just like any business traveler on a jet airplane! I'd call that progress, wouldn't you?"

"I suppose so," said Arden. "But I can't imagine a Cantling farmer going in for such luxury. The country folk can barely keep their children in shoes."

"But that's because you limit trade," said Frodd, rather warmly. He folded his napkin. "You hold back the tide. Lord Cant, may he rest in peace, held back the tide. I could never get that man to see the harm he did to this country. And frankly, Arden, I see you going down the same road. Holding back the tide."

Arden had swallowed a dry lump of muffin and it stuck in his craw. He sipped tea to wash it down, but the brew was tepid and left a bitter taste in his mouth. He frowned at Frodd.

"I don't know what you mean," he said. "The Cantling people have made more progress in the past month than in the past one hundred years. Where they were strangled by the greed of the nobles, now they breathe free. Forgive me, Pius, but it's wrong for you to suggest —"

"Arden!" Apryl Poke broke in. "Pius isn't suggesting anything of the sort! Why, you'd think he stepped on your sore toe, the way you go on!" She shook her head, as at a little boy who has thrown a tantrum, but at the same time laid her hand on his arm. "Of course Cant is better off now. And it's all thanks to you — the hero of your people! But won't you listen to what Pius has to say?"

Arden could refuse nothing to Apryl. His will melted at her touch. When he found the Wickwright girl he meant to put her under Apryl's care, so that the next Baroness of Cant would be a woman of the world, not some old-fashioned, horse-drawn relic to be mocked by the swells of Oxford. The Reverend Mr. Frodd exchanged a glance with Apryl and cleared his throat.

"I'm a guest in your fine country, and it's not my place to interfere," he said. "But I hear things, Arden. I've got contacts up at the frontier, at Fort Gustaf. They say the Commandant,

Fatty Trollopson, has done well in the gum trade. Vlad Orloff cut him in for a piece of it, I guess. He won't want to give that up, and he's got a lot of swords under his command."

"Sir Henry assures me he can take Fort Gustaf," Arden said. Sir Henry Wallow, a nobleman of Haslet March, commanded the Causist army. "Of course, we shan't attempt to capture the fort until the rest of the Barony is behind us."

"It'd be a lot easier if the Commandant came over to your side," said Frodd. "You'd spare everyone a lot of bloodshed, and you'd control Fort Gustaf that much quicker."

"Certainly. But how do you propose to do that?"

Again Frodd shared a glance with Apryl Poke.

"Simple," he said. "Let him go on skimming his bit off the gum trade. As long as a man gets his money, he won't care what side it comes from. You make him an offer and I guarantee he'll come over to the Cause like *that!*"

He snapped his fingers under Arden's nose.

"But this is madness!" cried the August Provisional Regent. He gaped at Frodd. "Are you suggesting I allow the gum trade to continue? The entire aim of the Cause was to bring it down!"

"Was it?" asked Frodd. He took from his pocket a copy of Arden Gutz's manifesto, the grand declaration of the Cause. "According to this," he said, "the problem with gum was that the nobles chewed it, but the working folks paid for it. The workers' taxes went up — what you folks call tithes — so the big-shots could have their gum. Those are your own words, Arden."

"Well, yes! That's why we must be rid of gum!"

"But, Arden," said Apryl Poke, "people are wondering when the tithes are going to go down. In Tenesmus they complain the

Causists are now collecting the tithes. The people must wonder if this rebellion was worth it, if they're no better off than they were under Lord Cant."

"We found the Baronial Exchequer in a shocking state," Arden explained. "I had heard there were rivers of gold in the bowels of Castle Cant, but we found only a little silver and those blasted engravings of Miss Cant. Sir Henry must pay his army, and so — on a strictly temporary basis — I have allowed the collection of tithes. The people must be patient! When we have defeated the Loyalists, they will thank us, I assure you!"

A man came in with a pot of fresh tea on a tray. The breakfast party fell silent while he put it down and cleared the table of dishes and cutlery. When he had gone, Pius Frodd plucked a flower from a vase on the table. He sniffed its perfume and then, snapping the stem a few inches below the bloom, placed it in his buttonhole.

"Arden," he said, "where other people see only a problem, the man of vision sees an opportunity. Lord Cant, if I may speak frankly, was a man of little vision. You're different. You've been abroad."

Arden Gutz nodded. How odd it was, he reflected, that in all the Barony of Cant these two outlanders best understood his virtues! He held out his teacup to Apryl, who filled it from the steaming pot.

"Now, you saw at Oxford that in the outlands anyone can chew gum," Frodd went on. "It's no luxury. Do you know why, Arden? One word: *volume.* The more of anything you sell, the cheaper it gets. So why not let the little people have gum? Slap a two-cent stamp on every pack and you'll rake in more cash than Lord Cant ever dreamed of. Volume, Arden. That's the ticket."

Arden frowned. It seemed madness to go into the gum trade in the middle of a war to abolish it. Yet, when the war was won, how would the servants be paid, how would the court do its work, how would the post roads be kept up without the revenue of the gum trade?

"But the gum sold in Cant is no ordinary stuff," he objected, seeing a flaw in Frodd's plan. "It's authentic chicle gum. The common folk could never afford it, no matter what the volume."

"Baloney!" said Frodd. "It's a scam, Arden. Someone's put plain old gum in a fancy wrapper to pull the wool over these noble fools' eyes. They'd buy sheep dung if you put a gold ribbon on it. Listen. Let me go up to Fort Gustaf and make a deal with the Commandant. With the fort under your control this war will be over lickety-split."

"I don't know. . . ." Arden hesitated. "How will the people take it?"

"You are their leader," said Apryl Poke. Her eyes — like liquid coals, Arden thought — gazed adoringly at him, and again she put her hand on his arm. "The thing is to act boldly, and with vision!"

"Lead, follow, or get out of the way. That's what we say back home," said Pius Frodd. "Here, I'll jot that down for you."

While he wrote this motto in Arden's notebook a Causist officer entered the room. Over a green tunic he wore a breastplate draped with yellow cords, and a heavy broadsword hung at his hips.

"Ah, MacTavish," said Arden, standing. "Just the man I wish to see."

"I'm sorry to trouble you, sir," said MacTavish, who served as Chief Lieutenant to Sir Henry Wallow. "A delegation has arrived from Tenesmus. Miss Wickwright's uncle is among them, along with Mayor Grunt and a number of the chief burghers. I gather they're upset by the recent collection of tithes. Shall I send them away?"

Arden looked at Apryl Poke. She gazed up at him, and in her eyes he saw the confident expectation that he would act boldly. It really was remarkable how these outlanders grasped his character! he thought. Almost it seemed they knew him better than he knew himself, for until he spoke to Pius Frodd he had only blindly groped towards a plan.

"No, I shall see them," he said. "MacTavish, I want you to provide an escort for the Reverend Mr. Frodd, who will be traveling to Fort Gustaf as my emissary. Two swordsmen should suffice. Pius, I'll write a letter to the Commandant after I've dealt with these townsfolk. You can leave today, if that's agreeable to you. I shall follow you when Sir Henry returns from the field."

"But sir, Fort Gustaf is a Loyalist stronghold," said MacTavish. "Indeed, we have every reason to believe that Fatty Trollopson is in Orloff's pocket. Begging your pardon, but what do you hope to accomplish by sending . . . this . . . *outlander* to trade words with him?"

Arden pulled back Apryl's chair, and his ladylove, rising, took his arm.

"Mr. Frodd will offer terms of surrender to the Commandant," he said, glancing at the battle map. "With Fort Gustaf under our control we will squash Gaspard Simone-Thierry like a flea between our fingers."

"Gaspard is a man, not a cootie!" said MacTavish. "With all respect, sir, I suggest you leave the military strategy to Sir Henry. How can you imagine Fatty Trollopson will surrender?"

Arden laid his hand on Apryl's where she held his arm.

"Sir Henry may wage this war as he pleases," he said, "but you will kindly leave the diplomacy to me. I have every confidence the Commandant will accept my terms. If war were only a matter of swords, MacTavish, there would be no end to the bloodshed. Swords may bring victory, but it is the man of vision who brings peace. Pius, will you join me in the Great Hall?"

Chapter 6

BACK for BACON

$\mathscr{P}$auline went with no little trepidation to meet the man who would be her regent. She remembered how Vladimir Orloff had lurked at her father's sickbed, gaunt and hollow of cheek. When Lord Cant died Orloff gazed hungrily at her, as though pining for some long-ago feast.

The swineherd had bound Lucy's wrists and he marched with his spear trained at the small of her back, to his hut a half a league away. Here he had laid stout timbers over thick turf walls, and over those more turf, so that his roof was a wild garden in which sparrows pecked for worms. On a log in front of this crude shelter sat a figure in a cloak and hood, his back turned to the marchers.

"There's your man," said the herdsman when they came in

sight of the hut. "That's the chap with the purse full of gold. He's been looking for you high and low."

Pauline sidled close to Lucy.

"What is our plan?" she whispered.

"I'm afraid we haven't got one," Lucy said glumly, "unless you've come up with something?"

"I'd counted on you for that," Pauline confessed. "Do you suppose we can fight them?"

"It would be two girls against two great men, and one girl with her hands tied," said Lucy. "I shouldn't like our chances." She peered at the figure by the hut. "But if that's Orloff, where is his arrow?"

"Hi! Hi!" the swineherd called. "Here she is! I've caught her!"

The cloaked figure rose and threw back his hood. No arrow protruded from his neck. What was more, he stood barely as tall as the hut's low doorway, and Pauline to her enormous surprise recognized an under-footman from the castle, Blaise Delagraisse. He was a great admirer of Lucy.

"Blaise!" Lucy cried. Delagraisse frowned at her.

"Well done, swineherd!" he said. "And you've found the Baroness, as well. Splendid, splendid! We've been . . . er . . . greatly worried about you, my Lady."

He bowed deeply to Pauline, with an urgent, sidelong glance at Lucy.

"Blaise?" the swineherd said. "What do you mean, *Blaise?*"

"Er — I meant to say . . . ," Lucy stammered.

"Oh, it's no use!" said Pauline, who saw the under-footman's game. "Cursing won't help matters, Lucy. We've been caught like two flies in a jam pot." She nodded coldly to Delagraisse. "Well played, Vladimir."

"Did she call you Blaise?" the swineherd asked the under-footman.

"The word she used was *blaze*," Pauline said. "She always was free with her tongue. Frankly, I'm glad you caught us, Vladimir. I've never been exposed to such foul language and bad manners as in the past days with this serving girl. I feel I want a hot bath and a plate of macaroons."

The swineherd look doubtfully at Lucy.

"What kind of cursing is *blaze*?" he asked. "Do ye mean to say *blast*?"

Pauline covered her ears with her hands. "Spare me!" she cried.

"Look here, swineherd!" said Delagraisse. "This is her Lady-ship the Baroness of Cant! Even a foul rebel knows better than to use words like *blast* in her presence." He glared angrily at the herdsman, who towered over him. "If you can't watch your tongue I shall have you locked up in the dungeon, where they're likely to pluck it out by the root and give it back in a jar of pickling salts!"

"Urngh!" the swineherd cried, clapping his hands to his mouth. He bowed awkwardly to Pauline. "F-f-forgive me, Lady!"

"Oh, it's too *much*!" Pauline wailed. "Kidnapped and driven like a beast, and now made to hear *strong oaths*! Has ever a body been subjected to such torments? Oh, boo hoo hoo! I feel I shall *faint* if I don't find something to eat!" She opened one eye and peeked into the hut, where a slab of bacon hung from a roofbeam.

"Please! Please, my Lady, don't cry!" begged the swineherd. "I've a lovely piece of bacon I can toast up for you. Forgive me! I don't know how to talk proper, being a poor, lowly drover, as you see. Mayn't I toast a bit of bacon for you?"

"I should very much doubt whether it's fit to eat," said Delagraisse.

"No, no, it's of the best!" the swineherd insisted.

"Shall I put him under arrest, my Lady?" Delagraisse asked.

Pauline sniffled and wiped her eyes with the back of her wrist.

"Perhaps I could force myself to eat a little, though it be rude, country fare," she said. She glanced at Lucy, and her eyes, though wet with weeping, merrily twinkled. Lucy with a great effort did not laugh.

"I shall start a fire straightaway!" the swineherd said. "Please to lie down in my hut, Lady. It's humble, to be sure, and not worthy of gentlefolk, but the fleas ain't come back after that hard winter, so it's not as bad as might be."

The hut was simply furnished with a wooden table and stool, shelves resting on sticks thrust into the walls, and a bed of piled straw covered with sheepskins. Firewood was stacked along the back wall. Pauline sat on the bed next to Lucy while the herdsman sawed off a great slab of bacon. Delagraisse perched on the stool.

"Bacon'll set the little lady right," the swineherd said when he had started a fire outside the hut. "It mayn't be lambchops and jelly, such as you eat up in your castle, but my ma brought up nine of us on bread and bacon, and it would've been ten if it weren't for the measles."

He speared the rasher with a sharpened stick and propped it over the flames. When the fire began to spit and smoke with bacon grease, Delagraisse left the stool and knelt next to Lucy.

"Well, haven't I found you at last!" he whispered, taking out a jackknife and cutting her bonds. "You are a sight for sore eyes, Lucy, and that is a fact. You as well, Miss Cant," he added.

"Thank you, Delagraisse," Pauline said. She moved closer to Lucy.

"What are *you* doing out here in the wilderness, Blaise?" Lucy asked.

"Why, I was looking for you, and now I've found you. I let on to the swineherd that I was Mr. Orloff, who *is* looking for you, Lucy." He looked at Pauline. "The rebels is offering a reward for you too, Miss Cant, but they're holed up in the castle."

"How did you ever convince him you were Orloff?" Lucy asked, for the under-footman was a lad of only twelve years, and spotty of face. A few children of noble persons held office in the castle, with grand-sounding titles such as Dame of the Darning Egg or Marshal of Leftovers, but they rarely traveled upon the business of the Barony.

Delagraisse grinned. He took from a corner of the hut his traveling bag and showed Lucy a great impressive scroll, full of seals, elaborate stamps, and ribbons. It authorized the bearer, Vladimir Orloff, to offer a reward of five gold pieces for the capture of Lucy Wickwright, who was declared a pox upon the Barony and a foul and cowardly traitor.

"I think it's the ribbons as does the trick," Delagraisse said. "Anyone might have a bit of sealing wax, and you could carve a seal from a bit of beet-root. But who in his right mind would throw away good ribbon to fancy up a piece of paper? He fell for it like a rotten tree!"

"That's wonderful, Blaise!" Lucy said. "And you carved those seals from beet-root?"

"Well, no. I was just giving a for instance. I took 'em from Orloff's office after the last of the Loyalists bolted from the castle." He showed them a number of official stamps and seals in the bottom of his bag, and then put away the impressive warrant. "I suspected as they'd come in handy for something," he added.

"Why, you've thought of everything!" said Lucy. Pauline frowned. She hardly thought it such a grand feat to steal a few seals from an empty office.

"It's good no one was there to stop you," Pauline pointed out.

"Aye," said Delagraisse. "The Loyalists ran out of gum, you see, so three nights ago they tied bed-linens together and climbed down from the southeast tower in the wee hours — even Orloff, and him with an arrow through his neck!"

Smoke from the bacon wafted into the hut and made Pauline's belly ache. She looked outside. The land fell away from the swineherd's hut to a shallow stream some furlongs distant. Two horsemen were fording the water, and when they had gained the nearer bank they spurred their mounts up the slope.

"No sooner did Arden Gutz take over than he sent Henry Wallow's men to collect tithes in Tenesmus," Delagraisse went on. "After all his complaining about the nobles!"

"Arden Gutz will lean however the wind blows," Lucy said bitterly.

"It made the townsfolk grumble, I can tell you. Finally

Mayor Grunt himself came to the castle with some of the masters of the guilds. Your uncle Hock came, Lucy, and Lu Mingshu as well."

The horsemen were making for the swineherd's hut. One had thrown back his cloak and Pauline saw that he carried a sword and pike. His companion's cloak stuck out strangely above his shoulder. His face was shadowed by a hood.

"I say, Lucy — ," began Pauline.

"Sh! Did you talk to Uncle Hock, Blaise?"

"I'm almost to that," said Delagraisse. "Gutz met the Mayor and the rest of them in the Great Hall. I happened to sneak in and hide behind a tapestry, so I heard it all. Mayor Grunt allowed as Arden Gutz had done a good thing by driving Orloff out of the castle. But he said they had no business sending men to collect tithes in Tenesmus, of which he was the duly appointed Mayor, thank you very much. And he wanted to know why this maidservant had run away, who was supposed to be Lord Cant's daughter."

"How could he listen to Arden Gutz and not know why?" said Lucy.

"I fancy he guessed it. Well, your uncle didn't like to talk in front of so many fine folk, Lucy, but the Mayor spoke for him. 'This good man,' he says — meaning your uncle — 'is next of kin to Lucy Wickwright, who is rumored to be the true heiress of this Barony. Who had put Gutz in office,' he asks, 'who called himself her regent? Was not the Privy Council supposed to decide these things?'

"Well, Gutz leans over to Mr. Frodd, who's sitting next to him, and they whisper for a while. I guess having gone away to school he gets along with outlanders. Then he stood up and poured out such a slew of hard words that I never hope to hear the like of it again, Lucy. I don't know what the half of them meant, but there was no mistaking his meaning, 'cause when he was done Sir Henry's men pulled out their swords and marched the whole lot of them down to the dungeons!"

"Uncle Hock!" Lucy gasped.

"I came out from where I was hiding and your uncle caught sight of me. 'Find Lucy!' he says, 'and tell her to fly! Flee this madness! To the outlands, if need be!' And here I have found you, Lucy," Delagraisse concluded, "and I'm telling you as I was told. Fly!"

Hooves pounded up the slope and the horsemen reined in their mounts.

"You, herdsman!" one of the riders yelled. "We'll have that meat, and any other provisions you can spare us. We're on the business of the Barony."

"Hide!" Pauline hissed. She dove under the sheepskins and made room for Lucy. Delagraisse threw himself against the wall beside the doorway. They heard the horsemen dismount.

"This meat is for my guests, and I ain't got none other to spare for no highwaymen," said the swineherd. "Be off with you, now!"

Pauline peeked from under the sheepskin. Beside an officer of the guard stood Vladimir Orloff. The rebel's arrow angled down from his throat, and blood had oozed through and stained the bandage around his neck. He strode up to the swineherd and put his hand on the hilt of his sword.

"It is your bound duty as a Cantling to give us aid!" he

hissed. "His Lordship is dead and his daughter kidnapped by a rebel. How dare you hinder our pursuit!"

"Looks like a rebel has been after *you*," the swineherd said, squinting at the arrow. "He had a good aim, too. But if you're thinking on collecting that reward for Miss Cant, you best think again."

"My reward will come when she wears the baronial cap!" Orloff said. "She and the rebel have been trailed these past days by a pair of tinkers in my service, and I do not intend to let them escape me. Now hand over that meat or I will cut you down!"

Lucy squealed.

"I *told* you we were followed!" Pauline whispered.

"Be off with you!" the swineherd said. "You'll get no meat and no reward. The rebel girl is inside, and the little Baroness, too. I beat you to 'em, mister. That gold belongs to me."

Orloff looked into the hut.

"Stand aside!" he commanded. He pushed past the swineherd, but Delagraisse stepped into the doorway and Orloff drew up short. The Postal Commissioner towered over the under-footman.

"Who are these fellows, Pa?" Delagraisse said.

"What?" the swineherd asked.

"Out of my way, boy!" said Orloff, but Delagraisse stretched out his arms.

"You don't want to come in here, mister," he said. "Ma's got the pox real bad. She's all over covered with boils, and they say that's when it's most catching." He went on in a low voice. "Pa's not been right in the mind since a horse kicked his noggin, when he was helping the smith to put a shoe on."

"I'm not his pa!" protested the swineherd. The guardsman strode up beside Orloff and grasped the hilt of his sword.

"You hinder us at your peril, boy," he warned.

"Suit your own self," said Delagraisse, shrugging. "Mind she don't cough on you."

He let them pass. Orloff stooped under the lintel and walked warily towards the bed, as though he sensed a trap. The guardsman followed. Orloff reached down for the sheepskin but, before he could throw it back, Delagraisse sprang to the guardsman's side and pulled the sword from his scabbard. The man cried out, and blood stained his tunic where the steel had cut him. Delagraisse gaped at the crimson edge of the sword.

"I-I-I'm sorry!" he stammered.

"Put down that blade, boy," said Orloff, letting go the sheepskin. The guardsman, sucking air through his teeth, put his hands over the wound. Delagraisse backed against the table, holding his weapon at the ready, and the Commissioner slowly drew his own long sword from its sheath.

"Lucy Wickwright!" Orloff cried. "I urge you to surrender and spare your mistress the sight of your spilt blood. But if need be I will cut you down for your treachery, and for this foul dart I carry in my person!"

"He lied to me!" the swineherd said from the doorway. He pointed at Delagraisse. "He said he was the Postal Commissioner, and there was five gold pieces in it for me if I brought him the rebel girl!"

"*That's* the Commissioner of Posts, you witless gob!" shouted the guardsman, nodding towards Orloff. He held out a hand dripping with blood. "Fetch me your spear!"

The herdsman had left the weapon outside, for it was too long to keep within his hut. Orloff's lieutenant took it at the doorway and leveled its head at Delagraisse. Lucy threw back the sheepskin and jumped up.

"Don't hurt him!" she said. "I'll surrender!"

She spoke too late. The guardsman lunged at Delagraisse, who threw himself on to the table to avoid a pincushion's fate. The spear's blade struck a stone in the wall and the long shaft split in two. Lucy, leaping from the bed, was nearly struck by the spearhead.

The table fell to pieces under Delagraisse and he dropped the guardsman's sword. Vlad Orloff saw his chance. He lifted his blade to make a bloody end of the under-footman.

Pauline covered her eyes and screamed.

But instead of the sound of a cocoanut being split — which is how she imagined a cloven skull would sound — she heard only a *thunk!* and felt herself pelted with debris. Orloff's weapon had struck a roofbeam, and there it was firmly stuck. The Commissioner cursed, blinded by a rain of soil and small pebbles.

"You'll pay for that table!" the swineherd yelled at Delagraisse. He picked up the shaft of his spear, which was sharply pointed where the head had broken off. "I'll teach you to lie to me!" he said.

Lucy lunged for the guardsman's sword and with it struck the spear's shaft. Delagraisse, now without a weapon, grabbed his bag of postal seals and swung it at the guardsman's belly, dropping the man like a sack of wet toads. The swineherd backed away from Lucy.

"Now, now," he said. "Girls oughtn't to play with swords, that they oughtn't!"

"Come *on*, Pauline!" Lucy urged.

Pauline leapt up. She wished *she* had been quick-witted enough to capture a sword. She picked up instead the broken-off spearhead and, waving it fiercely, ran past Orloff out of the hut. The Commissioner lurched for her but his eyes were too full of dust and he tripped over his fallen comrade.

Delagraisse had already mounted one of the horses. Lucy found her knapsack by the swineherd's fire, put it on her back, and tossed the guardsman's sword on to the blazing coals.

Pauline quickly mounted the other steed. Its stirrups were set far too low and she was hampered by the spearhead, but she had taken years of riding lessons and was an expert horse-woman. She took up the reins and spurred the beast around, meaning to reach down and pull up Lucy behind her, as she had seen the fancy riders do when they performed for her father. To her disappointment, Lucy had already climbed up behind Delagraisse.

"All settled?" Lucy asked her. Pauline nodded.

"We're off!" said Delagraisse, lashing his mount with the reins. The under-footman most certainly was *not* an expert rider. He bounced in the saddle like a baby on its grandfather's knee, and Lucy was hard pressed to hold on.

You'd have been better served to ride with me, thought Pauline, galloping after them. Was Delagraisse going to tag along with them now, she wondered, breathing through his mouth and gobbling what little food they could find?

Abruptly she reined in her horse. They had escaped, but they would not get far without food. By now Delagraisse had thrown his arms around the horse's neck and the animal ran wildly down the slope, Lucy bouncing on its rump.

Pauline reined the horse around. The swineherd had gone into his hut to tend the guardsman's wound, and his bacon still sizzled over the fire. She spurred her mount to a gallop and slid her foot down into the stirrup.

Something long and heavy hung behind her, beating against her leg, but she ignored it. Gripping the saddle with one hand, she leaned out and aimed the spearhead. She had seen the fancy riders pick up rings just like this, hanging from their horses and scooping the rings from the ground.

But they had not to contend with Vlad Orloff, who now ran out from the hut. Pauline speared the bacon with a victorious *"Ha!"* but was nearly thrown when the horse reared up at the Postal Commissioner. Whatever had been beating against her leg fell from the saddlebag and exploded.

Pauline had never heard such a sound in the Barony — nor, indeed, had anyone. Orloff, the importer of chewing gum, was also the first Cantling to bring a firearm across the frontier. The maddened horse bolted at the noise, and only by desperately clutching its neck did Pauline keep from falling.

"Come back!" cried Orloff. "Miss Cant, come back!"

Pauline struggled to regain the saddle. The horse galloped in a long curve as she hoisted herself up by its reins, so that by the time she again found her seat she was nearly back to the hut. Orloff had picked up the musket and fired it at the faraway speck of Lucy and Delagraisse. He dropped the weapon and waved his arms as the horse bore down on him.

"Your Ladyship! Pauline! I beseech you in your mother's name!" he rasped, clutching his neck. The arrow must have grated painfully when he yelled. "Quit that accursed traitor and come with me! Lead your people, dear child! Hellion, stop! Hellion!"

The last words were shouted at the horse, which would have trampled him had he not jumped out of its way. Without the use of stirrups Pauline could hardly stay on the animal's back. It raced down the slope towards the stream, swift and uncontrollable, its reins as useless to her as lengths of fancy ribbon. Astonishingly, she still held the speared bacon.

The horse forded the water and she spurred it along the bank, downstream towards the bog. When the swineherd's hut was well behind her she stopped and put the steaming bacon into a saddlebag. The spearhead she slid into the musket's empty holster.

Her legs shook so that she could barely stand. Her pony, Charlemagne, was a well-bred and courtly pet, often adorned with ribbons and bells, his mane combed and plaited like the locks of a lady-in-waiting. How different was this sweating animal, under whose churning hoofs she might have been ground to sausage! With a pounding heart she led it down to water.

What sort of person named his horse Hellion? she wondered. While fixing the animal's stirrups she saw the answer, for her mount's tack was embossed with the arms of Vlad Orloff — *argent a bordure wavy sable a serpent vert.** He had first brought the scourge of gum to Cant, and now the musket's savage blast. What other poison lurked in those fangs?

**A green snake on a black-bordered silver shield.*

A few hours of daylight remained. Somewhere Lucy and De-lagraisse would be looking for her, unless — and she hardly dared think it — that horrible, villainous weapon had done them harm. But where in the wide realm of Cant could they be?

For although the realm was small — so small that on a globe of the world the Barony could scarcely be seen — it held abundant space for two girls to miss each other. And already, alone and lost on the verges of the Great Bog, Pauline missed Lucy very much indeed.

She mounted the horse and, taking a guess at Lucy's last di-rection, set off.

Chapter 7

A FLY ON THE WALL

Lemonjello had never seen a castle like Château Simone-Thierry, which owed more to fairybook drawings, he thought, than to military logic. Gay pennants fluttered from its elegant towers, and rose vines leaved the walls like perfumed invitations to scale them. The drawbridge was down, and no one challenged him when he rode Guinevere over it. Colorful ribbons of crêpe twined through the iron spikes of the portcullis.

A young man sat on a barrel where the gatehouse tunnel opened on to the ward. He leaned against the wall, legs crossed at the knee, and buffed his nails with a woolen pad. Only when Guinevere's shadow fell on his hands did he glance up at Lemonjello.

"Oh. Where did you come from?" he asked. He sounded put out.

"I c-come from Castle Cant," Lemonjello said. "I wish to speak to your master."

"Gaspard is certainly in demand!" The guard sighed, then pocketed his bit of wool and took a final glance at his nails. "You're the second visitor the Baronet has had today. Is it the fashion to ride sidesaddle in metropolitan Cant?"

"Er, no. I b-b-borrowed this mule."

"It's not a handsome animal."

"She's a splendid b-beast, I assure you."

"I like the saddle," the guard confessed, "but it could use some gilding or a bit of fancy tooling. Perhaps I shall introduce the fashion of sidesaddles in La Provence. You must let on it's the done thing at Castle Cant."

"Sidesaddles are no more c-common at Castle Cant than in the rest of the Barony," said Lemonjello. "Is Sir Gaspard in residence?"

"Oh, you're no fun," the guard complained. "You must simply *let on* they're the fashion. Then I'll have introduced the latest trend, don't you see? As for old thunderpants, Gaspard is holed up with the last scarecrow to blow across the drawbridge. Are you growing moustaches?"

Lemonjello blushed and touched his face.

"Er, yes. I was t-told they might become me," he admitted.

"I believe they shall," the guard said. "What's your name?"

"Thank you. I am Luigi Lemonjello, Chief Astronomer at the Celestial Observatory. Now, if you'll k-kindly announce me to the Baronet?"

"I'm Swanson," the guard said, holding up his hand. Lemonjello held it for a confused moment, like a man given a mutton chop by a passing stranger. Handshaking was not the done thing at Castle Cant, where curtseys and bows still reigned.

"A p-p-pleasure, I'm sure," he said. "Now if you'll announce me —"

"Aren't you listening?" Swanson said. "Gaspard's engaged. The *first* visitor from Castle Cant wasn't as nice as you, I must say. He cursed like a hound and all but drew his sword on me until I announced him. He had a nasty, squinty lieutenant with him as well, scowling like a black cloud. Simply beastly, both of them!"

"You say they were from Castle Cant?" Lemonjello asked. This guard was so odd in his manner that the astronomer could scarcely follow him. "When did they arrive? Was it by chance a man called Vladimir Orloff? I must —"

"Oh, do climb down from that saddle!" wailed Swanson. "My neck's out of joint, staring up at you like this! Come, we'll have a nice milk tea and you can tell me all the latest trends."

Lemonjello dismounted. The courtyard at Château Simone-Thierry was not like the bare, rocky ward of Castle Cant, where guardsmen marched in formation and horses raced around the Stone of Justice. Here the ward was laid out in formal gardens, with neat gravel paths running between hedges of box elder and flower beds alive with tulips. Courtiers walked gossiping down these paths and lovers flirted on stone benches.

Nor had Lemonjello ever seen so many bulging cheeks, for every mouth not flapping with gossip was busy with gum. And the gum purses! The courtiers of Castle Cant offered gum from elegant cases, but at Château Simone-Thierry the gum purse had reached grotesque heights of luxury. The astronomer frankly gaped at the gilded, bejewelled designs.

After a groom had led Guinevere away, Swanson took Lemonjello's arm and led him to the servants' hall. A jowly cook poured out two mugs of weak milk tea and, with these in hand, the young guard led Lemonjello to a drawing room in the castle keep.

"You rest here," he said, putting down the mugs on a table that looked almost too fragile to support them, "and I'll tell old nastypants's secretary that you desire an audience. Have you a calling card?"

"I'm afraid n-not."

"Are they out of fashion?"

"N-no, it's just that I —"

"Oh, no matter, I'm sure the page won't forget your name. It fairly rolls off the tongue. Lu-*ee*-gi Lemonjello," he pronounced, drawing out the syllables. "Sit tight. I shall return in a trice."

With that he was off, leaving the astronomer alone in a drawing room whose silk-draped walls rose thirty feet or more, to a ceiling so flowered and beribboned by plaster moldings that he felt dizzy to look at it, as though he hung by his ankles over a vast wedding cake. From a distant room came laughter and the plunking of a harpsichord.

Over the fireplace hung a full-length portrait of Esmeralda, Pauline von Cant's mother. She could not have been more than fourteen when the likeness was taken, and she looked much like her daughter, with pale skin, fair hair, and the air of having her choice of good things to eat. She was dressed as The

Huntress in a smock girt with rope, and her tongue-toed foot rested on the neck of a fallen bear.*

There was nothing of the dark Adolphus in Pauline, Lemonjello mused, and perhaps that — and his desire for a male heir — explained Lord Cant's puzzling lack of interest in his daughter. Lucy Wickwright, on the other hand, looked very much a Cant, and had inherited the Baron's poor eyesight with his black hair and busy toes. It was a wonder that the Loyalists could not see the likeness.

Swanson returned presently and flung himself on to a chair.

"Sir Gaspard begs the favor of your patience," he said. "His noble pantsiness is closeted with the earlier distinguished visitor, and will receive the distinguished scientist as soon as blah blah blah blah blah . . . You know the rest. Sit tight and wait your turn. Listen!" he said, leaning forward. "I've something to tell you that will positively make you spit your tea. Are you ready? I've decided to grow moustaches!"

"Er . . . indeed?" said Lemonjello.

"Isn't it *mad*? But the more I thought of introducing sidesaddles, the less I liked it. The prospect is delicious, naturally, but then there's the expense. You know the price of gum has all but doubled, so I can't trust these little court popinjays to bear the expense of copying me. So I decided upon the moustaches. *Anyone* can grow moustaches . . . even some of the ladies, if truth be told. You inspire me, Luigi."

---

*Cantlings whose second and third toes grew together were called tongue toed, while those with six toes to each foot were busy toed. The rest of the population (including all tinkers) was considered plain toed.

"Well I — er, that is —"

"Swanson!"

Lemonjello jumped. A man in the blue tunic of Gaspard's men-at-arms stood at the doorway. His face was red, and a silver fleur-de-lis clasp at his throat suggested that he considerably outranked Swanson, who hurriedly gulped his tea before standing to attention.

"Good morning, Captain," he said.

"Good *morning*?" squealed the captain, his face going from red to purple. "Do you know that the gates to this castle stand open and unguarded?"

"Oh, dear," said Swanson. "Did I not lower the portcullis?"

For a moment the captain merely sputtered, unable to speak, and Lemonjello feared that he might go from purple to blue and burst like an overripe grape. Instead, he charged across the drawing room and grabbed the young guardsman by his ear.

"When I have done thrashing you, your own mother won't know you!" he vowed, dragging the whimpering Swanson over the parquetry. It must have been a familiar scene, for a passing courtier scarcely lifted his eyebrows at it.

Left alone, Lemonjello finished his tea and then went to admire the hall Swanson had led him through earlier. This eight-sided chamber rose to a stained-glass cupola, and in each of the panels stood a woman representing one of the civilized arts — Husbandry, Commerce, Letters, and so on. The uplifted spear of Warfare blazed like a flame, and she carried by its hair the head of a foe, whose neck dripped blood like a necklace of garnets. A few busts on slender pedestals were all the décor.

As Lemonjello gazed up, a draught blew into the hall and slammed shut the door behind him. He heard voices and, glancing down a corridor, saw walking towards him a man who could only be Gaspard Simone-Thierry. The Baronet's eyes flashed angrily at a man in a travel-stained cape beside him, whose bandaged neck was pierced by an arrow.

The astronomer threw himself against a wall. He was too late! Vlad Orloff had arrived before him, and in seconds his rival would find him out. Lemonjello tried the drawing room door but found its latch had fallen on the inside. His only route of escape led down the corridor where Orloff walked with the Baronet.

The voices came nearer. Looking about, Lemonjello saw a chandelier's chain that vined up from a bracket on the wall. An agile man might climb it and hang unnoticed at the feet of the Lady of Letters, he thought, while Orloff and Gaspard passed below. He did not consider himself especially nimble, but in fair weather he climbed a long ladder every night to reach his telescope. He had no fear of heights. He spat on his hands, rubbed them briskly, and leapt up to grab the chain.

Had he been less in a hurry he might have seen the flaw in his plan. His weight pulled the chain off its bracket, and as the chandelier fell from its well-oiled pulley the astronomer flew up. By chance his boot caught the bracket, but now he had become the weak link in the chain, and only his grip kept the chandelier from plummeting to the floor. Lemonjello trembled as Gaspard and Orloff entered the hall.

"My master must understand the difficulties of tracking the

girls with so small a force," Orloff said. The Baronet, who walked a few steps ahead of him, turned and glared at his former servant.

"Difficulties!" he cried. "I should think you'll meet difficulties when you begin by letting a young girl steal your horse — and she the very child you meant to rescue! Will your own mount not come when you whistle, squire?"

Lemonjello's heart pounded. He had not seen Orloff since the uprising began and he stared aghast at the arrow stuck through his neck. The astronomer's foot slipped in his boot and the chandelier fell an inch.

"The beast was startled by the musket," said Orloff. "I am no longer young, master. My lieutenant had taken a wound from the pretender's bodyguard, and I could hardly carry on alone and on foot."

"So you begged a ride in a farmer's cart and came to me," scoffed Gaspard. "You've come down in the world, Vladimir. If you sink any lower you'll end as you started — a beggar in a tinker's caravan, telling fortunes and mending shoes."

"This palace, I remember, was not so grandly furnished when I begged the honor of serving you," Orloff said. "I thought I had given satisfaction."

"I should hope to have some reward for my charity when I take in a tinker boy — when I feed and clothe him, and provide him tutors and the means to rise in the world. Indeed you gave me satisfaction, Vladimir," said Gaspard. "But you were greedy. It is a vice of those not born to riches. You asked too much."

Orloff looked darkly at the old man. "You possessed only one treasure I valued," he said, "and that you denied me."

"You asked too much," the Baronet repeated. He stood at the center of the hall, directly under the chandelier. "Esmeralda was my great and only treasure, Vladimir — the one gem in an old iron crown. You might with justice have asked for half my lands, for indeed you made me rich beyond measure. But I could not give you my jewel. Not Esmeralda."

"How better she might have fared but for her father's pride!"

"Silence!" said Gaspard. His voice rang so loudly in the echoing hall that Lemonjello flinched. The chandelier swayed. The astronomer splayed his toes to their widest, but his foot seemed determined to slide out of the boot. How he wished he was busy toed!

"I will remain silent no more!" Orloff rasped. "Do you not know your daughter sickened and died from loathing of Lord Cant? Her own father had married her to a man she despised, and she must see her child bear the name she hated. Esmeralda died of grief."

"So she surely would have died married to a tinker grown mighty in his mind! Do you believe a woman born to the house of Simone-Thierry would be long content as a letter-carrier's wife?"

The blood rose in Orloff's face. He crossed the stone floor and drew up so near to Gaspard that his arrow nearly pricked the old man. Lemonjello trembled, and the chandelier's chain faintly rattled.

"You are a fool!" Orloff spat. "Who but Esmeralda insisted that I remain at Castle Cant? It was for your daughter's sake that I served that spiritless prince Adolphus, and for the sake of her child that I did not slay him outright after Esmeralda's death!"

The Baronet stood his ground, though Orloff towered over him. A link of the chain slipped through Lemonjello's fingers.

"By my foresight that child now bears the greatest name in the Barony," said Gaspard. "You of all people should know the value of names, *Vladimir*. Had I given you my daughter's hand, my grandchild would now be seeking her husband among the fat burghers of Tenesmus!"

"Miss Cant bears his Lordship's name," Orloff said, "and that is all her inheritance. She has not his twelve toes. She has not his black hair, or his weak, squinting eyes. Fool! Are you as blind as he was? Esmeralda gave herself to no man not of her choosing. From her wedding to her death she allowed him not even a kiss. Your granddaughter is no child of Adolphus!"

"Lies!" Gaspard shouted.

"Miss Cant's father still lives!"

"You lie!"

Gaspard might have struck Orloff but for an ominous sound from above. He looked up, and the blood drained from his face as the chandelier's chain rattled through its pulley. Lemonjello had lost his boot.

Only the Commissioner's quick action saved the Baronet from a grisly end. Orloff flung the old man out of the way and fell upon him. The chandelier crashed where they had stood an instant earlier, its wrought bronze crumpling like cheap tin, its glass chimneys exploding. The hall rang with Gaspard's screams.

Lemonjello plummeted on to a bust of Glenden Galt and then tumbled across the floor, the poet's marble nose skittering after him. He could not have made a more ruinous entrance, and as the luckless envoy rose to his feet he saw that the Baronet would not soon be entertaining his appeal on behalf of Lucy Wickwright.

Gaspard lay shrieking beneath Vlad Orloff, who a moment earlier had cursed him as a blind fool, and tears of thin, ghastly jelly ran from the Baronet's eye where the arrow's shaft had pierced it. The Commissioner of Posts, all unwitting, had brought a message from afar. The first dart loosed in the Chewing Gum Rebellion, at Lord Cant's funeral leagues away, had found another victim.

Chapter 8

Little Girl Lost

$\mathcal{P}$auline woke with a gasp and looked around her. The sun had climbed clear of the hills but fog hung over the stream by which she camped. Three days had passed since she parted from Lucy and Delagraisse. She was hopelessly lost.

"Hello?" she hoarsely called.

There was no answer but the sounds of the wild — birds chirping, insects buzzing, the stream whispering under its blanket of fog. Pauline wrapped herself in the horse blanket, for she was sore and cold, and then went down to the stream to splash water on her face. She tightened the braid of her hair and climbed back up the slope to where Hellion's saddle, bags, and bridle lay on a flat rock.

"I'm afraid it's bacon for breakfast again," she said, opening the saddlebag.

A sliver of bacon remained, hardly bigger than a glove-lace.

"No use a-slicing *that* piece o' bacon," she went on in a rustic accent. "Finish it off, milady. You must keep your strength. I'm sure as I can find a dandelion to chew as we go."

Pauline was not used to being alone, so to keep up her spirits she had begun playing this game of pretend. When she wanted a voice to cheer her she played the part of Mrs. Selvage, a faithful old servant who was helping her mistress (a spoiled but beautiful princess) to escape her enemies. She had to keep a brave face in this role, for the princess was a helpless creature, unused to such hardships.

Pauline dutifully ate the meat, though she hoped never to see bacon again. When she had finished she wiped her fingers on the blanket and shrilly whistled.

"Hi, Hellion!" she cried in her normal voice. "Hi! Hi!"

Pauline had wandered aimlessly in her search for Lucy and Delagraisse. She was no huntress. Towards the end of the first day she had decided that the wise strategy would be to climb to high ground and wait. After all, her companions would be looking for her as well, and they might miss each other forever if both parties were on the move. So she had spent the next day scanning the horizon from a hilltop and patiently training Hellion to come to her whistle.

On the third day her plan's meek logic gave way to a loud cry for action. The same idea might have occurred to Lucy, after all, who could be sitting on a hill somewhere waiting for *her*. Lucy might think Pauline had forsaken her. The thought so frightened Pauline that she mounted Hellion and rode as the ground led her, yelling herself hoarse in tearful fits of panic. The bacon would soon be gone, and then what would become of her? When she came to a stream she had already forded twice she jumped off the horse and fell sobbing to the ground, overcome by fear.

That was when Mrs. Selvage arrived.

"It's not as bad as all *that*, milady," the faithful servant had said. "We're in a jam pot and no mistake, but we'll come out smellin' like berries in the end. Wash away those tears, now, and I'll cut you a nice piece o' bacon. Things'll look brighter on a full belly, that they will."

And things *had* looked brighter when Pauline (in the role of the spoiled princess) obeyed the trustworthy servant. Now she played at being Mrs. Selvage whenever things got dark again. At such times it was much easier to *play* at being Mrs. Selvage than to *be* Pauline.

"Hellion!" she called again. "Hi! Hi!"

A chevron of geese honked overhead and, a moment later, splashed into a finger of the Great Bog. No matter how Pauline had steered yesterday the land had seemed to lead her bogwards. Every stream and rivulet drained that way. When she turned back she found her path blocked by hills or impassable brush.

"Hellion!" she cried.

She cupped her ear but heard no hoofbeats, only a distant belching of bullfrogs.

"Give another whistle, mistress," advised Mrs. Selvage.

Pauline put two fingers between her lips and blew mightily, but to no avail. Hellion had run off. She was alone, without food or mount, in the forsaken wilds of a land she had once been destined to rule. She went to the now-useless saddle and kicked it.

"You stupid horse!" she cried.

"There's no call for cussing," said Mrs. Selvage.

"There is *so!*" Pauline said, kicking the saddle again. "That stupid beast should be made into wigs and glue! How will I ever find Lucy now?"

"The poor animal may be lying somewhere with a broken leg," answered Mrs. Selvage. "It may be in a far worse pickle than you are, for all your tantrums. Have you thought of that?"

Pauline stopped kicking. The old servant had never taken that tone with the princess before. She ought to be angry, but in her heart she knew Mrs. Selvage was right. She was not in the castle anymore, where screaming and kicking brought a host of servants to her aid. She might scream till her lungs burst, yet Lucy would never hear her. She sat down heavily on the saddle.

"I want to go *home!*" she said, tears starting in her eyes. "I want Lucy!"

"Now, that's all right," said Mrs. Selvage. "You have a good cry, mistress, and I'll think of what to do. This Barony ain't so big that we can stay lost forever, though we may starve in the meantime."

So Pauline wept for some minutes, and then dried her eyes and listened to her servant's advice. One of the saddlebags might serve as a pack, Mrs. Selvage suggested, with straps made from the horse's bridle. Pauline used the swineherd's spearhead to cut the leather. There was enough of the reins left over to attach the musket's holster to the pack, so she might carry the spearhead as well.

She found Orloff's gum purse at the bottom of the saddlebag. It was not as crusted with jewels as many noblemen's purses, but it was of pure gold and she might trade it for food in some village. She touched with her thumb the monogrammed

$$\mathbb{V}$$

on its lid. With it she put the horse blanket, Orloff's canteen and matchbox, and a notebook in which the Commissioner had kept a log of his search for the fugitives. A typical entry read, *"Outlandish" shirt report'd No. of G. Pillow. Pies taken fr. windowsill. Sent Retsch.*

Mrs. Selvage suggested leaving a note, so that if Lucy and Delagraisse came upon the saddle they might know she had been there. Pauline sharpened Orloff's pencil on the spearhead and tore out a page of his notebook.

Dear Rosie [she wrote],

I am lost and without horse or bacon. This may be the end of me. If it is my lot to die, I shall go to the dust confident in my belief that our Burony will be wisely led after the awful Forces of Gum have been defeated.

If it is vouchsafed me to live, I will not rest until I have found you, dear

Rosie. I cannot dream of reaching our destination alone, so I intend to skirt the Great B. and come at last to the Bogway, where mayhap some kindly soul will help me in this my Hour of Need.

WE ARE BUT TWO POOR TINKER GIRLS, yet our devotion and "pluck" may, someday, be the Stuff of Legend. I take heart in the knowledge that we shall meet again, if only in the poet's Deathless Rhyme. Until then I remain

Your devoted
"Pooter"

Pauline sniffled. The plight of the lost tinker girl so touched her that she could almost believe she was real. She dared not use Lucy's name, of course, lest Vlad Orloff or some other enemy find the message and come after her. After reading it again to make sure she had not let slip any clues, she folded the note and put it into the remaining saddlebag. Then she hoisted the improvised knapsack, took her bearings, and set off in a direction she hoped was west.

She had never been good at directions. Even in the familiar halls of Castle Cant she often lost her way and had to yell until some passing servant or courtier came and led her to a known corridor. But Pauline had read enough poetry to know that the sun rose in the east — where the bards called it Aurora and praised it with exclamations thick as ears of wheat — so she simply put the sun behind her and followed her shadow westward. At noon she would rest, enjoy a meal of succulent leaves, and then follow the sun as it fell.

Mrs. Selvage spoke little that morning. The land bordering the Great Bog was all ridges and glens, and the stout servant was hard put to keep breath in her lungs, never mind talking. The princess, on the other hand, had all her life climbed towers and fenced and danced and sported in a hundred ways (just as Pauline had done), so the going was easier for her. Finding Mrs. Selvage in no mood to talk, she amused herself by making a rhyme as she went (for, like Pauline, the princess fancied herself a poetess).

A theme was as near as her belly, and her figures came readily. Only when she reached the last lines did she have to mumble and count upon her fingers — for snapping shut a poem was hard work, like closing a chest filled with too many toys. When she had finished, she ran out in front of her panting servant.

"I've written a new poem," she announced.

"Why, bless you, child!" said Mrs. Selvage, sitting heavily and wiping her brow. "You were always clever as a clock. Let us hear it while I rest my poor feet. I'm not a spring lamb to be running over hill and dale like your Ladyship."

"You must promise not to judge it too harshly," the princess said. It was the custom in Cant to protest before reciting a poem.

"I'm sure you'll do wonderfully," said Mrs. Selvage.

Pauline needed no further prodding. She tidied her hair as best she could, smoothed her blouse, and put her right hand behind her back (for she was a left-handed girl and never gestured with the right). "The Hungry Wanderer!" she proclaimed.

For stealing a drumstick from Turkey
The sultan decreed my fate:
To wander alone, without even a bone
Or a crumb of stale bread on my plate.

O, how I repented my thieving
And dreamt with despair untold
Of rabbits and geese that sizzled in Greece
While I wandered hungry and cold.

If black tea is brewing in China,
Then off to the East I must go,
For I'm dying of thirst and I'm hungry and — worst! —
I don't know where marshmallows grow.

"Splendid!" said Mrs. Selvage, clapping her hands together.

"It's only a trifle," Pauline said, blushing.

"Nonsense. That was a proper mouthful, it was." The old servant stood with a groan and glanced at the sun. "It'll be coming on for noon 'ere long. We must keep our eyes sharp for somewhat to eat, now that you put me in mind of it."

Pauline had been hungry since breakfast. She tried to eat any number of leaves but not one of them proved to be succulent. And like countless poets before her she found that rhymes, while pleasing to the ear, did nothing to quiet a rumbling belly. Noon came, but not so much as a berry appeared on her path. Then Pauline remembered Orloff's gum purse and, on impulse, took it from her pack.

There were half a dozen tablets of gum inside. She had always opposed chewing gum — for it made her ears pop — but her mouth watered at the sight of its sugary coating. It reminded her of the hard frosting Mr. Broom (her cook) had put on filberts. Mrs. Selvage urged against it, but food was food as far as the princess was concerned. She put a tablet on her tongue.

"Now you've done it," sighed the servant.

"It's just to see me through," the princess replied.

The sugar did not fill her belly, but she chewed for the sake of chewing. After another hour's hiking she sat on a rock and let the knapsack fall from her back. The day had turned hot and her blouse was stuck to her skin.

"I'm *hungry!*" she moaned.

"I wouldn't say no to a nice bun," admitted Mrs. Selvage.

"I wouldn't say no to a boiled *skunk*," said Pauline. "You might boil it with coffin nails and old bandages and I'd *still* eat it — and finish with a cocoanut pudding!"

Pauline hated cocoanut.

"Let's hope it doesn't come to that, milady," said Mrs. Selvage. "Here, why don't you walk down by the water and find a bird's nest? A roasted egg'll set easier on your belly than boilt skunk, I dare say."

A watery tongue of the Great Bog glittered nearby. Pauline hiked towards it until the ground squished underfoot, all the while hacking through bulrushes and cattails with her spearhead. Her feet sank inches in the ground and left a string of boot-shaped puddles. The going was hard and she did not even pretend that Mrs. Selvage could follow in her button shoes. Often the water nearly overtopped Pauline's boots. The sun beat down and mites swarmed around her face.

Where were the birds' nests? Sweat pooled in her eyes and stung them, and when at last she found a duck's nest it held only broken shells. She saw chicks paddling after their mothers on the bog and realized that the time for eggs was past.

If the ground had been less soggy she might have sat down and cried. She stood among the cattails, legs shaking, and remembered the feasts where her father had sucked clean the bones of rabbits and geese, feasts that threatened to make her burst. With a sated hand she had waved away elaborate puddings and ten-storey trifles. If only her Papa had not died!

While she chewed on these despairing thoughts something plopped at her feet. A huge frog had jumped from the cattails and sat there puffing out its jowls. Pauline froze. She held the spearhead in her hand. The frog's legs were sleek and fat, and the frog was stupid with the sun, no doubt full of gnats and ready for its midday nap.

Very slowly, Pauline lifted the spearhead. She gripped the haft in both hands, sweat dripping from her palms. A bead of it slid down the spearhead and hung on the point like a jewel. Before it could fall and warn the frog, Pauline struck.

The resulting picture might have served as a plate in *Flora & Fauna of Cant*, for it was a textbook example of frog-sticking. The beast did not even quiver. The steel had gone through it like a draught of wine down a merchant's throat. Pauline looked for someone to witness this astonishing feat. If only Lucy could see! She had gone out with a spear and found food — a huntress!

She raced up the ridge with the frog held aloft, its legs flapping like a victorious pennant. Mrs. Selvage danced. Pauline unspeared the animal and, spying a nearby stand of hawthorns, gathered a bundle of dead wood for a fire.

When it came to preparing the frog's legs, however, she hesitated. Pauline had never gone into the kitchens of Castle Cant except on some whim or the other, and certainly she had done no cooking in them. She had never buttered her own toast. She laid the animal on its back and held the spearhead over it. It looked awfully like a dead frog.

"Here, let me do that, mistress," said Mrs. Selvage, and she hacked the frog without further ado, twisting its leg to sever the joint. "Nothing easier than frog's legs," she said, peeling back the skin. "Just chop 'em off and take away anything that don't look like dinner."

It was a paltry meal but it seemed a feast to Pauline. All it wanted was a pudding. She had surely earned the comfort of a sweet, she thought, so she took out Orloff's gum purse and chewed another piece. It made her ears pop awfully, but the sugar more than made it up. Worn out by her labors, she slept.

The sky was dark with clouds when she woke, but the meal of frog put some jump into her step and she made a good pace, hiking along the foot of a cliff that led steadily north-westwards.* The wind at her back smelled of rain. The path between the cliff and the bog narrowed as she walked, and

---

*This geographical feature was the site of a battle memorialized in Glenden Galt's historical ode, Threnody with Watercress. A stone marker on the cliff was toppled by failed republican putschists during the reign of Elvio, Lord Cant's grandfather.

when the rain came it churned up a terrific stench of rot from the water. A taste of charred frog climbed Pauline's throat. She might have been ill had she not chewed another tablet of gum.

"It'll grow dark soon," warned Mrs. Selvage.

Pauline pressed on, guided by the bolts that flashed from cloud to cloud. The rain fell harder, and she looked for a hole in the stone wall or even a boulder to rest under, but there was no place to hide. Ahead the ground rose steeply where a rock-fall had fractured the cliff. She decided to climb as high as she could and settle in for the night. Better to be struck by lightning, she thought, than to remain a prey to the sullen creatures of the bog, that might choke her with putrid slime or tear her limb from limb.

She climbed on her hands and knees, twice slipping on loose stones and tumbling all the way back down. Her shoulders ached under the heavy pack, and her clothes were torn. When at last she reached the summit she took out the horse blanket and sheltered under it.

Looking out, Pauline fancied she saw a light in the distance. Some isolated cottager, perhaps, was cooking porridge over a homely fire. Maybe Lucy had gone this way before and now sheltered in a woodchopper's hut, where she gazed forlornly into the storm, not knowing whether her sister lived or died. Yes, there — it was certainly a light!

Pauline plunged down the slope. Even if Lucy was not there, how much better to sleep in a warm cottage than to sit soaked to the skin under a wet blanket! She tripped and tumbled down in an avalanche of pebbles. The ground was spongy and yielding where she landed, and covered by some thorny vine that cut her hands. The blanket wound about her like a shroud.

She struck out for firmer ground but the vine snared her legs, and she remembered those tales of leech gatherers who sank in the bog, their bodies dug up generations later by peat cutters, preserved like wasps in jam.

Finally Pauline reached the foot of the cliff, but the water she poured from her boots there fell with a sound like mocking laughter. The blanket was soaked with mud, but she tied it over her head and pressed on. The bog had gripped her in its thorny claws, resenting her trespassing, her murder of one of its own. It wanted revenge.

She walked blindly, her hand on the face of the cliff. The cottage — if it was a cottage — seemed farther away than she had imagined, but the light led her on. She must get away from the bog!

When a frog belched near her feet Pauline threw off all caution, ran into the darkness, and pitched headlong into the bog. It was not deep but she screamed with fright, and the bog water, full of mud and putrid scum, filled her mouth and nose. Somewhere a hound forlornly wailed, and then lightning struck and showed frogs all around her. They moved forward in their ranks like the troops of an army, slimy and fat with malice. Pauline splashed to shore and the beasts threw themselves at her boots. She stumbled on, crushing them underfoot.

There! There was the light, which had seemed so far away. Now it was terribly near.

Alas! the light came from no homely cottage, but swung in the grip of a dreadful hand. The Great Bog had delivered

Pauline to its mistress. The lamp was borne by the drover of the frogs, their undying empress. Pauline walked to the flame as one enchanted, though the night dread of all Cantlings howled within her. The frogs screamed in the ecstacy of thralls. The ghastly crone grinned, and Pauline fell as one dead at the feet of the Bogwife.

Chapter 9

Interview with the Baronet

$\mathcal{L}$emonjello's prison looked over the gardens of Château Simone-Thierry. He slept on a straw mattress and was even given books to read, but he was not allowed a candle lest he set his cell ablaze. So when the sun went down he had ample time to reflect on what he had seen and heard as he hung from the chandelier's chain.

In those very gardens, perhaps, Orloff had courted Esmeralda. It was a disturbing thought, but the Commissioner's claims fitted so well with what Lemonjello knew, and explained so much that had puzzled him, that he could only believe they were true. Orloff's foul deeds sprang from thwarted love!

As he pondered this a torch threw its light on the wall, and keys jangled at the door. Two guards entered the cell. Bronze helmets hid their faces, and their eyes glittered under the cold masks, like worms in hollow skulls. One man held a pair of manacles.

"Hands out," said the other. "Sir Gaspard wants a word with you."

They led the prisoner down a covered walk to the castle keep. The Baronet received him in a drawing room hung with red curtains, where he lay under bearskins on a divan. An eye-patch, embroidered with a fleur-de-lis in white silk floss, hid his wound. It unnerved Lemonjello to look on that fanciful design while Gaspard's remaining eye fixed him in its gaze.

"You have a lively imagination, Mr. Lemonjello," said the Baronet, holding up several sheets of foolscap closely written in the astronomer's hand. "Your account of the goings on at Castle Cant is very entertaining, if not especially instructive."

Lemonjello had spent a day composing this manuscript — his "confession," as it was called. He did not respond at once to Gaspard's words but knelt on the thick carpet and bowed his head nearly to the floor.

"I was p-pleased to learn you suffered no fatal harm, sir," he said. "M-m-may I express my deepest regret regarding the in-fortunate uncident — er, I mean to say the unfortudent inci-nate — that is, the infuncinate accidunt —"

"Cease your groveling!" commanded Gaspard. He clicked his fingers at a footman, who approached and held to his master's lips a spoon such as the envoy from Castle Cant had never before seen. A hinged lid covered its bowl, and at the touch of a lever it opened to accept the nobleman's spent chewing gum. The footman snapped shut the spoon and carried the un-sightly cud to a pail by the fireplace.

"I spent much of yesterday in closet with Squire Orloff," Gaspard went on. "I cannot blame him for this infirmity. Indeed, his quick action saved my life. He tells me you are a kidnapper as well as a spy."

"A k-kidnapper! But — but — but! —"

"Silence! I have read your account of 'rescuing' my Pauline," Gaspard said. "A fine romantic tale! A known friend of the Causists would have me believe he is my granddaughter's savior — after he has abducted the child and sent her into the wilds with a Causist pretender."

"Sir, Lucy Wickwright is no pretender!" said Lemonjello. "Lord Cant confessed she was his daughter upon his d-deathbed. It was to save Miss Cant from exile that Lucy and I —"

"Squire Orloff has explained to me," Gaspard interrupted, "that at the time of her father's death, when Pauline was mad with grief, this Wickwright creature filled her head with such lies. I shall correct the girl when she is rescued from the rebel's clutches."

"But sir, even if Lucy Wickwright were not the Baron's child — and I assure you she is — Miss Cant cannot claim the baronial c-c-cap."

"What are you talking about?" said Gaspard.

"Why — why . . . begging your pardon, sir . . . Commissioner Orloff himself has confessed that Miss Cant is not the child of Adolphus's flesh. She cannot claim the barony!"

Gaspard flipped the pages of Lemonjello's confession, his one eye squinting.

"What new nonsense is this?" he asked. "I don't recall reading that here."

For a moment the astronomer could only gape at him.

"S-sir!" he finally said. "The Commissioner confessed! I was present at the time!"

The Baronet eyed him coldly.

"And you expect me to believe the word of a known spy?"

"But — but — but! —"

"You were caught in the act!"

"But — but *you* were there! Respectfully, sir! *You* heard him confess to it!"

"So say you!" Gaspard replied. "An admitted collaborator with Causists. A confessed abductor of little girls! Am I to believe the word of such a man?"

Lemonjello could almost believe he was the victim of an elaborate joke. He looked to the footman, but did not catch him smiling. The mouths of the guards were as hard and indifferent as their helmets.

"Sir," he tried again, "even if I had b-been spying, it would not change what Orloff said. The *Commissioner* wasn't spying. *You* weren't spying. What was said, sir, is what was said, no m-matter who reports it. Surely you see that?"

"You may twist words all you wish," said Gaspard, "but the truth remains that you were caught spying. How can you deny it? I saw you with my own eyes — and at that time I had two of them!"

"I d-don't *deny* I was spying — er, that is, I *do*, but that's not my point!"

"It is certainly mine!"

"Yes, but — but the subject at hand was your granddaughter. Miss Pauline von Cant. Vladimir Orloff claims she is no child of Lord Cant. She c-cannot inherit the baronial cap if she is not in truth the Baron's child."

"Coal!" said Gaspard. The footman added another brick to the fire, and another servant changed the warming dish at the Baronet's feet. Lemonjello was quite hot. The Baronet had called for coal, he suspected, merely to make him sweat.

"You call yourself a scientist," said Gaspard. "Your study is facts, and you believe that 'truth' is a thing that awaits your discovery of it. But I am a prince. My study is humanity. The prince knows that truth is simply what has *won*. When the history of these times is written, Mr. Lemonjello, Lucy Wickwright will be reviled as a pretender, and your own name will scarcely merit a footnote. History shall celebrate a great and glorious epoch of our Barony under Lady Pauline von Cant and her regent, Vladimir Orloff."

"What!" cried Lemonjello. He scarcely believed his ears. "But — but he betrayed you!"

"I am a forgiving man. Except in the case of spies."

"But Orloff is vile!" said the astronomer. He pointed to his confession. "Have you not read that he killed Casio Wickwright, a mere child, and Lucy's parents as well?"

The Baronet gazed at Lemonjello. His eye was scaly, unblinking. Almost it seemed that his feeling was expressed not through that organ but through the patch covering his wound, with its cold white silken device, the symbol of his line and his ambition.

"Vladimir has in some ways been a disappointment to me," he said, "but in dark times the foe of my foe is my friend. The gum trade is of vital importance, and I will not see it threatened by Causist blackguards."

"But, but it's an outlandish luxury," said Lemonjello. A bead of sweat crawled with madding slowness down his face. "The people are far too burdened by tithes. They cannot support it!"

A gleam came into the Baronet's eye. He threw back the bearskin, and a footman hurried to put a pillow behind his back. Gaspard beckoned the astronomer to come closer.

"You call yourself a scientist," he said. "I too am an amateur of science, in a small way. Have you considered the remarkable character of gum, Mr. Lemonjello? I have made a study of it. Its skin or shell is simply sugar, flavored with some oil or essence. This dissolves and leaves behind the inner meat, which may be chewed for hours without losing its substance.

"When the sweetness has worn off," Gaspard continued, "what remains is utterly lacking in flavor. But it is also indestructible. My steward once kept a girl on staff whose sole duty was to scrape the stuff from the bottoms of chairs and tables. When I considered its properties, I gave orders that chewed gum should henceforth be collected in pails, such as you see by the fire. The gum-meat, after all, serves only to carry sugar to the mouth. Why could not it be used for that purpose a second time? Or, for that matter, a third or a fourth?"

"But – but – but . . . you can't mean —"

The Baronet's lips turned up in a dreadful smile.

"I am not deaf to the people's hardships," he said. "Indeed, under my granddaughter's rule their burdens shall be lifted. By making use of the spent gum-meat, we shall reduce the cost of gum to the nobles, who will then have no cause to increase their rents and tithes. Vladimir saw at once the wisdom of my plan. He has left for the Vale of Kandu, there to arrange matters at the gum plant."

"But this is madness!" Lemonjello cried.

"A new day dawns, Mr. Lemonjello," said the Baronet. "While Vladimir works in Kandu, I shall muster my swords, and upon his return we shall lay siege to Castle Cant and put down the rebels forever. Guard!"

"And what of Lucy Wickwright?" Lemonjello pleaded.

"The girls will be found. I have prepared a broadside offering fifty guilders' reward for Pauline's safe return to me. Her kidnapper shall spend the rest of her days in the dungeons of Castle Cant, the fate of all pretenders. You shall join her there when I can spare men to escort you. In the meantime, I trust you will enjoy my little birdcage. Take him away!"

He snapped his fingers, and the guards dragged Lemonjello from the room. How long before Lucy and Miss Cant arrived? he wondered. He had not mentioned their destination in his report — his spying had brought that good result — but still they were coming, and he could not warn them off while caged like a bird in the Baronet's garden. As an envoy he was worse than useless.

The guards, perhaps longing for air in their stifling helmets, led him to the gatehouse by way of the ward. Blue and red lanterns hung from poles, and between them the stars shone cold and white. Young ladies danced with ribbons in celebration of the Shearing Festival, watched by hungry-cheeked young men, and fat courtiers who gnawed the bones of chops.

The guards and their prisoner entered the gatehouse and went up a broad stair. On the second landing one of Lemonjello's escorts fell behind, and the astronomer was startled to see him take a knob-headed mace from a suit of armor. The noise alerted the other guard, who stopped. The man with the weapon approached him.

"Here, what are you about?" the other guard asked.

In answer his comrade swung the mace down on his helmet with a tremendous *CHANK!* The guard swayed like a tree after the fatal blow of an axe, then toppled backwards, his helmet bouncing *clank-CLANK! clank-CLANK!* as he slid down to the landing. Lemonjello cowered at the feet of the attacker. He had thought the blow was meant for him.

"Goodness, you *are* a scaredy-pants!" the guard exclaimed. "How did you ever get to be a spy? Spies are supposed to be chesty and brave and so forth. You're like a little girl!"

"Swanson?" said Lemonjello.

"At your service," Swanson said, taking off his helmet. "O, I hate these things! I'm sure my hair looks like grass in a hailstorm. You don't suppose I've killed Charles, do you?"

Lemonjello looked at the fallen guard.

"He seems to b-be breathing."

"That's all right, then. I wasn't certain how hard to *strike*, you know? They never taught us how to knock out a man in training camp. It was always 'Kill! Kill! Kill!' So in the end I just hit him as hard as I could."

"It appears to have b-been the correct strategy."

"Thanks. It felt good, I must say. Charles was a bit of a bully, frankly, always barking and shouting and scaring the new recruits. I used to call him Sir Manley Strideforth to tease him. He's not barking now!"

"Er, no."

"Shall we escape, then?"

"What!"

Swanson looked perplexed.

"You *do* want to escape, Luigi?"

"Why — why *yes*, but — but — but —"

"Well come along then, before old pepper-pants wakes up and raises the alarum." Swanson took a key from his pocket and unlocked the astronomer's manacles, leaving them and his helmet on the stairs. Taking up a lamp that burned on the landing, he led Lemonjello down an arched passage. "I've packed a few things and saddled Guinevere," he said. "She *is* a sweetheart, Luigi. I'm sorry I ever said a word against her."

Lemonjello felt quite in the dark.

"When you say 'Shall we escape?' do you mean to say . . . *we?*" he asked. "P-plural? The two of us?"

"That is the meaning of *we*, I'm told."

"Well, yes. But — but why do *you* want to escape, Swanson?"

Swanson took the astronomer to a brattice overhanging the moat and put down the lamp in a loophole. He seemed hesitant to speak. He twisted the hem of his tunic.

"Luigi," he said, "is it true that you know Miss Cant?"

"Why, certainly," said Lemonjello. "She used to look through my t-telescope."

"You lucky man, I *hate* you! Is she as beautiful as they say?"

"Er — ah —," stammered the astronomer. "As beautiful as *who* says?"

"Why, everyone!" Swanson said. He took a wallet from his tunic and, opening it by the lamp, unfolded a square of paper.

It was Pauline von Cant's birthday portrait. Every year before his death, Lord Cant and Pauline had had their likenesses taken by an engraver. The prints were sent to all corners of the Barony so that, for the price of a shilling, all the Baron's subjects might admire their ruler and his heiress. Lemonjello read the familiar caption:

THE ADORED & HON'BLE PAULINE VON CANT

"She is a *dream!*" sighed Swanson.

Lemonjello thought of Miss Cant's pastime of sliding down the coal chute, and of her many whims (such as inflating a pig's bladder in a roast goose so that the bird exploded when the serving man began to carve it), and her tantrums of such magnificence that — even across the distance of the ward and from the height of a tower — the sound of shattering teacups sent chills up his neck.

"Miss Cant is a high-spirited young lady," he murmured.

"A *dream!*" Swanson repeated. "May I confide in you, Luigi? I know I can. I felt there was a bond between us the moment you rode up to my post. The truth is, I never wanted to be a guard. Since I was a boy I've dreamt of moving to metropolitan Cant and being a dressmaker!"

The astronomer blinked rapidly several times.

"I'm sure it is a n-noble ambition, but —"

"We're *years* behind the fashion in La Provence!" Swanson wailed. "It's inhuman! When this wretched war is over you must introduce me to Miss Cant. You see how they've stuffed her into that horrid bodice?" He held up the engraving and shook it. "Why, it doesn't suit her at all! She wants ruffled sleeves and a pannier gown! Oh, *do* take me with you, Luigi! I want to dress Pauline von Cant!"

The astronomer hardly knew how to answer.

"Er . . . shall we make our escape, then?" he asked.

"You *will* take me with you? Come, then, let us off!"

Swanson put the lamp on the floor and lifted the iron ring of a trapdoor. Stars twinkled in the moat below. Lemonjello was not afraid of heights, but neither was he fond of falling from them. He judged the drop to be about three fathoms.

"You have a rope, of c-course?" he asked.

"No, we'll have to jump for it," said Swanson. "Don't worry, the water's quite deep."

"I see. Shall I go first?"

"Luigi," Swanson gravely said.

"Yes?"

"Aren't you going to say anything?" Swanson asked.

"Er . . . hurrah? Long live the Baroness?"

"No, you awful beast. Don't you notice anything?"

He held up the lamp and Lemonjello peered intently at his face. A down of fine hairs covered the young guardsman's lip.

"Are you g-growing moustaches?" asked the astronomer.

"Isn't it a lark?" squealed Swanson. "We shall look a pair of dashing highwaymen!"

Before Lemonjello could reply, a voice called from the gatehouse.

"Ho!" it said. "Who goes there?"

Swanson sucked in his breath.

"It seems they're on to us!" he hissed. "I was rather loud!"

"Yes!"

"Off you go, then. I'll be right behind you!"

"Yes!" said Lemonjello. He dangled his feet through the hatch and looked down at the glimmering water. Lucy Wickwright, he recalled, had jumped from a much greater height into the moat of Castle Cant after she recovered the Causist manifesto. But Lucy was a much braver soul than he.

Footsteps approached. Lucy must be warned away from La Provence, and once again the astronomer was the only man for the job. Swanson put out the lamp. Lemonjello steeled himself against the shock of cold water, and dropped into the shimmering stars.

Chapter 10

Lillian Fungwich

*P*auline's funeral was a tawdry affair. The woolen shroud scratched her and the coffin pitched as though its bearers had been recruited from the stumbling tosspots of a tavern. She would be thrown into a shallow grave, her bones turned out of the coffin so that another poor child might use it after her, as countless others had done before.

She willed herself to wake. If a single tantrum remained in her marrow-bones she would spend it to protest this treatment. She belonged in the marble vaults of Castle Cant, not among the unmourned bones of the paupers' field! But when her eyelids fluttered open she realized she had dreamed her funeral. The Bogwife's lantern swung from the coffin's lid. The old crone was not done with her yet.

Pauline lurched up. She rode in a covered wagon filled with

jars and cages and the smell of drying herbs. A cat dozed in a basket at her feet. Pulling aside a curtain at the back, she saw Hellion following at the end of a rope. She had never heard of the Bogwife's traveling in broad daylight, or beyond the Great Bog. Evidently she had been captured by a horse thief.

It would have been the work of an instant to loose the rope, mount Hellion, and escape, but her captor had thwarted that chance by taking her clothes. Pauline could ride bareback, but she drew a line at galloping through Cant without a stitch on herself. She let fall the curtain and found an old smock hanging from a peg. It was too short for riding, but it answered the needs of modesty.

The jars held roots, or ribbons of fragrant bark, or nothing at all, but in one she found a dozen purple truffles, a prized delicacy of Cant. She brushed the soil from a large one and ate it. Further searching uncovered her knapsack and spearhead. With her belly filled and a weapon at hand she felt she could face even the Bogwife, so she pushed aside the curtain and called out the back of the wagon.

"Ho!" she said.

"Ah, she's woke up," a woman said. "Took her dear time about it."

"Who goes there?" Pauline asked.

"Listen at her. She thinks she's a knight o' the realm."

Pauline did not like this woman's tone. She climbed up the back of the wagon, still clutching the spearhead, and looked out over the roof. The driver had tucked her hair into her bonnet, and her exposed neck was sunburnt and scrawny. A lop-eared hound sat beside her.

"Answer me!" Pauline insisted. "Who are you, and where are you taking me?"

"I could hear the dear thing better," the woman confided to the hound, "if she'd quit her caterwauling and say how-do-ye-do. A little lamb oughtn't to roar like a great big bear. It ain't natural."

Grumbling, Pauline crawled over the roof and sat beside the hound.

"Good morning!" she said curtly.

The old woman glanced at the spearhead and smirked. Pale whiskers glinted at the corners of her mouth, but she had no wart at the end of her nose, so Pauline knew she could not be the Bogwife. She wore a knitted shawl, and her face was so lined by the elements that she seemed the carved figurehead of a ship, draped with a shawl of seaweed.

Her hound turned its muzzle to Pauline. It sniffed the air curiously, then pressed its wet nose to hers and licked her mouth.

"Uck!" Pauline said, pushing the beast away.

"Been at my truffles, has she?" the woman asked. "Well, I call that a fine return of my charity! If I'd known she was a thief I'd a-left her lying in the rain and mud."

"I was hungry!" said Pauline.

"She was hungry, she tells us!"

"Yes, I was! And you've no right to talk of thieving after stealing my horse!"

"Stealing!" cried the old woman. "Why, I've never been so beset and insulted, Roto! You treat people nice and they turn about and spit in your eye. Enough to make you sick, it is."

She turned and spat a string of brown juice over the side of the wagon. (Chewing seeds or flavorsome bark was common among Cantlings of the lower orders, though it was considered uncouth and bestial by the gum-chewing nobles.)

"You haven't told me your name, child," she said. "Did your ma never teach you manners in your life?"

"She did not!" Pauline answered hotly (for her mother had died when she was one year old). "I'm a common little orphan and I does as I please! My name is Clementine Violetta de Gama Ortiz, but —"

"But your friends call you Pooter," the woman supplied. "And if that's what your friends call you," she added, "I'd hate to hear what your enemies say. Very likely it would curl my ears."

Pauline's grip tightened on the spearhead.

"How do you know my name?" she demanded.

"Ha! Maybe I'm a witch, my darling."

"Someone has told you! You're a friend to that swineherd!"

"Swineherd!" scoffed her captor. "When has a tinker and a herdsman ever been friends, I'd like to know? They'll ring wedding bells for a wolf and a sheepdog before that happens!"

"You've spoken with him, at least," Pauline insisted. "You must have done. I've given my name to no one else."

"Is that so? A big girl like you, and only one drover knows your name?"

"Of course not!" said Pauline. "That's not what I meant!"

"You meant he's the only one what knows you as 'Clementine' and all the rest of it," said the tinker, "but there's more than him as knows who you be, my sweet peach. You're known the length and breadth of Cant, I daresay."

A cold sweat broke out on Pauline's brow. If the old woman had talked to the swineherd, she must know her true identity, for the herdsman had learned it from Orloff. Or perhaps she had met Orloff himself and now scouted for him, as Marci and Sammy had done. A poor tinker would not turn up her nose at five gold pieces.

So be it, thought Pauline. She would teach the old crow to respect the house of Cant!

"Enough of these games!" she said, brandishing the spearhead. "I've not come through dungeons and bogs to bandy words with a horse thief! I am Pauline von Cant! I ask you again — who are you, and where are you taking me?"

The old woman cackled.

"I liked you better as 'Pooter,' my darling," she said. "As to where I'm a-taking you, I'm taking you with me, unless you care to run off half-naked and barefoot as a goat, with nothing but that broken-off toothpick to fend off the wolves. I am Lillian Lungwich, Miss Cant, but you may call me Lil."*

Pauline was in no mood to be familiar. The truffle sat badly on her stomach.

"I shall call you Mrs. Lungwich if I must call you anything," she snapped.

"As you please."

"I demand that you direct this wagon to the Bogway."

"And who put you in charge?" asked the tinker. "I'm about getting tired of your sass, Miss Pooter. Why, if you was my kid I'd spank your butt all the way to River Leech, I would!"

---

*"Lungwich" is pronounced "lung-itch" in the dialect of western Haslet March.

"If I were a tinker's child I'd jump in it!" said Pauline. The hound, as though wanting no part of the conversation, jumped to the wagon's roof and stretched out in the sun. Pauline wiped sweat from her brow. Somehow the mention of the river had made her seasick. "I *insist* that you take me to the Bogway," she added.

"Pah! You can't give me orders, little princess," said Lil. "Indeed, after meeting you, I fancy I'll bend my knee to that Wickwright girl. She won't offer to boss me around like a maid-of-all-work!"

The wagon abruptly lurched. For three days Pauline had eaten nothing but cold bacon, scorched frog, and a newly unearthed whole truffle. She was not a delicate girl, but that diet would have tried a stomach of iron, so she leaned out now and spewed her breakfast over the side of the wagon. Too late she saw that Lil had hung her clothes there to dry.

"Must've been some bile in the wee thing's belly!" Lil cried to her hound, who covered his muzzle with a paw. "No wonder she was so sassy! Here," she said, taking a wineskin from under the board. "Swish some 'o that over your choppers. Mind you don't put your lips to it!"

Pauline uncorked the nozzle. She had drunk from wineskins before — on "rustic" picnics with other folk from the castle — but the tinker's skin held no pale mead of the country. The liquor burned like a hot coal and she at once coughed it out. Lillian Lungwich roared.

"That's the true poteen!" she said. "It'll burn a hole right through ye!"*

---

*Poteen: a colorless beverage unlawfully distilled by tinkers.

Pauline's eyes filled with tears. The poteen's vapor scorched her nose, and the drop she swallowed burned down her throat like melted wax. When it hit her belly she felt she must be ill again. Lil took back the wineskin and handed her a coarse sack in its stead.

"I expect raw truffle is too rich for a little lady's belly," she said. "Nibble a bit of soda bread and see if that don't put you right."

"I was never made ill from a truffle!" gasped Pauline. She felt dreadful but she would not admit to being a "little lady." "I had nothing to eat yesterday but bacon and two frog's legs — that is, the two legs of one frog. It must have been a poisonous breed."

"I wonder you didn't make a supper of cattails, as you were hard against the bog."

Pauline broke off and chewed a piece of soda bread. It was hard as cork.

"Are cattails good to eat?" she mumbled.

"Good to eat?" cried Lil. "Why, you walked through the tinkers' greengrocer and came out starving!" She laughed merrily. "A body needn't ever go hungry as long as cattails grow in Cant!"

"I didn't know!" wailed Pauline. "Lucy — that is, my friend Rosie, has the guidebook. Please, missus," she added miserably, "won't you tell me where you're taking me?"

"Sh!" said Lil, pointing up the road. "Don't be giving away any names now, my sweet. Here's the constable upon us. You keep shut your mouth and let old Lil do the talking. And put away that toothpick!"

Pauline did not want trouble from a lawman. A lap rug lay under the riding board and she hurriedly hid the spearhead within its folds. The rug was wonderfully soft and fine — indeed, too fine for a tinker's cart, she thought — and on looking closer she saw it was her own mourning dress, which she and Lucy had carried in their pack.

So that was how the tinker knew her name! She had found Lucy. Perhaps she had already collected a reward for her from Orloff and now — the double-dealing crone! — she meant to sell Pauline to the rebels. When the constable had gone away, Pauline vowed, she would demand answers from Lil — at the point of the spearhead, if need be.

The lawman rode a bay mare and wore a badge sewn with the arms of the local gentry. Pauline recognized the rush-and-badger emblem of Lady Harpen-Hasten, Baronette of Bogside. She must have hiked farther last night than she knew.

"A word with you, Lil!" he said.

Lil cried "Whoa!" to her mule. Roto growled at the lawman.

"What a delight to see you, Jack!" said Lil. "And ain't it a grand morning in Cant?"

The constable rode by this hello without a word. He looked closely at Hellion, stroking the horse's coat and then sniffing his fingers. He used his sword to push aside the curtain at the back of the wagon. Pauline heard the cat's hissing.

"Is there something you're a-looking for?" Lil asked.

"Whose horse is this?" the constable demanded.

"Why, it's mine! You know old Lil does a little horse trading."

"Aye, and she does a little horse thieving, as well," the lawman replied. He rode back to the front of the wagon and gazed suspiciously at Pauline.

"Ah, I was young and troublish long ago, but I'm an honest woman now, Jack," Lil said. "You know us tinkers can turn our hand to anything. When I have made a little money gathering simples, I buys a horse cheap and sells it dear. It's a hard life, but virtuous."

"Aye, you're an example to us all, Lil," the constable scoffed. "Whose child are you, lass?" he asked Pauline.

"That's little Pooter," said Lil. "She belongs to my brother Dick. I'm teaching her the ways."

"Can she not speak for herself?"

"No, there's the pity, Jack. The poor child is simple. Has never spoke a word, but she's sweet as a pig for all that. We hope she may learn to be a leech-gatherer, as she has good, strong, sturdy legs. Of course, she'll never find a husband, but there be worse fates, don't you agree?"

The constable gave Lil a dark glance.

"And why is she half nekkid?"

"Did I not tell you the poor child is simple? It takes her half a morning to climb into that smock, much less put on boots and a bonnet and such nonsense. But she's sweet as grubworms and I do trust I can teach her the ways and keep her out the poorhouse. It's the least I can do for dear Dick."

Pauline feared the constable would recognize her, for her portrait hung in almost every tavern of the Barony. She tried to act "simple" and, in fact, it wanted very little acting. Her hair was tangled and unwashed, her face grimy. The poteen had unfocused her eyes. The constable spared her no pity but spat out a seed and spoke again to Lillian Lungwich.

"I'm taking you in on suspicion of horse thieving," he said.

"I never!" cried Lil. "You're cruel and mean, Jack Stonefeather!"

"That's as may be," the constable said, "but I have my orders from Lady Harpen-Hasten. She spoke to a man from the castle last night who changed horses at the Toad & Tumbler. His own horse was stole by rebels in these parts not four days ago, it seems. I'm to fetch it and keep it until he comes back, along with any rebels I may find."

"Rebels!" Lil said. "And why are you pestering me? Can you not tell a rebel from a poor old tinker woman?"

"A body may be both a tinker *and* a rebel, Lil," said Jack Stonefeather, "just as he may be a tinker and a horse thief, too."

"I never stole that horse!"

"You can tell that to him when Marshal Orloff comes back."

Pauline gasped. The constable scowled at her.

"What's got into the lass?" he asked.

"Ah, she twitches now and then," said Lil, looking crossly at Pauline. "I thought as I'd whipped it out of her, but I can see I wanted a bigger cane. Her backside must be as dull as her wits."

"Och, my uncle Henry is a twitcher," said Jack Stonefeather. "Beating only makes it worse."

"As you say. Now, Jack, what's this nonsense you're about? If I'm supposed to have stole this feller's horse, let him stand with me before the magistrate. Orloff, you called him? Is that even a Cantling name? You can't take me in on the word of some fly-by-night outlander!"

"I can and I will," the constable said. "There's a war on, Lil. This fellow ain't some jack-in-the-box with a paper sword. Gaspard Simone-Thierry has made him Supreme Commander of the Loyalist Army. He'd rode all night from La Provence and he hadn't got time to bandy words with an old horse thief! You'll stay in my gaol until he comes back."

Pauline moaned, but the constable must have taken it as another show of simpleness. He shook his head, turned his horse, and rode off without a word. Lil let go the wagon's brake and whipped her mule. The tinker suffered a fit of coughing when they entered the hamlet of Dragonfly-on-Bog, but Pauline was too dispirited even to pound her back. Moments later she climbed down from the wagon and followed Lil into Jack Stonefeather's gaol.

Chapter 11

BARBER BLAISE

*L*ucy's disguise was Blaise's idea, or Blaise's fault, depending on how one looked at it. Lucy took the latter view. She stormed tearfully into the cottage, leaving him in the garden with the shears, a cast-off sheet, and the better part of her hair.

In the past days his devotion had been sorely tested. He supposed it was a foretaste of what it meant to be married. You started almost bursting with warm feelings for someone, but then, living cheek by jowl, you began to see your idol in a different light. Who knew that Lucy could be peevish?

"I almost had it evened out," he called through the cottage window.

"Go *away!*" Lucy wailed.

Naturally she was upset. Three days they had searched for Pauline, but after ranging far and wide in upper Haslet March they had found only Vlad Orloff's horse, missing its tack and tied to the back of a tinker's wagon. Lucy had been wary, at first, of Lillian Lungwich. Her experience with Marci Frelock had given her a dubious opinion of tinkers, and she frankly suspected the old woman might have killed Pauline.

But Mrs. Lungwich swore with many oaths and crossings of her heart that she had found the horse wandering. She finally earned Lucy's trust when, hearing about the encounter with Marci and Sammy, she cursed the clan of Frelocks as being the sort of thieving rascals who gave tinkers a bad name.

"Imagine 'em taking food from a couple o' orphans!" she said. "As if there wasn't great herds and flocks of rich people to steal from, that have enough and to spare!"

She fed them soda bread — thereby earning the gratitude of Blaise, who had fared worse than Lucy on a diet of cattails and Blacksmith's Beard — and when she had teased their whole tale from them she took it upon herself to track down Pauline. Her hound could sniff out a button in a field of mint, she said, and she took for a scent Pauline's mourning dress, which Lucy still carried in their knapsack. She would not allow them to go with her, but directed them to the cottage of a friend who lived in the hamlet of Dragonfly-on-Bog.

There Blaise was introduced to Lucy's peevish side. She had held up bravely for three days in the wilderness, but now — with a roof over their heads and food in their bellies — she had utterly broken down. Blaise looked sadly at the little pile of her hair.

"Do you fancy a bit of cold pie?" he called out.

"*No!*"

The under-footman sighed and went in search of a whittling stick. He was hungry, but as an only son among sisters he had learned to stay out of the house when a girl was "in a state" (as his mother put it).

They were lodging at the home of Mrs. Harriet Holstein-Quack, who served as midwife and herbalist to the people of Dragonfly-on-Bog. When she was not pulling out babies or tending sore teeth, Mrs. Quack (as she was known) supplied the villagers with all manner of tinctures, tonics, and balms, and in that capacity she did much business with Lillian Lungwich, without whose poteen her love potion inspired only a mild fondness.

She had welcomed Lucy with great enthusiasm. By now the rumor of Lord Cant's secret child had reached even the smallest of villages, and Mrs. Quack — an avid reader of romances in which humble girls rose to wear crowns — was a whole-hearted supporter of Lucy's claims. She went so far as to curtsey before her, and declared that if Lucy wanted anything of her, she need only speak the word of command.

Lucy had blushed at this speech, for she was saddle sore and dirty and felt hardly worthy to sit on a clean cushion, much less be treated as a lady. But she curtseyed in turn to the midwife and hesitantly asked, "Have you a pair of shears?"

"Aye, I have shears," said Mrs. Quack. "What needs a-cutting?"

Lucy shook her head and her hair fell down over her glasses. She had begun to wear a fringe on her forehead before she left the castle, but it had grown out since then and she was constantly having to push back her hair. Mrs. Quack nodded and opened the dresser.

"I'll fix it myself," she said. "Come to the garden and I won't have to sweep."

She carried a stool outside and tied an old sheet around Lucy's neck, but scarcely had she combed out her hair when a man came yelling down the high street. His wife's time had come to bring forth their first child, he said, and he gave such a blood-curdling account of her screams that the midwife judged there was no time to linger.

"Run home and boil water, and send down to the tavern for a pint of ale," she told him. "I'll be along shortly! Remind her to breathe!" She ran into the cottage and came out moments later with her bag and a shawl. "I'm sorry, children, the barbering will have to wait. There's a cold pie in the dresser. Expect me when you see me!"

"Why do you need ale, Mrs. Quack?" Blaise asked as she raced down the path (for he was a youngest child, and had only the vaguest notions of what went on during a woman's confinement). The midwife did not break her stride.

"Pulling out a baby's thirsty work, lad!" she said.

Lucy sat with the sheet tied around her neck. She hardly looked herself without her glasses, thought Blaise. She picked up the shears from the grass and held them out to him.

"You may as well do it," she said.

"Me?" asked Blaise.

"I don't expect to look like a lady. I just want it out of my eyes."

Blaise took the shears. If there was any hair he longed to touch it was Lucy's, yet he hesitated. They had slept at arm's length for three nights, and straddled a horse together for as many days, but he blushed in the presence of a bedsheet. He took a lock of hair in a trembling hand.

"How – how – how long?" he asked.

Lucy shrugged. "Just use your fingers as a guide," she said.

Blaise took Lucy's fringe between two fingers. It seemed a pity to cut it. Never had he felt anything so soft and fine. He squeezed the shears and the strands fell on to Lucy's lap. She stiffened.

"Blaise, what did you do?" she asked.

The under-footman uneasily swallowed. Lucy now had half a fringe.

"I d-did as you said," he told her. "I used my fingers and cut the rest."

Lucy's eyebrows rose in alarm.

"I meant you to leave it the *length* of a finger!" she said.

"But you said 'fingers,'" said Blaise.

"I assumed you knew what I meant!" said Lucy.

"I assumed you meant what you said!" Blaise answered. "Here, it's not so bad." Timidly he combed over what was left of her fringe, trying to cover the blank expanse of forehead. Lucy swatted the comb out of his hand.

"That won't do!" she moaned. "Just cut it even!"

It went from bad to worse. With her fringe gone the hair on top of Lucy's head looked absurdly long, so Blaise helpfully tried to blend it into the shorter part. Having done one side to his satisfaction he moved on to the other, but there he took off too much and had to go back for symmetry. Somehow, hair of equal length stuck out *more* on that side. He came to the startling conclusion that Lucy's skull was lopsided.

By now she was in a panic. She sent him to fetch a looking-glass from the cottage, and when she saw what he had done she burst into tears.

"I look like a clown!" she wailed.

It was a low moment in Blaise's life. Lucy threw off the sheet and ran into the cottage, where she cast herself sobbing upon the midwife's bed. He tried to console her, but no sooner had he entered the room than he was struck in the face by a pillow. Lucy, he gathered, needed time alone.

So he whittled in the garden until Mrs. Quack returned and made a bed on the floor for him. In the morning, over a breakfast of cold pie, he proposed to Lucy his idea of dressing her as a boy.

There could be no putting back her hair, he reasonably pointed out. Orloff's broadside described her clothes, so a change of costume was certainly wanted. What better disguise than hiding in plain view as a boy?

"Why, if you left off your glasses, even I'd never know you!" he said.

"If you never knew me, I'd still have my hair," muttered Lucy (who had come to breakfast with the hood of her jumper pulled up). Yet on further thought she had to admit the wisdom of his plan. Mrs. Quack, as it happened, had a grown son whose old clothes could be turned to the purpose, so when the table was cleared she took Lucy to the garden and properly cut her hair.

"I'd take you for a lad myself, if I didn't know better," she said when she had finished, admiring her handiwork. "What do you think, Master Blaise?"

"Aye, you look every bit a boy, Lucy."

"Splendid," Lucy grumbled.

"Well . . . I mean to say, you make an uncommonly *pretty* one —"

Lucy scowled and stomped into the cottage, and moments later loud sobbing was heard. Mrs. Quack, having folded the bedsheet, laid a consoling hand on the under-footman's shoulder.

"Never you mind," she said. "If she didn't care for you she wouldn't bother to pout. Can you handle a needle and thread?"

"Aye. Better than shears, anyway."

"There, you can make yourself useful. I've a pair of Harvey's old trousers that wants hemming up to fit her. You take my advice and make yourself small. She'll come round soon enough."

Blaise suspected Lucy would never "come round" until Miss Cant was found, but a "good cry" (to use his mother's term) seemed to do her some good. When he had finished hemming the trousers he sent them in with Mrs. Quack, and some minutes later Lucy emerged wearing them with a tunic, turnshoes, and a muffin cap. The midwife had sewn a pocket in the tunic where she might hide her glasses, so from head to toe Lucy looked a common scamp.

"Well?" she asked.

Blaise hesitated. He did not want to put Lucy in a state by suggesting she passed for a boy.

"No one will know you," he eventually said.

"We'll soon find out," said Lucy, peering down the road. "Hurry, fetch my pack!"

Blaise was glad to take orders, for it meant Lucy was at least speaking to him. When he returned with the pack Lucy took from it the copy of Orloff's broadside and ran down to the road, where two men approached on the most disgraceful-looking mule Blaise had ever seen.

"Please, sir!" Lucy called.

A man with the scruffy look of a peddler held the reins. He rode on a sidesaddle, and behind him sat a younger man in the soldierly frock of a man-at-arms. Lucy held the broadside up to them. "Please, have you by chance seen Miss Cant?" she begged. "They say her Ladyship's been kidnapped by rebels!"

The peddler had to twist around to look (for his saddle faced the other way), and had his friend not grasped his tunic he might have fallen. He pushed his spectacles up his nose and gazed wonderingly at Lucy.

"Why – why – why this is most curious!" he stammered. "Do I know you, lad?"

Lucy squinted at his blackened eyebrows.

"Mr. Lemonjello?" she asked.

"Lucy!" the astronomer cried. This so startled Lemonjello's friend that the latter lost his grip and Lemonjello tumbled from the mule, pulling Lucy to the ground. Blaise ran over and helped the scientist to his feet, whereupon Lucy leapt up and threw her arms around him.

"I thought you were in the dungeon!" she cried. "How did you? —"

"Shh!" said Lemonjello. A girl hanging up laundry at a neighboring cottage stared curiously at the wayfarers. "We m-mustn't draw undue attention," the astronomer warned.

"Come inside!" said Lucy.

A glad reunion took place in the midwife's cottage. Blaise even dared to hope his offence might be forgiven, for, upon being introduced to Lucy, Mr. Swanson declared that her haircut was "absolutely stunning."

"You must wear a *severe* gown with it," he advised. "For jewelry, a pearl around the neck, nothing more. You have the eye-lashes for it, dear. The ladies will die of jealousy."

"What nonsense you talk, Mr. Swanson!" said Lucy, grate-fully blushing.

The astronomer insisted on hearing Lucy's tale before giving an account of himself, and Mrs. Quack brewed a welcome pot of tea while Lucy told all that had happened since she and Pauline left Castle Cant. Blaise served bread and butter, adding his own comments when he felt that Lucy had understated her resourcefulness and heroism. Lemonjello listened gravely, and when she had finished he took from his sleeve a folded sheet of paper.

"We m-may at least be certain Miss Cant was not harmed by Orloff's weapon," he said, giving it to Lucy. "Mr. Swanson dis-covered that note in a castoff saddlebag while I d-dozed this morning, having ridden through the night from La Provence."

Lucy eagerly read the note.

"Without horse or bacon!" said Blaise, looking over her shoulder.

"We couldn't understand why she fell behind," Lucy told the astronomer. "Imagine her going back for that bacon! But how is it that *you're* looking for her? And whatever took you to La Provence?" She glanced at Swanson, as though the guardsman was some exotic pet Lemonjello had adopted there.

"I was recruited for my m-mission by Dr. Sauersop," said Lemonjello. "He suspected that Vlad Orloff would seek the aid of his old master, and his suspicion was well founded. I bring grievous t-tidings, Lucy. Orloff and Gaspard are now in league."

"How dreadful!"

"It's worse than you imagine," said Lemonjello, looking away. "You see, though I failed as an envoy I succeeded all too well as a spy. It . . . it pains me to tell you this. I can't bear to think of telling Miss Cant."

"You don't mean to say her grandfather has turned against Pauline?"

"Worse than that," said the astronomer. "I've learned that Miss Cant's f-father is still alive."

Lucy gaped at him. "But we watched him die!" she said.

"Lord Cant is dead," said Lemonjello, "but he was n-no father to Miss Cant."

Haltingly, he told of his arrival at Château Simone-Thierry. Blaise whistled in admiration when Lemonjello described climbing the chandelier's chain, and Mrs. Quack frankly shivered as it slipped through his fingers. Lemonjello stammered so badly when recounting Orloff's love for Esmeralda that Swanson was obliged to pound his back. On Gaspard's wound the scientist touched only lightly, and he left to another time the Baronet's plans for the gum trade.

"I'd always marveled that Lord Cant t-took so little interest in his daughter," he said. "I was loath to believe Orloff's tale, but it explains much. I can only conclude he spoke the truth."

"It doesn't mean he's Pauline's father," insisted Lucy.

"He said, 'Her father still lives,'" Blaise concurred. "It could be anyone."

"I wish I c-could agree," said Lemonjello. "But I gave the matter much thought while I sat in Gaspard's prison. Lucy . . .

I hardly like to ask . . . but did you never wonder why Orloff let you live, on the d-day when . . . when . . ."

"When he killed my family."

"Yes. Why kill them, only to let you live? He'd learned when arranging Lord Cant's marriage to Esmeralda that the Baron had fathered a child. He insisted that it . . . that you . . . be left in the wood to die. Why, then, when he discovered years later that you'd survived . . . why did he not kill you outright?"

"I . . . I don't know. I don't see what this has to do —"

"It was because of Miss Cant!" said Blaise. Lemonjello nodded.

"Precisely. Though Pauline von Cant bore another man's name, she was Orloff's child, and he was determined that she should someday rule the Barony. Had he killed Lucy he might have provoked a c-counterstroke from Adolphus, who could disown Pauline as a child of adultery. Esmeralda was by then dead, and her dowry safely in the Baron's coffers. So Orloff slew your family, Lucy, and brought you to the castle, where he trusted you would never learn the truth."

"But it's too awful!" cried Lucy. "Poor Pauline!"

"My sole good luck till now was meeting Mr. Swanson," said Lemonjello. "Without his help I would still be Gaspard's p-prisoner. But perhaps our meeting signals a change in all our fortunes. With Orloff now bound for the Vale of Kandu, we may p-perhaps hope that — Great stars! Were you expecting a patient, Mrs. Quackstein?"

Through the doorway of the cottage came a sound of horrible coughing, like a goose being slaughtered with a dull sword.

The startled midwife hurried to a window and looked out, then turned and beckoned to Lucy.

"Come see!" she hissed. "Didn't Lil tell you Roto had a nose on him?"

Lucy ran to the window and the others gathered behind her.

"It's Pauline!" she yelped. Mrs. Holstein-Quack clapped a hand over her mouth.

"Shh!" she said. "And ain't it the constable riding along before her?"

Pauline sat glumly on the board next to Lillian Lungwich, who coughed and coughed but cast only a sidelong glance at her old friend's cottage. Roto slept atop the wagon. He had found his quarry, and now he rode with her to the kennel of Jack Stonefeather's gaol. Swanson breathed an enraptured sigh at this first glimpse of his idol.

"She's more stunning than I imagined," he whispered. "But if I ever find the person who dressed her in that smock, blood will flow!"

Chapter 12

How Dick Lungwich Made His NAME

"Supreme Commander of the Loyalist Army!" Lillian Lung-wich fumed, pacing the dirt floor. Mrs. Stonefeather had brought a dish of porridge, and though she served it with neither treacle nor cream, Pauline ate with a will. The affair of the truffle had left her feeling hollow.

"Aren't you going to eat, missus?" Pauline asked, scraping her porringer.

"I've no appetite," Lil said. She took her wineskin from a peg on the wall and swallowed a draught of poteen. "You gobble it up, now. You want your strength."

Pauline gladly scooped the rest of the porridge from the pot. Mrs. Lungwich had proved to be an ally, after all. She had not come upon Pauline by chance, she admitted, but had been led to her by Roto. The hound now whimpered in a kennel beyond the door (the gaol being simply a walled-off part of Jack Stonefeather's stable).

"I oughtn't to have teased you," the tinker allowed, "but you came at me so headstrong, waving that toothpick like a boy playing at knights. I couldn't help but have bit of fun with ye."

"Please, where is Lucy?" Pauline asked. "Were you really taking me to her?"

"Aye, that I was. And you might have made a good getaway, had not the Supreme Commander of the Oiliest Army pushed his nose into things. Imagine him being in league again with Gaspard Simone-Thierry!"

"But where is Lucy? Is she still with Delagraisse?"

Lil sat beside her.

"Miss Lucy and Master Blaise are stopping with a friend of mine, not a pig's whistle from here," she said. "I met them yestermorning. Their horse recognized your'n, which I had found wandering, and 'finders keepers,' I say. Horse thief, pah! Your friends had been living off cattails for three days and they looked like what my cat brings home."

Pauline's heart leapt.

"We'll soon be free!" she said. "Lucy will rescue us!"

"She's a sharp-witted lass," Lil granted. "I might have been pulling a healthy tooth, getting anything out of her. She thought I'd killed you and stole your horse. He-he-he! Do I look like a murderess to you?"

Pauline politely shook her head. She knew only one murderer — Vladimir Orloff — but in fact Lil did bear a striking resemblance to the Postal Commissioner. Only now had she noticed it.

"Well, I convinced her I'd found the horse," Lil went on, "and then she wants to know what side I'm on, Loyalist or Causist? Ha! Lil ain't on nobody's side, 'cause neither the rebels nor the nobs is on the tinkers' side. I'm on Jock Shaver's side, and beggar all else!"*

Pauline nodded, her mouth full of porridge.

"By good chance they carried your dress, so I sent 'em to Harriet and set out. The wind was easterly, which was good luck for Roto." Lil looked at the floor and frowned. "Though not so lucky if it blew the head of the Oily Army this way. What's that rascal about now, I wonder?"

"Orloff is after Lucy and me," Pauline said. "He nearly caught us in the swineherd's hut. That's when I got lost. You see, I knew we'd not get far without food, so I turned back to steal the bacon. It was a rash act, but that's my nature! So I —"

"Orloff!" Lil broke in. "Why, his name's as false as his lying tongue. Never was there such a double-dealing, good-for-naught rapscallion born as Vladimir Orloff — as he calls himself!"

Pauline swallowed a lump of porridge.

"Why do you say, 'As he calls himself'?" she asked.

"Because it's so!" Lil said. "He took his name from a story-book, I'll wager, and put it on like a fancy cap, only it didn't fit him then and it don't fit now. He wanted to rise in the world, he said, and make his name. Hah! The tall corn falls to the scythe, same as the short, only it falls that much farther. Better to be a weed, I say. We don't rise far, but always we thrive."

---

*Jock Shaver: legendary bandit and grandsire of the tinkers. (See A Cyclopædic Dictionary of Cantling Folklore, Ernst Englottogaster, ed.)

"You talk as though you know him," said Pauline.

"Know him?" Lil said. "And ain't he Dick Lungwich, my own kid brother?"

"What!"

"You may well say 'What!'" said Lil. "Wee Dickie Lungwich he was, till he rose to be a lickspittle to Sir Gaspard, who calls himself your granddad. Dick knew he'd never get nowhere with a tinker's name, and so he started calling himself 'Vladimir Orloff.' Well, you may call a skunk a rose but it still smells like a fart, and so it is with Dick. I needn't tell you that!"

"I pray you won't!" said Pauline, blushing.

"Forgive me, child! I talk as my head leads me, and I ain't used to speaking with gentlefolk. But you take my meaning. Your Lucy told me the horrible thing he done. Well, I am right glad he changed his name, for never was there a murderer in the clan of Lungwich. I take back every kiss ever I gave him."

"I *thought* he favored you about the face!" said Pauline. She stared wonderingly at Lil. "To think he began life as a tinker, and now he has the effrontery to call himself my regent!"

"He was ever trying to climb to power up a woman's skirts," said Lil. She spat the chewed husk of a seed to the dirt floor. "He thought he would marry Esmeralda, and so take her pa's place as the big nob of La Provence. But no matter how rich Dickie made him by trading gum, Gaspard wanted no tinker as a son-in-law. So didn't he sell off Esmeralda to Lord Cant, and made Dickie the go-between to rub his nose in it?"

Pauline pushed away the porringer. Her face was troubled.

"Dickie used to talk to me before then," Lil went on, "and

get me a bite of food out of kitchens in the hard winters. But when he went to Castle Cant he shut his face to the tinkers, even to his own sis that used to change his nappies. That's what ambition will do to a man."

"Do you mean to tell me Vladimir Orloff asked for my mother's hand?" asked Pauline.

"Eh?" Lil said absently. Then she clapped a hand to her brow. "My stars, Esmeralda *was* your mum, weren't she? I forget who I'm a-talking to. Aye, Dickie courted her, and they say she was sweet on him too, though he was old as dust even then. A woman's heart is blind as a turnip, Pooter. And many's the girl that fell in love with a fork."

"My mother never loved Vladimir Orloff," said Pauline. She pushed back her stool and stood up. "Mother deeply loved Papa. I am very surprised you don't know it. Why, surely even a tinker hears the popular tunes! Do you know 'Their love was as a bloom of spring, fleeting as the linnet's wing?' It's a lovely air. It was written about Mother and Papa."

"Oh, darling, I'm sorry I spoke," said Lil. She put her hand on Pauline's shoulder. "Of course she loved him. Don't every ma and pa love each other, and their baby, too? It's only natural."

Pauline pushed Lil's hand away.

"They *did* love each other!" she insisted. "Papa was crushed when Mother died. I suspect he turned to chewing gum in his grief, to help him bear the agony. He loved me deeply and he would have . . . he would have . . ."

Her voice trembled.

"He . . . he would have spent more time with me, had not

affairs of state weighed upon him so! People don't know the burden of being a ruler, how affairs press upon one so that . . . so . . . so he c-couldn't spare an hour for . . . for his own daughter!"

She sat on the stool and sobbed. She had been too long hungry, too long in the cold and in fear of the Bogwife. Now to hear this! She could bear with being an orphan — she had Lucy's example for that — but she could not bear to think that her mother had loved Vlad Orloff. For it explained too much. If Papa had shown little interest in her, if he had let her run wild and take a maidservant as her friend, was it not because he saw in Pauline's features the image of his wife — who loved another? Everyone said she was the image of her mother. She buried her face in her hands. Tears fell and turned the floor to mud.

Lillian Lungwich knelt beside her and said "Tut-tut" and "Shh!" and "There, there." She held Pauline to her bosom and stroked her hair. Pauline's voice trembled with fear and grief.

"What if . . . what if he didn't love me?"

"Shh. Your pa loved you, girl. What are you thinking? Don't you know a man loves his daughter more than any girl that ever was? She's the light of his eyes, and oh! I bet he spoilt you like a pail of cream!"

"But if he didn't love Mother . . ."

"Now, don't you listen to an old goat like me! You must never pay any mind to gossips and wagging tongues, Pooter, or your head will go and spin off like a top. Your mother was the fairest gal in the land. Who could not love her? I saw her riding out once and it was like the sun coming up over the hills."

Pauline sniffled. "She was very beautiful, wasn't she?" she asked.

"Oh, the pictures don't do her justice!" said Lil, wiping tears from Pauline's cheeks. "And aren't you her girl from top to tongue-toes? Why, a prettier lass I've never seen, under all the dirt and grime. I reckon we could both do with a wash and a brushup. Here, I've a comb in my bag. Let's tease out that golden hair."

She fetched the comb and unwove the tangled braid of hair. Pauline, who a month ago had dropped soiled kerchiefs for the chambermaids to launder, now wiped her dripping nose with the back of her hand.

"Papa said I had Mother's eyes," she said. "They're a rare shade of violet."

"Ah, I never was near enough to look at her eyes, my doll."

"And you're mistaken on another point. Mother was a plain-toed woman."

"No, I always heard as she was tongue toed," said Lil, "such as those people are in La Provence."

"But that's nonsense," said Pauline. "You see?"

She held out a foot and wiggled its five plain toes.

"Papa was busy toed," she explained, "and to have plain toes you must have at least one plain-toed parent. So Mother could hardly have been tongue toed."

Lil, like all tinkers, was plain toed. She frowned at Pauline's bare foot.

"Oh, dear stars," she said in a whisper. "I heard wrong, I fancy. Yes, you must have had a plain-toed parent. Well, whatever else she left you, your ma gave you a rare head of hair. If you're ever down on your luck, I know a wigmaker in Bogsend who'd give a pretty penny to take the shears to you. Why, it's like running the comb over an ermine's belly!"

She seemed anxious to leave behind the topic of toes. For her part Pauline had never objected to flattery, and after a lifelong diet of it she was starved for such attention. With her belly full of porridge she began drowsily to tell about the fantastical coiffures she had worn in the castle. Before one banquet, Rocky (her hairdresser) had woven a cage into her tresses with a real songbird inside, and another time he had hung her hair with bells so that, by pulling the braids in proper order, she could play "Nutting Time" and other familiar airs.

Her memories of Castle Cant so pleased Pauline that she did not hear the unbolting of the door, and only when Lil stopped combing did she glance up to see Jack Stonefeather scowling in the doorway. The tales of grand banquets died in her mouth. How long had he stood listening? she wondered.

"Simple, is she?" the constable asked.

"Aye," said Lil. "Grand, ain't it? She's finally learnt to talk!"

The constable sourly shook his head.

"You've done it this time, Lil," he said. "Horse thieving I expect from a tinker, but not kidnapping!"

"What does he mean, Aunt Lil?" Pauline asked.

"It's no use pretending, my Lady," Jack said. "They warned me you'd try to spin a tale, being all deceived and befuddled by the rebel girl. And you might have gone on fooling me, had I not heard you with my own ears. You looked a proper tinker girl, you did."

"You were eavesdropping!" Lil said. "That's cheating!"

"Call it what you may," Jack said. "Like I told you, there's a war on, Lil." He held out his hand to Pauline. "Please to come with me, ma'am. My missus will draw you a bath."

Lil stood between the constable and Pauline.

"And who's to say you're not a rebel, Jack Stonefeather?" she demanded. "For all I know you mean to take this poor girl and slit her throat! There's a war on, as you say."

"There'll be no throat slitting," said the constable, pushing her aside. "I've just served tea to a delegation from the Loyalist army, what's come to take the girl in hand. She'll stay with her kinfolk on Lake Poltroon till these Causists have been dealt with. *Then* we may see some throat slitting, if there's any justice in this Barony."

He took Pauline by her arm, but before he led her off she broke away and kissed Lil's cheek. The old tinker whispered "Be brave!" but Pauline felt she had used up her small store of courage long ago.

$\mathscr{P}$auline plotted her vengeance in a tin bath by Mrs. Stonefeather's kitchen fire. The lawman had cheated by eavesdropping, and it would serve him right if she threw a tantrum in his parlor. Even a village constable must own some trinket worth breaking. Astrid, the kitchen girl, served Pauline cakes from the village baker while she laid her plans.

When the constable's wife had pinned up her hair, Pauline climbed from the bath and Astrid dried her with a sheet. Mrs. Stonefeather brought out a chemise and an old-fashioned kirtle that had belonged to her daughter (now married), along with a pair of poulaines with turned-up toes. The deep green kirtle had been often, though neatly, mended.

The Stonefeathers' tea service sat on a table in the parlor. Pauline was debating whether first to smash the creamer or the sugar bowl when she realized that the Loyalist delegate was none other than Luigi Lemonjello. Her father's astronomer now wore moustaches and burnt-cork eyebrows, and with him stood a man in the livery of Château Simone-Thierry.

"Ah, h-here she is now," said Lemonjello. "Hail, Lady Cant!"

What a lot of imposters I know! thought Pauline. First Delagraisse had claimed to be Vladimir Orloff, and now here was Lemonjello looking like a villain from a comic operetta. She knew at once he must be plotting her rescue. Good old Luigi!

"What is the meaning of this?" she demanded. At the castle Pauline had begged to act in masques and other entertainments, and now she threw herself with relish into the role of a headstrong fugitive.

"My Lady," said Lemonjello, "how g-gladding it is to find you well. I am Captain Lemonjello of the ad hoc Loyalist Army. I bring greetings from my Lady's grandsire, Sir Gaspard, who is d-deeply concerned for her welfare."

"And do you always go about with a kept baboon, Captain?" asked Pauline. She pointed to the guardsman, who had bowed his head nearly to the floor. "Kindly tell your lieutenant to get up. I grow dizzy simply looking at him!"

"I b-b-beg your p-pardon, my Lady!" bleated Swanson. "And may I s-say how *deeply* honored I am to — to —"

"Oh, hush!" said Pauline. "I have no patience for flattery!"

"Forgive me!" Swanson begged.

Lemonjello unrolled a parchment, and Pauline recognized on it those stamps and seals that Delagraisse had stolen from the office of the Postal Commissioner. So Luigi and Blaise were in league!

"I have here a warrant from Marshal Orloff, my Lady," he said, "granting me authority to escort your Ladyship to a safe refuge of my ch-choosing, where you may remain until our forces have defeated the Causist rebels, and restored the rule of the house of C-cant."

"Insolence!" said Pauline. "I shan't be led by a man who doesn't recognize the rightful claim of my dear sister Lucy." She turned to Jack Stonefeather. "I demand that you put these men in irons and flog them without pity."

"Eep!" said Swanson.

"I'm sorry, my Lady," the constable said. "I have my orders from Lady Harpen-Hasten, who spoke with Marshal Orloff only yesterday. You must be taken in hand until you come to your senses."

"Do you suggest I've taken leave of my senses?" Pauline cried.

"Sometimes I think the world has took leave of its senses," said Jack Stonefeather, sadly shaking his head. "They say the nobles are rioting in Goatshank for want of gum." He turned to Lemonjello. "Have you seen a nobleman deprived of his gum? You might as well take away the air from his nose!"

"Precisely," said the astronomer. "The Causists would p-plunge the Barony into chaos."

"What utter bosh!" snorted Pauline. "Let the nobs chew paraffin if they insist on being a herd of stupid cows. Chewing gum is an outlandish custom that has no place among civilized people!"

"Och, that rebel girl truly has turned your head around!" lamented the constable.

"La dee da!" said Pauline, putting her fingers into her ears.

"Well, I c-commend you for your swift action, constable,"

said Lemonjello. "Indeed, all of Cant owes you a d-debt of gratitude. I should n-not be surprised to learn you have risen to the knighthood when this rebellion is put down."

"Thank you, sir!"

"Now, regarding Lady Cant," Lemonjello continued. "I shall commandeer that t-tinker's cart and take her Ladyship to Villa Martlet, where her people have set up a g-government-in-exile. Marshal Orloff's horse I shall leave in your care. I'll take the tinker's mule, however, as my own beast is untrained to the yoke."

"La dee da dee da!" Pauline sang.

"Very good, sir," said Jack Stonefeather. He hesitated, then stepped close to Lemonjello. "Er, forgive me, Captain, but I was given to understand a reward was offered for the little lady's return. A sum of fifty guilders, I believe it was."

"Fifty guilders!" screamed Pauline (who in a lifetime of tantrums had developed the uncanny ability to hear through her fingers, even while *la-dee-da*-ing at the top of her lungs). "Why, that's highway robbery! You should demand at least one hundred guilders. I'm not a musty old piece of horseflesh!"

"Ah, er, yes, the re-reward!" sputtered Lemonjello. "Yes! Yes, of course!"

He grinned anxiously, and Pauline saw he was unprepared for this turn of events.

"Shall I fetch the boy, Captain?" asked Swanson.

"What? Ah, the b-boy!" said the astronomer. "Yes, Swanson. Be quick about it!"

Swanson bowed deeply to Pauline and then raced out of the

constable's house. She watched from an open window as he sprinted down the high street of Dragonfly-on-Bog.

Jack Stonefeather, meanwhile, asked "Captain" Lemonjello about the progress of the war, and the astronomer blustered vaguely about bowmen, blockades, and cavalry. The rebels would soon meet a bloody fate, he assured the constable. Then Swanson returned with Delagraisse. The under-footman presented a sheet of parchment to Lemonjello, who read the document over the top of his spectacles before handing it to Jack Stonefeather.

"What's this?" the constable asked.

"Your voucher," said Lemonjello. "On behalf of the Loyalist Army, may I be the first to c-congratulate you, my good man. Your service will not be forgotten."

Pauline pecked at the document. She had to admit Delagraisse had been clever to burgle Orloff's office. All Cantlings were impressed by fancy seals, and the boy had a good hand with a pen. She fancied Swanson had dictated the words to him:

By authority of **Vladimir Orloff,** Esq., Supreme Marshal of the Army and Honorable Regent to her Ladyship, Baroness Cant:

Be it known, that whosoever bears this voucher, by virtue of having restored the Merciful Shepherdess (saved from the Machinations of those vile and perfidious Rebels) to her People, shall be entitled to recompense in the sum of Fifty ~50~ Guilders, to

be paid from the Baronial Exchequer, within Six
~6~ Months of the Capitalization of our Beloved
and Celestial Pauline;*

Whereof we stand in witness, this 26th day of the
Interregnum,

Romney Festschrift   Abelard Festschrift

"Who are Romney and Abelard Festschrift?" the constable
asked.

"The witnesses," said Swanson. "Honest, sober men, I assure you."

"You mean I don't get my fifty guilders until you've driven
out the rebels?"

"I'm afraid it c-could hardly be otherwise," said Lemonjello.
"The sum is to be paid from the Baronial Exchequer, which is
within the castle, which is held by the rebels. You might apply
to them for payment, but they are offering only twelve shillings
for the capture of Miss Cant."

"Twelve shillings!" screamed Pauline.

"Of course, that would make you a t-traitor," added
Lemonjello. "We should have to take off your head for that."

"I see," said Jack Stonefeather, staring glumly at the voucher.
He knitted his brows. "Say, why is this wax soft?" he asked,

---

*Barons of Cant wore a four-tufted cap rather than a crown, and thus the ceremony of their
assuming power was termed a capitalization rather than a coronation.

showing the document to Lemonjello. His thumb had left a mark in the sealing wax. Blaise Delagraisse stepped forward.

"I beg your pardon, Captain," he said. "I put it in my blouse so it wouldn't get crumpled. With the day being warm, it must've acted upon the wax."

"Ah, that explains it," Lemonjello said, giving the voucher back to Jack Stonefeather. "See that it d-doesn't happen again, Delagraisse."

"No, sir. That is, yes, sir."

"C-constable, I thank you again for your heroic service to our Barony," the astronomer concluded. "P-please to give my compliments to your missus for the tea and biscuits."

"Aye," Jack Stonefeather grumbled. He slid the voucher under a saucer on the tea table. "Well, I'll help you get that mule in harness. Lil's not going to like this one bit, but I reckon her Ladyship can't be expected to walk to Ramsford and beyond. Come along."

He led them past Lil's wagon to the stables, where the mule stood in a stall between the constable's horse and Hellion. With help from Delagraisse the constable put the beast between the shafts while Swanson tethered Guinevere to the back of the wagon. Pauline knelt by Roto's kennel to say goodbye. She had not the heart to knock and tell Lil she was leaving her behind in the gaol.

Roto licked her hand, his tail whipping the straw of his bed, and Pauline noticed that the peg had fallen out that held shut his kennel door. She went to slip it into the rings but the hound growled warningly at her. The peg, she saw, could never have fallen out on its own. Seeing the constable's back turned, Pauline slipped it into her chemise.

"Please to c-come along, my Lady!" Lemonjello called. "Are we ready, Swanson? Delagraisse? My Lady, would you ride upon the board or in the wagon?"

"I shall ride on the board," Pauline said. "It's bad enough to be bought and sold like a prize sheep. I refuse to be penned like one. Please to help me up."

"Allow *me!*" cried Swanson, dropping to his hands and knees. With Lemonjello's help Pauline climbed on to Swanson's back and from there to the riding board. The astronomer followed and took up the whip and reins. Swanson clambered up to sit on the other side of Pauline, and, when Delagraisse had crawled into the wagon, Lemonjello struck the mule's flanks.

"Fare well, Jack Stonefeather!" he said. "Truly you are a Cantling of the finest m-mettle! I hope you shall be a knight indeed when n-next we meet!"

"Aye," the constable grumbled, "and fifty guilders richer."

Word had spread in Dragonfly-on-Bog that Lord Cant's daughter was found, and the high street was lined with excited villagers. Matrons waved kerchiefs at Pauline and squealed like schoolgirls when she waved back. Old men gaped like upset pails. Lemonjello could hardly steer a path through the crowd in the village square, where young girls went into ecstasies at the sight of the Baron's daughter. They screamed and clutched one another, their cheeks wet with tears.

At the far side of the square, on the steps of the guild hall,

Astrid the kitchen girl stood behind a plank that rested on two barrels. The enterprising young woman had set up shop and was doing a brisk business. Behind her a sign was tacked to the door of the hall, crudely painted on butcher paper in letters as big and black as fire grates:

REAL BARONIAL BATH TOWELLS!
That wiped the Adored & Onerable
PAULINE!
The price of only
2 - Shillings - 2
WET PARTS - 5 SHILLING!

She worked with a pair of shears, cutting into small squares the sheet she had used to dry Pauline. Customers thronged towards her with coins clutched in their fists, and a stout, perspiring man pressed through the crowd, crying "Save a wet part for me!"

"I barely used a corner of it," sniffed Pauline. "Those people are being cheated."

"My mother used to say that some p-people have more money than they have sense."

"But how did you find me, Luigi? And where is Lu —"

"Shh!" said the astronomer. "Let us get c-clear of the village."

The crowd reluctantly parted. A dozen children followed the

wagon well beyond the last houses, waving branches and shouting Pauline's name. They finally turned back when Lemonjello threw a handful of pennies among them. When the wagon had gone some distance farther, Swanson climbed on to its roof and looked behind.

"I don't believe we're pursued," he said. "Have you seen anything, Blaise?"

The under-footman's head poked out of the wagon.

"Nothing but birds, sir."

"To work, then!" said Lemonjello. He leapt down from the riding board and Pauline followed him to the back of the wagon. When Delagraisse had climbed out the astronomer reached underneath and pulled a hidden pin. The floor opened within, and Lillian Lungwich rose from among jugs of poteen, her bones popping loudly as she climbed from her hiding place.

"Ah, I'm getting too old for these tricks, Pooter!" she said.

"Lil!" cried Pauline, throwing her arms around the tinker. "I almost gave you away by knocking on the gaol door!"

"Well, aren't you the little lady!" said Lil, touching Pauline's hair as a milliner might admire a bolt of flaxen cloth. "La, you're young and want only soap and water to look pretty. When I heard all that uproar and clapping in the village I says, 'What's got into 'em?' And Lucy says, 'Why, it's Pauline.' And I says, 'They're clapping for that little rag doll?' But you do look a sight, even in a plain old kirtle."

"One might bring *back* the fashion of kirtles!" sighed Swanson.

"But where is Lucy?" said Pauline.

"The question is, Where have *you* been these four days?" Lucy asked, wiggling from the hingeless side of the wagon's floor. "I don't approve of your running off like that, Pauline von Cant. You can't expect me to go on without you!"

"Lucy!" cried Pauline. Lucy leapt upon her and together they tumbled into the tall grass beside the road. In their happiness they might have been two kittens of Lil's cat, who left off washing her paws to watch their antics.

"Don't I look like a boy?" asked Lucy, jumping up and showing off her costume. Pauline thought Lucy too fair to really look like a boy, even with her hair cropped, but she gladly agreed. She leapt up and squeezed her again.

"Oh, Lucy, I hunted a *frog!*" she said. "I built a fire and toasted frog legs and left a secret note in case you found it. I hadn't the sense to eat cattails, and I believed Lil was the Bogwife, but I vowed I would find you and I *did!*"

"Aren't you brave!" said Lucy.

"I . . . I . . . fell into the bog, but I vowed I would find you . . . I would! . . ."

She could not finish, for now, at the summit of joy, she burst with every tear she had swallowed in the valley of fear. She had been sorely tried and beset and had never paused to reflect that she — Mrs. Selvage's spoiled princess! — had got through her trials bravely.

"We lived off cattails, Miss Cant," said Delagraisse. "Lucy's book said you could eat 'em, but if I never taste one again it'll be too soon for me. Fancy you cooking up frogs' legs while we was eating old ditch weeds!"

"We must remember to bring salt next time we camp!" said Pauline, wiping her cheek. She turned to Lemonjello and — for the first time in her life — curtseyed to someone other than Lord Cant. "But you've rescued me out of prison again, Luigi! Is saving damsels in distress something they taught you at star-gazing school? However did you find us?"

"That is a long story, Miss C-cant," said the astronomer, bowing. "But — but I don't like to stop to tell it. The constable seemed very doubtful about that warrant. I should like to b-be well away when he learns that seal is for third-class postage."

"Let us ride in the back," Lucy said to Pauline. "I must hear all your adventures!"

Pauline noticed a strong scent coming from the wagon, but she could not place it. She coaxed Lil's cat into her arms and put it back inside, then unlaced her kirtle and took out the peg from Roto's kennel.

"Was this your doing, Lucy Wickwright?" she asked.

"Naturally."

"I knew it! I almost put it back but Blaise was there so I *knew* it had to be you!"

"We couldn't leave old Roto behind, could we?" said Lil, climbing to the riding board.

"But where *is* Roto?"

"Look!" cried Delagraisse.

The under-footman must have had eagle eyes, for at first Pauline saw only a little cloud of dust on the road behind them. Soon she could make out legs, however, and then a wagging, eager tongue. A few minutes later the hound stood panting beside the wagon. It put its paws on the shaft and barked at Lillian Lungwich.

"That was *my* idea," said Delagraisse. "There weren't room for him to hide in back with Lucy and Mrs. Lungwich, so after

they climbed in I rubbed the wheels with coal tar. A blind poo-
dle with a stuffy nose could follow that scent!"

"Coal tar!" said Pauline, sneezing. "*I* scented it!" she added.

The hound whimpered at Lil.

"You'll have to ride in back, boy," she said. "We've three of
us on the board."

"I'll ride with Miss Cant!" Swanson volunteered.

"As you wish," said Lil. "Come on, Roto!"

Swanson leapt down and the hound took his place on the
board.

"All aboard back there?" Lil called.

"Blissfully so!" cried Swanson.

"Off we go, then. Giddy-up, mule!"

Lil flicked her whip, and the mule, straining against the weight
of six passengers (not counting Roto and the cat), pulled the
wagon creaking down the road. Guinevere followed at the end of
her tether, seeming quite pleased not to be between the shafts.

Chapter 14

The Congress of Smuts

*O*n Lil's advice the wagon turned off the Bogway before Muckleston, where the fighting was fierce between rebels and Loyalists. A country lane led the fugitives to a tinkers' camp near the village of Smuts, where, among campfires and sighing larches, they might rest and plan their next move.

When the wagon had been propped up and the mules watered, Lil chose a jug of poteen and set out to barter, returning shortly with onions, turnips, carrots, and a meaty pig's knuckle. Blaise and Swanson carried Lil's cooking pot to the stream, where at that hour the grandfathers sat with fishing poles. The young men carried the pot back between them, water splashing at their feet. Pauline and Lucy had volunteered for the chore but Lil would not hear of it.

"Let the menfolk do it," she said. "Why would I yoke a goat

to my plow when I've got a good strong ox in the barn? Remember that, if you grow up to be married, girls. Never let a man put a ring on your finger unless you've first put one through his nose. Otherwise he'll treat *you* like a beast of burden, then complain when you start to look like one."

"It doesn't seem fair that a husband should do *all* the work," objected Lucy.

"Have you ever had a baby, lass?" Lil asked.

"No, ma'am!"

"Nor are you likely to, being dressed up as a boy like that. Well, I had a little one once, Lucy, and I can tell you that washing out nappies is plenty of work for a woman to do, and she don't need to be hauling the water besides. So unless you find a husband who likes to wash nappies and sing lullabies — and that Mr. Swanson seems a likely candidate, come to think of it — you make sure he knows his place is between the shafts, pulling you and the young 'uns along."

"Is your husband long dead?" asked Pauline.

"Eh? I had no husband, darling. The rascal I was to marry ran off when the baby came along. You see, I was foolish and didn't place a ring through his nose. Harriet helped me, though. She looked after little Sally whilst I gathered my simples, and lo if Sally didn't end up getting hitched to Harriet's boy, Harvey, whose old britches Miss Lucy's a-wearing."

"And does Harvey have a ring through his nose?"

"Aye, and apron strings for a tether, Pooter. Don't let anyone fool you. Fellers are happiest when they've got a wife to boss 'em, however they may groan. Elsewise they'd hardly know what to do with themselves after they'd ate and farted. Begging your pardon, milady."

Lil hung the pot over the fire and Pauline insisted on peeling the vegetables. If she meant to live as a fugitive, she reasoned, she had better learn to feed herself. Roto, lured by the smell of pig's knuckle, snapped up the turnip skins as they fell. The cat had come out to hunt, and stalked crickets among the wildflowers.

When the broth had come to a simmer Lemonjello called a congress.

"It is incumbent upon me," he said, "as the d-duly appointed envoy to La Provence, to give an accounting of what . . . of that which . . . Oh dear, I've started too grandly. I'll never m-make an orator, I'm afraid."

"Plain speech is the coming style, I'm told," encouraged Swanson.

"V-very good. Well, then. I was sent b-by our trusted friends — Dr. Azziz, Mr. Splint, and Dr. Sauersop — to thwart any attempt by Vlad Orloff to turn Gaspard against Lucy. In that I have failed, and I have earned Gaspard's wrath into the bargain, for he rather b-blames me for the loss of his eye. Your grandfather has no great love for Orloff, Miss Cant" — here the astronomer blushed — "but their love of money has made them allies. If Lucy goes to La Provence, I fear she shall be imprisoned, as I was."

"The constable said Dickie was in these parts yesterday — him as you call Vlad Orloff," said Lil. "Has he come a-looking for the girls, do you fancy?"

"I suspect he's long gone by now," said Lemonjello. "Gaspard is determined to revive the gum trade, and he sent Orloff to arrange the matter. I g-gathered from our interview that the Vale of Kandu is the source of the stuff. Gaspard spoke of a g-gum plant."

"It's true!" said Lucy. "At least, Arden Gutz claimed that gum comes from a plant."

"If Gaspard's plan succeeds, our woes will multiply," said Lemonjello. "He means to collect spent gum-meat and use it a second, even a third or fourth time, by putting on a new c-coat of sugar-icing. A lucrative scheme!"

"Do you mean to say he'll use the gum-meat *again*, after it's been chewed?" asked Pauline.

Lemonjello grimly nodded.

"He showed me a b-bucket of the stuff, collected expressly for that purpose."

"Ugh! That is re-*volt*-ing!"

"I'm surprised Dickie didn't think of it first," said Lil. "He was a nose-picker, growing up, and he never let his pickings go to waste, if you take my meaning. Leave it to Dickie to go into the gum trade."

"I am going to be *ill*!" shrieked Pauline.

"No d-doubt we all share your distress," said Lemonjello. "The question is, what are we to do? We c-cannot apply to the Causists for aid. Despite his grand words and pamphlets, Arden Gutz has softened on the question of gum, I gather, now that he has gained control of the castle."

"We must first stop Orloff," said Lucy. "He still controls the gum trade. We ought to follow him to Kandu and rip up the gum plant by its roots. When that was done we could deal with Arden Gutz."

"I second that!" said Pauline.

"That would be most welcome," said Lemonjello, "but we must consider the here and the now. My concern is for your welfare, Lucy, and for yours, Miss C-cant. You have acted with g-great fortitude and courage, but — but — but you are children and you must . . . if possible . . . be spared the intrigues and violence of men. I have given the matter much thought, and c-consulted with Mrs. Lungwich. Miss Cant, I have concluded, may best escape the Causist threat by going to her kinsmen, who dwell at Villa Martlet —"

"*No!*" cried Pauline.

"— where a government-in-exile has b-been established. I see no other recourse."

"I should have to live with *Eugenia!*" Pauline wailed. Her cousin Eugenia, the elder daughter of Sir Clarence Martlet and Lord Cant's sister, Petunia, was the sort of girl who wore gloves to play croquet.

"We all m-must prepare for sacrifices, Miss Cant."

"You needn't call me *Miss Cant*, Luigi," Pauline pouted. "Lucy is the heiress. I'm but a younger sister, a girl of no account, to be hidden away in some relative's attic like a second-best bed!"

"Forgive me, Miss C-c-c — er, that is, Miss Pauline. Old habits —"

"In any case, I refuse. I *stoutly* refuse. Eugenia makes me *ill.* Why, you could bake a cake with the amount of powder on her face! And my uncle Clarence is a puffed-up pig's bladder, simply *full* of heraldic hoo-haw. He would very likely put Lucy in bonds as a pretender. You certainly aren't very long-sighted, Luigi, considering you're an astronomer!"

"B-begging your pardon, Miss — er, Pauline, I have considered the threat to Lucy. Mrs. Lungwich has agreed to return with her to D-dragonfly-on-Bog, where she may lodge with Mrs. Holstein-Quack until order has been restored in the Barony."

"*No!*" cried Lucy and Pauline together.

"But — but I see no alternative —"

"No," said Lucy. A gust of wind blew sparks from the tinkers' campfires, and Lucy looked away, as though embarrassed at having to cross the astronomer. "I can't allow it," she added.

"But — but Lucy! —"

"I never wanted to be a Baroness," Lucy said. "I hoped that if I served Pauline well she might reward me with a dowry, so I could open a chandlery when she came into her inheritance. But Lord Cant claimed me as his child, and as such I have a duty to my sister, and to the Barony. I will not hide while Cantling fights against Cantling."

"But — but what can you do?" asked Lemonjello. "What resort has a child against t-two armies? Whoever wins this war must have a Baroness in Castle Cant. When the dust has settled you may come forward . . . or Miss Pauline . . . and p-perhaps exercise no little influence . . ."

"Whoever wins this war will still profit by the gum trade," said Lucy. "Arden Gutz is no less greedy than Vlad Orloff. And so all of Cant will be the loser. War will settle nothing, not even the dust."

"That is well put!" said Pauline.

"But — but what are we to do?"

Lucy took the astronomer's hand.

"You must talk to the people of Cant, Luigi. They want no part of war! But they're scared of armies and rebels, and they want someone to give them courage. You must rally them! There can be no war if the people won't take up arms."

"But – but – but –"

"Ride down the North Road. Swanson will go with you. And when you reach the castle you must set free my uncle Hock. He'll be able to deal with Arden Gutz when the time comes."

"But – but, Lucy!" pleaded Lemonjello. "I have a c-considerable c-c-catch in my speech! Surely you have n-noticed that! I am not an orator, to rally the p-people of C-cant!"

"Neither was I a spy, Luigi," said Lucy. "I simply pretended."

"And what do *you* p-propose to do?"

Lucy looked into the fire. "My business is with Vlad Orloff," she said.

"Don't say such a thing!" hissed Lil. "You don't know Dick Lungwich, child! He has a stone where his heart ought to be, and I say it as his sis that changed his nappies! You don't want him as your enemy!"

"But I do know him, ma'am," Lucy said. "Your brother killed my family. And he will be my enemy as long as I draw breath." In the hush that followed this avowal Swanson leaned over to Pauline.

"Forget floating sleeves!" he whispered. "She wants a suit of armor!"

Lucy pleaded until the fire burned down to coals, but Lemonjello held firm. With her uncle in the dungeon it fell to him to assume the role of grown-up in her life, he argued. The fugitives would travel together to Ramsford, but then she must turn back with Lil and remain in hiding with Harriet Holstein-Quack until the Barony was at peace again.

Pauline boiled up nearly to a tantrum, steadfastly refusing to live with her cousin Eugenia. But Lemonjello used her own words against her. She had declared herself to be a girl of no account, he said. Very well. That m-meant she must defer to authority, and not presume to interfere in the matter!

Pauline was so stunned by this retort — who knew that the astronomer was such a wily debater? — that she got up in a huff and went to sulk in the wagon. She was unused to being spoken to in such a manner, and Lil's broth, furthermore, had made a most unsatisfactory meal.

How good a tablet of gum would taste! she thought. She took Orloff's gum purse from her pack but found she had chewed the last piece. Vainly she searched in the bottom of the pack, hoping perhaps a tablet had fallen out as she hiked. The situation struck her as wholly unfair. She could have chewed gum all day long while her father lived, but now, when she certainly deserved the consolation of a sweet, she must do without.

You ought never have chewed that gum, milady.

Nonsense, thought Pauline. She had been lost in the wilds and quite starving. She had wanted her strength — Mrs. Selvage had said so herself. (Or had that been Lil?) In any case, she *had* wanted her strength, and the gum had given her a needed boost. She had little choice in the matter.

Then why do you want gum now? Mrs. Selvage asked. Your belly's full, ain't it?

She didn't want *gum*, Pauline explained, rather warmly. Why did Mrs. Selvage insist on twisting her words around? She simply wanted a *sweet*, and as Lil had offered no pudding after supper, she thought she might make do with a tablet of gum.

You ought never've chewed it, said Mrs. Selvage.

"Oh, hold your tongue, old woman!" snapped Pauline.

"Who are you talking to, Miss Cant?" asked Blaise.

Pauline started, and her head struck the ceiling of the wagon.

"Ow!" she cried. "Blast it, Delagraisse! Why must you sneak up on a person?"

"Pauline, what's wrong?" Lucy asked. She stood behind the under-footman, a troubled look on her brow. Lil's lantern swung from its hook and threw dizzying shadows.

"Nothing's *wrong*," Pauline said. "He startled me, that's all."

"That's no reason to cuss," mumbled Blaise.

"Who *were* you talking to?" Lucy asked.

"I . . . I was playing with the cat," said Pauline. That animal yawned in its basket and blinked like a worker caught napping on the job. The knapsack lay open, with Orloff's gum purse and its other contents beside it. Pauline hurriedly put them away. "Forgive me, Delagraisse," she said. "It's just that you startled me, that's all."

She avoided Lucy's eye.

"Why did you say 'Hold your tongue'?" Blaise persisted.

Pauline's hands trembled so she could hardly buckle the pack.

"I was *playing*, I told you! Honestly, Delagraisse, have you no imagination at all?"

"I'm just saying!"

"Pauline is tired, Blaise," Lucy said, climbing up into the

wagon. She took the pack and hung it on the wall. "Goodness, you've been lost, and found, and put under arrest, and rescued again all in a day. It's a wonder you don't fall over!"

"Yes — yes, of course you're right," said Pauline. She was simply tired and peevish; that was all. "But I'm an awful, spoilt, willful creature and I *know* you'll forgive me, Delagraisse."

"Oh, you're not as bad as that," said the under-footman. He took a blanket from his pack and went to sleep with the men by the embers of the fire.

"Come, lie down, Pauline," said Lucy. She unrolled the blanket they shared, and when Pauline had lain down beside her she spread it over them. Pauline, as was her habit, curled up on her side and put her head on Lucy's shoulder. She had grown up sleeping on pillows, and Lucy was the nearest thing to a pillow in the wilds.

Yes, she was simply tired. That was why Mrs. Selvage had come. But now Lucy was here and Pauline had no need of the old servant and her foolish warnings about gum. Besides, Mrs. Selvage was a figment. One would have to be daft to pay a figment any mind.

Chapter 15

*L*ucy had never been so far abroad, and when the wagon turned down Dock Street in Ramsford she frankly gaped at the mighty River Leech. The only boats she knew were the punts and rowboats that folk from the castle used on Micklewood Pond, and she gazed dumbstruck at the tall-masted vessels that rested at anchor or cleaved the broad river under billowing sails.

They had been three days traveling from Smuts, and on this their last night together Lemonjello had agreed to take rooms at an inn. Dock Street smelled of tar and rotting fish, and its cobbles nearly shook the wagon to splinters. None of the inns looked respectable. Their shingles bore crude paintings of sea serpents and bosomy mermaids, and leering sailors loitered at their doors, their arms tattooed with anchors. Cats skulked in alleys or bolted from the dockside with fish guts in their jaws.

Finally the travelers stopped at the Carp and Caper, which had a slightly more wholesome aspect than its neighbors. Lemonjello went in with Swanson and, some minutes later, they returned with a stable boy.

"I have t-taken two rooms on the first floor front," the astronomer said. "Swanson will show you the way while I see to the animals with Mrs. Lungwich. Please to remember," he added in a whisper, "that we are *incognito.* Answer to nothing but Jams and Pooter, even among yourselves. There may be bad elements about."

Lucy, disguised as a boy, could no longer travel as "Rosie," so Pauline had given her the name "Jams." It was, she insisted, a common name among tinkers. (Lil had snorted.) To disguise herself, Pauline had corked her eyebrows and tucked up her hair into a bonnet.

The rooms looked over the docks, and after weeks of camping they seemed great luxury to Pauline, who in the castle had slept on a feather bed so grand it wanted four maids to turn it. She threw herself on the straw mattress and flung out her arms.

"I'm going to sleep for a fortnight!" she said.

"Then please to lie on your belly, or your snoring will keep me awake the whole time," said Lucy, who would share the bed with her and Lil while Blaise and the men slept next door.

"I don't snore, Jams," said Pauline.

"You do a good imitation, anyway."

Pauline sat up. Lucy had somehow got into her head the absurd notion that she (Pauline) was a snorer, and she (Lucy) was always poking her (Pauline) with an elbow at night and begging her (Pauline) to roll over. It was tiresome because Pauline did not like sleeping on her belly. One woke with wrinkles on one's face.

"I'm afraid it's true, Miss Pooter," said Blaise, who had lingered when Swanson carried his pack next door. "It ain't a bed-shaking snore, such as my old man used to make who could wake the dead, but more of a 'flubbity' sound — like a wee lost lamb."

"*Flubbity?*" cried Pauline, springing from the bed. "Why, that's not even a word!"

"That's how it sounds, all the same."

Pauline threw open the window and looked out over the docks, fuming. She could not deny that Delagraisse had proved useful, both in the castle and since, but in her view he was far too familiar. To name one example, Lucy was rightfully the Baroness of Cant, and yet the boy continued to address her as "Lucy" rather than "Lady Wickwright," as befitted an under-footman. And whenever some misunderstanding arose — this absurd accusation of snoring, for instance, or her talking aloud to Mrs. Selvage at Smuts — the boy always tried to turn Lucy against her.

They must soon bid farewell to Blaise Delagraisse, in any case. Lucy and Pauline had made plans while lying in the wagon at night. They did not mean to be separated. In Ramsford they would sneak off and somehow make their way to the Vale of Kandu. The rebels claimed Lucy as their Baroness and the Loyalists stood by Pauline, but both sides, it was clear, cared chiefly about the gum trade. Pauline and Lucy meant to find the gum plant and lay an axe to its roots.

They had not discussed what to tell Blaise — indeed, in their plotting they had never mentioned him at all — but

Pauline thought now was as good a time as any to inform the under-footman that his services would no longer be required.

"Delagraisse," she said, turning from the window, "I must have a word with you."

"I'm sorry, Miss Pooter. I shouldn't have said 'flubbity.'"

"It's not about that. It concerns —"

She was interrupted, for at that moment Lillian Lungwich came in, followed by Swanson and Lemonjello. Lil carried a shawl and a jug of poteen and cried "La-dee-da!" when she saw the grandeur of the room.

"Ain't we living like nobs!" she said, putting down her shawl on the washstand. "Would you care for a snort, Mr. Lemonjello? Mr. Swanson? Riding on that dusty road has given me an awful thirst."

"Thank you, no," said the astronomer. He turned to Lucy. "I saw a barber's pole some doors distant, so we will leave you in the care of Mrs. Lungwich. I *strongly* suggest you not stray from the inn, or t-talk to anyone, or use your proper names." He gave her a few shillings from his purse. "This should suffice for a meal. The landlord assures me his stew is harmless."

"Thank you, sir," said Lucy.

Lemonjello whispered *"Incognito!"* and opened the door for Swanson. A moment later Pauline saw them emerge from the Carp and Caper and make their way down Dock Street. Lil uncorked her jug and drank at length, then lay down on the bed with a deep, contented sigh.

"Ah, this is grand," she said. "I fancy a bit of a nap before dinner. You children go ahead without me. And take care to bridle your tongues, as Mr. Lemonjello said. Ramsford is all full of river rats, my dears. They'd snitch on their own mothers for a penn'orth of ale. Be sharp!"

With this warning she closed her eyes and at once began to snore. Pauline pointed urgently to her open mouth — as though to say "You see my point!" — but Lucy had already tiptoed out of the room, and Blaise Delagraisse merely shrugged.

"Aye, Lil snores," he admitted as they went down the gloomy stairway, "but she don't snore flubbity. That's the point I'm trying to make."

A crude table and benches took most of the space in the common room, which was black from decades of coal fires. The once-pink roses on the wallpaper looked like the mouths of filthy drains. A dozen fishers crowded the benches, but beyond them, in a nook by the fireplace, a man sat at a smaller table. He looked up and, catching Pauline's eye, indicated that they might sit with him.

"You are travelers, I surmise?" he said, standing.

"Thank you, sir, yes," said Blaise, bringing stools from the fireside. The stranger wore a clean if rumpled tunic and had a thin beard that stretched from ear to ear along the line of his jaw. His cheeks and lip were clean shaven.

"I am Primo Furstival," he told Blaise. "I have traveled from Boondock."

"Boondock!" Blaise marveled. That town was nearly as far from the castle as one could go in Cant, and its name was a byword for all that was curious, provincial, and uncouth.

"A Boondocker born and bred," said Furstival with pride.

"My great-great-grandsire settled in Boondock when it was only a fishers' village — before it was named Boondock, indeed. It wasn't then the grand town it is today. And with whom have I the pleasure of speaking?"

"I beg your pardon, sir," said the under-footman. "Blaise Tooey's my name, and this here's my brother Jams, and that's our little sis, what we call Pooter."

"Well-brought-up children, all of you, I can tell," said Furstival. "You have an artist's face, Jams. Very fine and sensitive, with a mouth many women would envy. And Pooter, why, you're as pretty as your name suggests. Was it your parents I saw you with earlier?"

"No, sir," Lucy quickly said. "We've just come from the shearing in Great Pillow and the lady was kind enough to carry us in her wagon. We're casting about for work. Blaise looks after us."

"Three bowls of fish stew, if you please!" Furstival called to the serving girl. Pauline begged Lucy to order a bottle of squash, for she badly craved a sweet, and after counting their silver Lucy asked the girl to bring a bottle with three tumblers, for sharing.

"I believe I shall have a squash, as well," said Primo Furstival. "What a delightful suggestion, Pooter. I say, if you children are looking for work, you might consider coming Boondock way. We want strong backs in our part of the Barony."

"Is there work to be had there, sir?" asked Lucy.

"There soon will be!" said Furstival. "We've not always prospered, away in Boondock. I'll not pretend otherwise. No doubt you've heard people mocking us as being backward, poor, uncultivated folks."

"'Dull as a day in Boondock,'" quoted Blaise, adding "Ow!" when Lucy kicked him.

"No, no, he's right," said Furstival. "That is our reputation. I shan't deny it."

"I'm sure it's merely idle talk," Pauline politely said.

"Not only idle, but wrong!" the Boondocker replied. "Boondock is ready to boom, Pooter. We've come up with a plan to lure folk from all over Cant to spend their money in Boondock — from as far away as Tenesmus!"

"Indeed?" said Pauline. "Why would they go to Boondock?"

"Sightseeing!" proclaimed Primo Furstival.

In the stunned silence that followed, the serving girl returned with their squash. She poured out a bottle between Lucy, Pauline, and Blaise, then put Furstival's bottle and blackjack next to his plate.* The squash made a disappointing puddle in Pauline's tumbler, but before she could feel cheated the Boondocker made up the want from his bottle.

"Ah, that's fine!" he said, tasting the drink. "It doesn't compare to the squash of our Boondock inns, of course, but you'll find nothing like that in all the length of Cant. I," he went on, "am the chief traveling delegate of the Boondock Town Assembly, popularly known as the 'Boondock Boosters.' Our aim is to buck up the fortunes of Boondock by encouraging the sightseeing trade."

"And you imagine folk will come from Tenesmus?" asked Pauline, wiping a dribble of squash from her chin. Lucy and

---

*Blackjack: a drinking vessel made of leather covered with tar.

Blaise were spooning up the stew, eating their proper meal before enjoying the squash, but Pauline had never learned such restraint. As the Baron's daughter she had drunk from bottomless goblets. She ate the good things first, then stopped. Furstival seemed charmed by her greed.

"When folks learn of all there is to see in our vicinity they will *flock* to Boondock, Pooter. No doubt you've heard of the tongue baths at Dwelft, which is not half a league distant? But did you know that the baths are but a fraction of a great region of hot springs, some of them fizzy? And a half day's carriage ride from Boondock brings one to Dundandilly Glacier, site of year-round tobogganing. In Boondock proper, of course, the chief attraction is the dock itself, which is recognized as one of the Seven Wonders of Cant."*

"They say it is grand," admitted Blaise.

"And it is only the first of many worthy sights," Furstival said. "There is the Fish Palace, naturally, and the Museum of Vegetable Taxidermy, and for the truly adventurous the renowned Zeitszchnitzsche Mole Preserve. And at the end of an exciting day of sightseeing one retires to a welcoming inn and enjoys a squash worthy of the name. That is what we are really selling — our famous Boondocker hospitality!"

"I should like to see the mole preserve!" said Blaise.

"But I had no idea Boondock was such fun!" said Pauline,

---

* *The immense dock extended far into Lake Poltroon. According to legend the town got its name when a boatman, lost in a storm for several days, fell to his knees and kissed its planks upon reaching port. "Tis a boon dock!" the boatman reportedly cried, and the epithet (meaning "good dock") soon passed into common usage.*

who now felt cheated by her father. She had gone with Lord Cant to many corners of the Barony, but always they stopped at some nobleman's estate, where she endured tedious evenings of quadrille dancing. She wished they had gone to Boondock, instead. "Are there *giant* moles on the mole preserve?" she asked.

"As long as this!" said Furstival, holding his hands wonderfully far apart.

"I simply had no idea!"

"And that is our challenge, Pooter," said the Boondock booster. "How to inform folk of all our town offers?" He opened a satchel and placed before them a folded pamphlet, such as the orphans peddled at the American Mission. "We intend to send these to all the towns and villages of Cant," he explained. His tablemates leaned over to read the title:

VISIT FARAWAY BOONDOCK!
"The Tenesmus of Trans-Poltroon"

Below these words an engraving showed a Cantling family walking hand in hand down a great boat dock. The artist was a master of perspective and had made the dock dwindle to a point on the horizon behind them.

"I don't understand," said Lucy (who without her glasses had leaned nearly into her stew to read the italics). She unfolded the pamphlet and looked at its drawings and descriptions. "Why do you call it 'The Tenesmus of Trans-Poltroon?'"

"It's a way of speaking, Jams. A figure of speech."

"Yes, sir. But why?"

"Why?" The Boondocker seemed taken aback. "Well,

Tenesmus is the great town of metropolitan Cant, Jams. Folks come from all parts to hear the bells of the guild hall, or to see the colossus of Gustaf I. Now, Boondock is the great town of Trans-Poltroon. We want folks to come see *our* attractions. Boondock is to Trans-Poltroon as Tenesmus is to metropolitan Cant. That's what you call an analogy, Jams."

"But if you give away these pamphlets in Great Pillow or Muckleston," Lucy persisted, "won't folks think it's much easier simply to go to the *real* Tenesmus, instead of making a great long voyage by boat to see the Tenesmus of Trans-Poltroon? You admit yourself it's far away," she said, pointing to the title.

Pauline impatiently snatched the pamphlet from her.

"What utter nonsense you talk," she said. "*I* understand, Mr. Furstival. I think Boondock sounds absolutely *buckets* of fun. As soon as the war is over I intend to visit the mole preserve."

"I meant no disrespect to Boondock, sir," Lucy said.

"No, no, Jams, it's quite all right. Perhaps the copy does want revision."

"I shouldn't change a thing," Pauline insisted. "Is that why you're stopping at Ramsford, Mr. Furstival? Do you mean to give out pamphlets?" She took another drink of squash and put down her blackjack next to the Boondocker's bottle. He again topped her up.

"Ah, now you've touched a sore spot, Pooter. We're having to start all over again with the pamphlets," he said. "A merchant I know, who trades in the outlands, offered to have them printed there cheaply. Alas, save a penny, lose a crown, as they say. Look on the other side!"

He jabbed his finger at a map of Cant on which a guild hall, representing Boondock, showed the town as being quite distant from Lake Poltroon, and indeed on the wrong side of the Trans-Poltroon post road. But it was the word printed next to it that made Pauline's eyes pop out.

"*Boondook?*" she screamed. The fishers looked up from their stew.

"*Boondook!*" wailed Primo Furstival. "How does one misspell Boondock on a pamphlet for the Boondock Town Assembly? That's what trading with outlanders will get you. By good fortune a member of the Assembly, Mrs. Tittle of the Turtle Tavern, spotted the error. If not for her sharp eye, 'Boondook' would now be the laughingstock of Cant."

Blaise turned over a fold of the pamphlet.

"They spelled it right on the front," he noted.

"It's simply baffling," said Furstival. "I can only guess the printer's apprentice copied from some outlandish map and his master failed to check the work. Or there may be strong drink at the bottom of it. In any case, I find myself obliged to travel to the Vale of Kandu to set the matter right."

Lucy, who had almost finished her stew, froze with a spoon in her mouth.

"You're going to Kandu, sir?" she asked (after removing the spoon).

"There's nothing else for it, I'm afraid," sighed Furstival. "And the dashed thing is, I'll have to go by road from here. I hired a boat to take me to Fort Gustaf, but then made the mistake of giving my crew part wages when we docked at Ramsford. The blackguards bolted for the rum shops, and I've not seen the hide of them since. I daren't hire a crew off the docks unless I want to end with my throat slit, so tomorrow I shall board the post coach. It's a great nuisance."

"Why, if you want a trustworthy crew you needn't look further!" said Lucy, with a sidelong glance at Pauline. "Our brother Blaise is an expert boatman, aren't you, Blaise? I've been after him to teach me the way of it. I should love to see the river!"

Furstival turned to Blaise.

"Indeed!" he said. "You've got your sea-legs, have you, Blaise?

The under-footman, who had got lost in the picture of the mole preserve (and who had never gone more than waist deep into Micklewood Pond), looked up from the pamphlet with an expression of deep anxiety. Pauline could not believe her ears. Lucy meant to bring the boy with them!

"I shouldn't say I've got my *sea-legs*, exactly," Blaise protested.

"Oh, blushes! He's an accomplished sailor, Mr. Furstival," said Lucy.

"Mostly punts and rowboats, really," said the under-footman, naming the only kinds of vessel on which he had ever before laid his eyes. "Pole-work and oar-work, you know."

"There'll be none of that on the river," warned Furstival, "but of course I'm going downstream, so if you're not an expert with sails we should still end up at the same place."

"Even a cork can sail *down*stream," said Lucy.

"What say you, then?" asked Furstival. "You've only one proper sailor among you, but you strike me as an able lad, Jams, and I'm sure little Pooter can manage the washing up. I'll give you ten shillings per day for the three together, payable at Fort Gustaf, as well as your return fare on the post coach."

"Washing up!" wailed Pauline.

"She wants to be a boatman, too," Lucy hurriedly said. "She always was a tom-boy, Mr. Furstival. But, Pooter, you know you're too little for any such thing, and, besides, you're a girl. I think Mr. Furstival's offer is very generous, Blaise."

Delagraisse blinked. He was breathing through his mouth again, Pauline noticed, and though her heart was sinking she felt an almost irresistible urge to kick his shin. The boy was so used to following Lucy that he'd forgotten he was their elder brother, and must appear to make the decisions.

"There's nothing more bracing than river air," said Furstival.

"And I should love to see Fort Gustaf!" added Lucy.

Delagraisse blinked again, like a chicken grown dizzy in the hot sun. Pauline wanted to scream. She was certain that Lucy and she could have floated a boat down the river without this ridiculous boy's help, and now he was so dull with fish stew and visions of the mole preserve that he could barely keep his head upright. Say something, you great baboon! she thought.

"I shall lay in several bottles of squash for the journey," said Furstival, evidently taking the under-footman's hesitation to mean he must sweeten his offer. Pauline could not let Delagraisse upset their mission. The words stuck in her craw like a fish bone, but she cleared her throat and coughed them out.

"Please, Blaise," she begged, "may we ship with Mr. Furstival and see Fort Gustaf?"

Understanding dawned at last on the under-footman's face. He looked at Lucy, who nodded her head the tiniest possible fraction of an inch.

"Aye," he said, "aye, we'll accept your offer, Mr. Furstival. That is, if you're certain you're up to it, Jams."

"Oh, yes!" said Lucy. "Imagine, we're going to see Fort Gustaf, Pooter. Isn't it grand?"

"Aye, grand!" sighed Pauline, who would serve as scullery maid while Lucy played at being a boy and the under-footman breathed the bracing river air. What a tumble she had taken!

She snatched the map from Delagraisse. Her cousins lived across the river at Villa Martlet, where she would have been welcomed as the rightful Baroness and stuffed with finger cakes while Uncle Clarence plotted her restoration (and his own place in the Paulinine order). But there Lucy would have been arrested as a pretender. At Castle Cant, meanwhile, the Causist rebels would hail Lucy as their ruler, but lock Pauline in the dungeon. Nowhere in the Barony could they be safe together. So the Adored & Honorable Pauline would go with Lucy into exile.

With her finger she followed the Leech past Fort Gustaf to the frontier, where it disappeared into the mountains. On maps of the olden days the lands beyond the border were marked with dire warnings — 𝕳𝖊𝖗𝖊 𝖇𝖊 𝖉𝖗𝖆𝖌𝖔𝖓𝖘 was typical — but Pauline had learned that monsters were not nearly as fearsome as the greed of men. Perhaps, she thought wistfully, one or two mythical beasts still lived somewhere in the Vale of Kandu. She pictured Blaise Delagraisse sliding headfirst through a dragon's jaws, and she felt a little better.

Chapter 16

On the River Leech

"I can't say what we shall find on the river," said Mr. Furstival, "but I have neither gum nor anything else worth stealing on my boat, so I shouldn't fear any acts of piracy against us. I have brought a sword, nevertheless."

He had told frightful stories of his voyage from Boondock. Causist pirates now sailed Lake Poltroon, he said, boarding traders' ships and stealing their cargoes of chewing gum. The price of gum had soared in Boondock, where the rebels sold their loot on the black market. The noble houses had raised militias, and their fleets contended with the rebels for control of the lake.

Fog settled on Ramsford that night. Blaise promised to keep awake, and when the first birds sang he crept down the corridor and whispered at the girls' door. They would sail at first light. Lucy hated to leave without a word to her friends, so when she had gathered her things she slid a note under the astronomer's door and then barefooted down the stairs after Pauline.

My dear L. [she wrote],

Cant wants level heads and true hearts in these times. I beg you not to follow us, but to take the path I suggested. In Tenesmus you may confide in Penelope, Uncle H.'s maid-of-all-work. After you have rescued Uncle H. you must rouse the people of Tenesmus. Remember that we have eyes and ears within the enemy's stronghold.

Be brave, my friend! It is not your tongue but your heart that will serve the people of Cant. Written this 30th day of the Interregnum by

your devoted
"Jams"

The streetlamps cast but little light in the fog. Blaise groaned when he saw the knocker-up at work, who with her long pole was tapping upper windows to rouse the dockmen and other early risers.

"I might have paid her to wake me instead of staying up all night," he said.

"But that would have woken Luigi, as well," Lucy pointed out.

"Aye," admitted the under-footman. "My head's dull from want of sleep. I can't be blamed for saying stupid things today."

And what about every other day? Pauline wondered, but if she meant to travel to Kandu with Delagraisse she supposed she must learn to hold her tongue. Lucy would only take his side, anyway.

The docks blazed with torches and braziers, for the ships must be loaded, fog or no fog. Mr. Furstival's boat was moored between two larger vessels, and they might have walked past it had he not called out to them. The Boondocker, holding a spyglass, stood on the forward deck.

"Ahoy, my swabs!" he cried.

"Ahoy, sir," said Lucy. The gangplank was narrow, and Pauline clung to Lucy's tunic as they walked over the water. Blaise tripped on a cleat and nearly fell overboard before ever setting foot on deck.

"You must call me 'Cap'n,' Jams," said Primo Furstival. "You're a boatman now."

"Yes sir, Cap'n."

"May I be called 'matey'?" Pauline asked. She loved sea stories and had begun to look forward to the voyage, on which she hoped to see a pirate ship, a sea serpent, a shipwreck, and (if such creatures really lived) a beautiful enchanting mermaid.

"That you may, lass," said Furstival. He turned to Blaise. "Stow away that plank now, Master Blaise. Cast off the forward line and weigh anchor. The pilot will be along presently to take us out. Pooter, you may bring the bags below deck."

"Matey," Pauline reminded him.

"Hop to!" barked the Boondocker. Pauline guessed he was

teasing but nonetheless she flung their knapsacks over her shoulders and followed him down the hatch. The cabin was close as a hen coop. Hammocks hung to right and left, and beyond them a lamp swung over a nailed-down table and bench. Pauline stowed the gear in a locker, and Mr. Furstival showed her where the provisions were kept.

The voyage would be cramped and uncomfortable, the food wretched, her labor hard. Pauline was ecstatic. Already she felt like a true "swab." Their boat, the *Unicorn*, was wonderfully old and weather-beaten, its prow thickly bearded with algae. Pauline went "topside" and explored the deck while Blaise, with much help from Lucy, prepared to cast off. Primo Furstival joined Pauline on the forward deck.

"I believe the fog is lifting, Pooter . . . er, matey." He raised the spyglass to his eye and scanned the river. "We should soon have a breeze off the lake, and then we'll see what kind of sailors your brothers will make. Ah, here comes the pilot."

"May I see, Cap'n?" Pauline asked. Furstival gave her the glass and she looked out over the river. A boat hove into view. Two men plied its oars, and another, his beard plaited in braids like a ram's curled horns, stood with his foot on the gunwale. The pilot and his crew would tow their vessel into the shipping channel, casting off when it had cleared the hidden rocks that might breach its hull.

"*Unicorn!*" the pilot cried. "Throw us a line!"

"Master Blaise!" said Furstival. "A line, if you please!"

Blaise found a coil of rope and was about to toss it to the pilot when Furstival held his arm. The line must first be made fast to the *Unicorn*, he explained. Pauline rolled her eyes. When the rope had been tied to a ring under the bowsprit, Blaise threw it to the pilot, who pulled it hand over hand until his boat bumped against the *Unicorn*'s hull. He hung a boarding ladder over the railing.

"Give us a hand up!" he growled, and with Furstival's help he climbed on deck. Over his dirty blouse he wore a tight-fitting waistcoat of pig leather, from which he took a small notebook and pencil. After consulting his watch he noted the time in his log.

"This ain't the crew you sailed in with," he said, scowling.

"No, Mr. Salt," said the Boondocker. "I'm afraid they jumped ship."

"All fast!" cried an oarsman in the pilot's boat.

"Cast off your line!" barked Salt. Blaise ran aft to obey this order, and when it was done the oarsmen began to pull the *Unicorn* from the quay. Lucy had joined Pauline on the foredeck. The pilot limped over to Pauline, his step booming on the deck, and he thrust out his horned beard at her. She would have tripped over the rail had he not grabbed her arm.

"What's your name, girl?" he demanded.

"Pooter, sir!" she said. His grip was frightfully strong.

"Whose child be ye?"

"My — my father is dead . . . and Mama, too," she stammered.

"The elder lad is her guardian," said Primo Furstival. Lucy had stepped forward when the pilot grabbed Pauline, and now she glared at Salt.

"And who're you?" he asked.

"Jams, sir. I'm her brother. And I'll thank you to keep your hands off her."

The pilot growled but Lucy stood her ground. Mr. Salt had been drinking spirits, Pauline suspected. His eyes were red and his breath reeked of juniper. He turned again to Furstival.

"This here's the crew that's taking you downriver?" he asked.

"Yes, as far as Fort Gustaf."

"I shouldn't trust 'em to paddle me over a duck pond," the pilot said. He leered at Lucy and touched her cheek with his knuckles. "This lad wouldn't know a razor from a cheese knife!"

Lucy slapped his hand away and Salt threw back his head, roaring with laughter. Pauline clenched her fists. She wanted to push the great bully into the river but she dared not.

"Ah, you're truly a boatman, Jams!" said the pilot, wiping his eyes. "All full of sauce and ready to fight over string and moonbeams. Well, pick your battles wisely, lad. A lesser man than me would've slain you for that, but lucky for you I'm sweet natured. Here! Can you not stroke it, you great warts?" he cried to the oarsmen.

"And aren't we stroking to break our arms?" one of them yelled.

"Then stroke to break your backs, you ugly toads!" screamed the pilot.

Fog hung like torn rags over the water but the light had risen. Soon the sun would come up. The pilot scratched between the horns of his beard and glared darkly at Pauline. She seemed to vex him.

"You're a pretty little thing," he said accusingly.

"She doesn't need to hear flattery," said Lucy.

The pilot lifted his finger.

"I told you to pick your battles wisely, Jams, and you oughtn't to pick this one!" he warned. "What kind of folks were your ma and pa, girl?" he asked Pauline. "How is it they died?"

"They . . . they were chandlers. They died in a fire."

"Chandlers!" the pilot said. "I've made port in Ramsford since Urbano wore the Baron's cap. I don't recall no chandler's shop a-catching fire."

"Not ship's chandlers," said Pauline. "They were candle makers. We hail from Tenesmus."

Salt's eyes narrowed.

"And how did you end up in Ramsford?"

"See here!" said Primo Furstival. "What is the meaning of all these questions? You've brought us into the shipping channel. Please to cast off your boat, and we shall be on our way."

"I know my duty, Boondocker!" said the pilot. "It's my business to keep an eye open for smugglers and cut-throats and such as washes up to our docks. And since the fall of the house of Cant there's been every kind of rat boarding ships."

Pauline hid her trembling hands in the pockets of her kirtle. "The house of Cant is not fallen!" she said.

"Oh, it ain't?" mocked the pilot. "Well, ain't you behind times! Ramsford is a Causist town, and it stands behind the house of Wickwright, little girl."

"The house of Wickwright!" Lucy gasped.

"Aye! And I don't mean to let no Loyalist spies ship through my port!"

"You can't mean my crew!" said Furstival.

"Did you not think to ask where these ragamuffins came from?" the pilot asked. "Or where they might be going, with a war on and all of Cant in an uproar?"

"Sir," the Boondocker said warmly, "I am a delegate of the Boondock Town Assembly, not some slippery ne'er-do-well fellow. I can vouch for the character of my crew! They have come from the shearing in Great Pillow."

"Come from the shearing, have they?" scoffed Salt. He grabbed Pauline's wrist and showed her palm to the Boondocker. "Why, her hand's as white and soft as mushrooms! You couldn't plant a mustard seed in the dirt under her nails!"

"I had a wash-up!" Pauline said.

"And did ye wash the horn off your palms, my little princess?"

"What are you implying?" demanded Furstival.

"Are ye blind, man?" asked Salt. "If these kids make up a family their ma must've been a friendly woman! One tow-headed child, one black haired, and one brown. Mama whelped in any old kennel, it seems. Avast!" he called to his oarsmen. "Hard about!"

"You can't talk about our mother like that!" said Blaise.

"Silence!" said the pilot. He flung away Pauline's arm and drew a short sword. "I've been long enough a river man to know a rat when I smell one. Mr. Chubb!" he called. "Board this vessel and secure any weapons you may find. Mr. Elias, stand guard while I search below. Cut down anyone who offers to stand!"

"This is sheer piracy!" protested Furstival.

"Sit down!" said Elias, scrambling up the boarding ladder. "Down, the lot of you!"

Pauline, who had looked forward to seeing pirates, sat miserably next to Lucy. With no hand at her tiller the *Unicorn* turned sideways on the current. Elias stood watch on the roof of the cabin. Primo Furstival sat down with his back to their guard.

"I shall have that pilot sacked for this!" he assured them.

Pauline touched Lucy's arm.

"We can't keep Mr. Furstival in the dark," she whispered. "We need his help!"

Lucy nodded. She glanced around to make sure Salt's men were out of earshot, then leaned over towards the Boondocker.

"Mr. Furstival — that is, Cap'n, sir," she said, "we've not been entirely forthcoming with you, I'm afraid." She hesitated. "You see, I've never liked to lie or steal but since the war began it's not been so simple. There are lives at stake. And the grown-ups have gone simply mad!"

Primo Furstival waited.

"For example," Lucy went on, "we *have* come from Great Pillow, just as we said, and it was shearing time, to be sure, but we had nothing to do with it. We quite frankly deceived you."

"But why, Jams?" said Furstival, obviously confused.

"Oh, *hurry!*" Pauline urged. "They'll be back soon!"

The oarsman Chubb had opened the hatches astern and was lifting boxes out of the hold. Belowdecks the pilot searched the cabin. Elias scowled at their whispers, but Mr. Salt had said nothing about forbidding the prisoners to talk. He had his orders. If they got up to no good it was the boss's fault.

"What are you trying to say, Jams?" Furstival asked.

"Oh dear," said Lucy, wiping her nose on the sleeve of her tunic. "Cap'n, the truth is Pooter's not a spy. It's worse than that. She's the Baron's daughter, sir. Pauline von Cant. We're helping her to escape."

"What!" Furstival cried.

"Shh! Yes, sir. And I'm afraid Mr. Salt suspects us."

The *Unicorn* spun in the current, the pilot's rowboat knocking against her hull. Downriver a line of rocks stood close to the shipping channel. Mr. Salt climbed laden with packs from below and spoke to Chubb in the hold, then came forward and dropped his burdens on the deck. Primo Furstival collected himself. He spoke to Salt in a tone that Pauline fancied he normally reserved for meetings of the Boondock Town Assembly.

"I must lodge a strong protest against your handling our personal effects," he said.

"Duly noted," said the pilot. He took the spearhead from Pauline's knapsack and flung it down so its point sank into the deck. "You kids use that at the shearing, did ye?" he asked.

"It's to save us from blackguards who bully children!" said Lucy.

"Har har har! You're full of sauce, Jams!" He shoved his arm into the knapsack and brought out Vlad Orloff's gum purse. Its gold gleamed in the first rays of dawn.

"Here, what's this?" he said. "Here's a pretty trinket for a poor orphan kid!"

"I stole that!" Pauline blurted. "You put it back!"

"Stole it, did you?" Salt asked. "And who is V.O.?" He pointed to the monogram with his cracked yellow nail.

"That's O.V.!" said Pauline. "Yes . . . Otis was the name . . . Otis Vineflower. He started the fire that killed our parents. I slew him with my spear and stole his gum purse!"

The pilot roared.

"Ha!" he said. "Your wit's as sharp as your spear! Chubb!"

"Sir?"

"Bring that box here!" the pilot ordered.

"Aye, sir!"

The water swirled and foamed around the rocks downstream. The *Unicorn* now floated stern foremost, the line of the pilot's boat tangled under her hull. Elias, on the cabin roof, saw the rocks ahead and ran aft to man the tiller. As Salt searched through the knapsack, Pauline exchanged glances with Lucy, Mr. Furstival, and Blaise. Furstival inclined his head towards the rowboat.

"Your Mr. Vineflower got about, he did," said the pilot, who had opened Orloff's journal. "*Struck out from East Rd. in pursuit of Wickwright*, he says. *Sent Retsch and Wilcox ahead to G. Pillow.* That means Great Pillow, I daresay. Where you kids came from."

"You've no right to read a dead man's journal!" said Pauline.

"Nor have you any right to steal it, Pooter — as you call yourself. Put it on the deck, Mr. Chubb," he instructed the oarsman, who had brought forward a small wooden box from the hold, "Let's see what manner of cargo these folks be shipping."

Chubb had already used his sword to prise open the box. The pilot lifted off its top and Pauline saw that it held hundreds of copies of "Visit Faraway Boondock!" One of the stacks of pamphlets had got turned upside down — it was obvious Chubb had tampered with it. The pilot lifted the pamphlets and from the bottom of the box took out a packet printed with the legend TWITE'S SUPERIOR CHEWING GUM.

"As I suspected," the pilot said. "Smugglers!"

"That's absurd!" said Primo Furstival. "You put that gum there!"

"Aye? And did I put Pauline von Cant on your ship as well?"

"I don't know what you're talking about!"

The pilot put the gum into Orloff's purse. It fitted snugly as a finger up a nose.

"Here is a purse belonging to Vladimir Orloff, Miss Cant's regent," he said. "Here's his journal. And here's a tow-headed darling what never scrubbed a pan or wrung out a sheet in her life, by the look of her hands. If that ain't Pauline Cant then I'm the Roman Emperor!"

The *Unicorn* listed to starboard. Elias had taken the tiller and was trying to bring the boat about. The box of pamphlets slid across the deck and Mr. Furstival barely managed to catch Orloff's gum purse and journal before they fell overboard. He hid them in a pocket of his tunic.

"Avast!" cried the pilot. "Are you trying to capsize us, man?"

"The rocks, sir!" said Elias, pointing downriver.

"Blast!" Salt cursed. He looked to the top of the mast, where a pennant showed the breeze coming off Lake Poltroon. "Mr. Chubb, let out that sheet. Elias! Bring her athwart the current. We shall tack into the wind. We're taking this ship back to Ramsford, men!"

"I object!" said Furstival, standing.

The pilot again drew his sword.

"Sit!" he commanded.

"You *can't* believe the daughter of Lord Cant has shipped as a mate on this boat!" the Boondocker said, standing his ground. Salt's boat thumped against the *Unicorn*'s hull, and the sail, as Chubb let it out, began to snap in the wind.

"That's no common girl!" the pilot said, pointing his sword at Pauline. "Who is she if not the Baron's whelp? And unless I'm blind she's not the only girl aboard this tub."

"What!"

"That is Lucy Wickwright!" said the pilot, pointing with his sword.

Furstival gaped at him.

"You are a madman. A madman!"

"If I'm a madman I shall soon be a rich one," the pilot said. "Lady Wickwright is devoted to her old boss, they say, and is helping her willingly. Well, there's a fat purse of gold waiting for the man who brings her back to Castle Cant, and I intend to claim it, by Neptune's beard! Sit, you spinster's son, or I shall strike you down!"

"But Jams is a boy!" said Furstival, yelling over the turmoil of water. Downstream the Leech surged and foamed around the threatening rocks.

"In a pig's eye he's a boy!" the pilot laughed. "Maybe your boys in Boondock have such pretty mouths, but I think I know a girl when I see one! Mr. Elias! Bring this tub about, I tell you!"

"She won't answer to the helm, sir! I think the rudder is caught on our line!"

"You can't believe Jams is a girl!" Furstival exclaimed. "He has no bosoms!"

"Chubb! Let out that sheet, blast your eyes, and swing round the boom! Hard at it, Elias!" The pilot scowled at Furstival. "A girl that age has no more bosoms than two fried eggs on a griddle. You're under arrest for kidnapping and giving aid and comfort to a fugitive!"

The spearhead stood close to Pauline, and she was tempted to stick the pilot's belly like a frog. He certainly deserved it, for Lucy had blushed a deep crimson at the mention of fried eggs.

But Pauline would be outnumbered in that fight — each of the oarsman carried a sword. She would let wind, wave, and time be her weapons.

"Enough of this charade!" she cried, leaping up. "It's no use, Mr. Furstival! He's caught me fair and square."

"But Pooter! —"

The *Unicorn* yawed wildly and the Boondocker fell to the deck before he could finish his thought. Chubb had got the sail unfurled and was unwinding the boom's line from its cleat.

"I knew it!" yelled the pilot. "Full and by, Mr. Chubb!"

"A hand if you please, sir!" cried Chubb, for the wind threatened to pull the line from his hands.

"Yes, it's true!" said Pauline, grabbing Salt's sleeve. "I meant to raise funds for the Loyalist Army by smuggling gum among those pamphlets. Long live the house of Cant!"

"Please, sir, a hand!" said Chubb. The *Unicorn* pitched up and Elias, at the tiller, fell down. The pilot kept his balance only by using his sword as a staff. He stared suspiciously at Pauline.

"You didn't put that gum in there," he said.

"Not I, but Mr. Orloff! He's hidden in the cabin!"

"What nonsense is this?" Salt asked.

"Vladimir!" cried Pauline, looking behind him. "It's no use! We're found out!"

She scarcely believed her own nerve. Even Lucy, who was trusting as a lamb, had long ago stopped falling for that old trick. But the pilot looked around, and that was all the chance Pauline needed. She yanked the spearhead from the deck and then leapt to the cabin's roof and slashed the boom's line. The

Unicorn had turned wind abeam and the boom swept out over the foredeck. It struck the pilot's chest and flung him overboard, weightless as a pamphlet in a breeze.

"Pauline!" yelled Lucy. "Behind you!"

Chubb had fallen with the line slack in his hands but now Elias drew his sword. The oarsman was twice her size, but Pauline had spent countless hours with a fencing master at Castle Cant, and her efforts repaid her now. She easily parried his artless hacking. The great difficulty was keeping her feet, for the *Unicorn* had nearly reached the rocks and was pitching madly. Mr. Salt cried from the waves before the surging foam sucked him down.

"I move that we abandon ship!" yelled Primo Furstival. He crawled over the foredeck and took up the pilot's sword, pointing it tremulously at the fallen Chubb while Blaise flung knapsacks into the pilot's boat. The wind whipped Pauline's kirtle around her legs.

"Hurry, Miss Cant!" said Blaise.

Pauline held off Elias until Blaise had pulled Lucy into the rowboat, and then she expertly struck the oarsman's blade from his hand. Salt sailed over the rocks, his cries drowned by roaring water. Chubb dodged the swinging boom and lunged at Primo Furstival, but Pauline thrust the spearhead between his legs and he fell heavily to the deck. The *Unicorn* pulled the pilot's boat towards the rocks.

"Jump, Cap'n!" Pauline cried.

Mr. Furstival flung himself over the rail, and as Pauline climbed it to follow him the ship struck the rocks, throwing her headlong into the rowboat. The torrent rolled the *Unicorn* over to its side, and the rowboat, tethered by its line, rode up on the larger vessel's hull.

"We're sunk!" yelped Blaise.

As Pauline struggled to her feet the hull gave way with a frightful, splintering roar. Half-blinded by jets of water, Pauline staggered to the prow and swung her blade at the tow rope. The severed line whipped her head, and the boat, like a sled poised over a snow hill, rode down over the *Unicorn* and shot through the surging rapids.

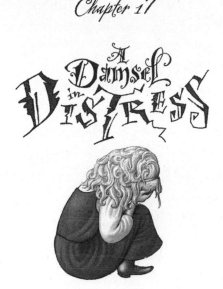

Chapter 17

A Damsel in Distress

"*T*o think I'm traveling with the heirs of Adolphus von Cant!" said Primo Furstival. "I confess I was perplexed by your want of a squire's nut, Jams . . . I mean to say, Miss Wickwright . . . but I had put it down to your youth.* Fancy my not being able to tell a boy from a girl!"

"We're not so different, I suppose," said Lucy, blushing.

The day was hot and Pauline's hands sweated on the oar. They had drawn lots to decide who should row, and Pauline was paired with Delagraisse for the first shift. When her partner was not looking she furtively chewed a tablet of the Twite's Superior Chewing Gum that Mr. Salt had put into Orloff's gum purse. It felt wonderfully soothing to her throat. Furstival,

---

*Squire's nut: Cantling term for the laryngeal cartilage, or Adam's apple.

who had saved the purse from going overboard, sat behind her in the prow with Lucy.

"And you're to be our Baroness!" marveled the Boondocker. "Now, I favored the Loyalist side in this gum rebellion, I admit. It's not that I endorse gum chewing, mind you, but I can hardly promote sightseeing in Boondock when Lake Poltroon is crawling with pirates!"

"Swimming with pirates, I should say," offered Pauline.

"Yes, of course. Very clever of you, Pooter. But as I was saying, Jams — er, Miss Wickwright — when these Causists talked of a maidservant claiming the barony, I put it down to sheer moonstruck hogwash. But if his Lordship claimed you, I think I may safely speak for the Boondock Town Assembly in promising that we shall bend the knee to no one else!"

"That's very good of you, sir," Lucy said.

"Why, you must feel you're in a fairy tale!" persisted Furstival. "One day you're sweeping cinders from the hearth and the next you're the Baroness of Cant! Think of it! You'll have every knight of the realm begging for your hand."

"Oh, no sir!" Lucy protested.

"Of course you will! You'll be quite fair when you dress like a girl again."

"I want nothing to do with knights, please, sir," begged Lucy.

"Lucy was spurned in love by Arden Gutz," said Pauline, more for Delagraisse's benefit than for Mr. Furstival. She had been roundly praised for saving the day and she thought she might be forgiven a little teasing. "She's lost all interest in boys and means never to marry."

"I did not love Arden Gutz!"

"Of course, that will mean the end of the house of Wickwright," Pauline went on, "so I suppose my eldest son will become the Baron after Lucy dies, and I'll be Baroness Dowager. I intend to have twelve children, Mr. Furstival, each one named for a sign of the zodiac."

"I feel sorry for Sagittarius," muttered Blaise.

"Pauline is making fun," Lucy told the Boondocker.

"She's a spirited lass," Furstival said. "I had rather worried when you children said you meant to travel to the outlands, but when I think how little Pooter handled that oarsman . . . Why, it's the outlanders who ought to worry! Can you handle a blade, Master Blaise?"

"Aye, sir! At least, we used to fight with broomsticks when I was a boy."

"Good lad!"

"I've had three years of fencing lessons," said Pauline, who thought Delagraisse had no call to be boasting of broomsticks. "I daresay I could cut a man to ribbons if I had a mind to. You saw how I toyed with that oarsman!"

"You swung a handsome blade," admitted the Boondocker.

"They say the sword has fallen from favor in the outlands," mused Pauline, "so I'll have the advantage of any highwaymen we may meet. You needn't worry about *us*, Mr. Furstival. I'll not let Lucy come to harm."

"But the outlanders have muskets," Blaise pointed out.

"Pah! Vlad Orloff had a musket and I stole bacon from under his nose!" Pauline said. "If you ask me, the outlanders rely too much on muskets and rocket ships, and have forgotten the virtue of a good, old-fashioned fight. Give me plain Cantling steel or, better yet, my bare fists!"

"Fists!" exclaimed Furstival. "Did you have fighting lessons as well, Miss Pooter?"

"No, but I've wrestled a greased pig and won!" Pauline boasted. It was true. At a fair in Twee the Baron had let her enter a greased-pig contest with the village children, and Pauline had caught hold of the porker's ears (which had missed the grease) and been dragged around the pen until the poor beast fell over panting.

Her hands were blistered from the oars but Pauline felt topping. What fun it was to be adventuring again! The gum had given her a lift as well. Of course, she chewed it only because she was parched. Gum was useful in times of crisis, much like the laudanum Mr. Splint had given her after Papa died, but when the war was over — when she knew from one day to the next where her next meal was coming from — she would no longer have any need of it.

When Pauline's turn at the oar was over, Mr. Furstival hailed a passing ship and, after haggling with the skipper, bought two jugs of cider and a casket of biscuits to see them through to Fort Gustaf. They pulled to shore to rest and eat. The biscuits were dry as dust and the first jug of cider barely touched the ground. By the time they had eaten their fill it was empty.

"It's unusually warm for this early in the year," Furstival observed. The travelers had rested in a stand of larches but even in the shade the air was stifling. The boat was tied at the mouth of a stream that fed the Leech.

"I added up the days yesterday and realized it was summer!" said Lucy.

"It will only get hotter this afternoon," said the Boondocker. "Perhaps we should find the source of that stream and fill this jug with fresh water. We don't want to get sun-struck."

"I'll fetch water!" said Pauline, jumping up.

"But don't you want to rest, Pooter?"

"Pshaw! We'll be penned up in that boat all day. I want to stretch my legs." She picked up her pack, which she had brought from the boat. "I've the canteen I took from Orloff, as well."

"I'll bring our canteen from the boat," Lucy said, getting up.

"No!" Pauline said. "I'll get it. It's your turn to row next. You should rest."

"If you insist!" said Lucy, throwing herself on her belly. "Thank you, Pauline."

"Perhaps I should come," said Furstival. "These are wild lands. There may be wolves."

"I have my spear," Pauline assured him.

"Well, don't go far. Scream if you need help."

Pauline hurried to the boat and hung the second canteen by its lanyard over her shoulder. The stream was little more than a rivulet. She followed it through a meadow full of wildflowers and bumbling bees, and then into a wood where squirrels rustled the branches. Fallen trees and thick vines made the going harder here, but she pressed on. The stream was no wider than her arm; its source must be at hand. From above came the warbling of her favorite bird, the purple-throated doggerel.*

---

*Scientific name Avis poetaster. *The species is native to Cant.*

In the deepest shade of the wood she found the moss-circled spring and filled the jug and canteens. Then, looking around as though the squirrels might give her away, she reached into her pack and took out the gum purse. Her hands trembled as she opened the package and put a tablet into her mouth. She hesitated — for gum chewing always made her ears pop — and then bit down on the white lozenge.

Oh, sugar! Pauline quivered to her feet. The gum's shell shattered like a delicate teacup and the sweet shards pricked her mouth. Her tongue wanted to sing. She crunched the sugar and sucked greedily at the gum-meat, her jaw working like a happy cow's.

Soon she had sucked all the sweetness out of the gum. When the war was over she would eat puddings and lollies and sticky buns — things that were sweet right through, not merely frosted — but until then gum would suffice. When she had spat out the spent gum-meat it occurred to her that the others could not know how far she had walked, so she might enjoy another tablet before going back. She opened the packet of Twite's Superior and threw a piece into her mouth.

That's three pieces o' gum you've ate, milady, said a familiar voice.

Nonsense, thought Pauline. I've had only two.

I counted three, all the same, said Mrs. Selvage.

Pauline looked at the package on her lap. She had chewed one piece on the boat while rowing. Twite's Superior came in a "12 Count" package, so there ought to be nine pieces left. She slid out the little paperboard tray that held the gum, and counted. Eight tablets remained.

Didn't I tell you? the old servant asked.

Pauline shivered. Had she chewed three pieces at the spring? She remembered only two. Perhaps the Twite's people had cheated and put in only eleven. But no. The package had been full when she opened it, twelve tablets neatly aligned in the tray.

Suddenly she remembered her father as he looked on his deathbed — gasping, sweating, determined not to chew again but tortured by the craving. Mr. Splint discovered afterwards that his gum had been prepared with some physic that made him crave it even as his teeth rotted, even though his hands trembled when he put it into his mouth.

An awful fear seized her. Did all gum inspire the craving? In her young life Pauline had probably eaten her weight in frosted filberts and suffered no ill effect. She could not imagine any harm in a lozenge of gum. Besides, she had only wanted a sweet! She was not a gum chewer!

I told you, milady. You ought never have done it!

"But what shall I do?" Pauline begged. "I don't want to die!"

Hush! said Mrs. Selvage. You shan't die. But you'll want help!

"Pauline?" came a distant voice.

"Lucy!" Pauline cried. She snapped shut and hid the gum purse. Lucy was there, climbing over a fallen log, and Pauline had never seen a more welcome sight. However bravely she had acted that day, however fiercely she had brandished her spear, she now was a damsel in distress, as locked up in the gum purse as she had ever been in the dungeon. Lucy would come to her rescue.

"It feels wonderful in this wood!" Lucy said, falling beside her. "What a lovely spring!"

"Yes, it's cooler here," Pauline said. With her tongue she

pushed the gum to her cheek. She ought to have spat it out and confessed at once, but the moment was not right. Lucy cupped her hands and drank of the spring.

"I left the men snoring," she said.

"We always seem to take up with snorers! You heard how Lil trumpeted."

"You were wonderfully brave this morning, Pauline."

Pauline blushed. She had finally done something truly outstanding, but now she felt unworthy of Lucy's praise.

"I hope Mr. Furstival's not too upset at the loss of his boat," she mumbled.

"Nonsense. He owes you his life. We all do."

Pauline shrugged. "One tries to be helpful."

"Pauline!" Lucy laughed. "Why, if I didn't know you better I'd think you've become humble! Stop it! Next you'll start being quiet and obedient and I shan't recognize you at all!"

Pauline forced a smile. "Did you suffer dreadfully when you were my maidservant, Lucy?" she asked, the smile fading. "You must have cursed me a thousand times."

"Nonsense. You forget I was bound for the American Mission before you took me in. I should have had to answer to Miss Poke and watch Mr. Frodd perform as a clown. And I'd have missed all the fun we had!"

"You don't regret giving up the baronial cap to help me?"

"I will never be Baroness if it means forsaking a friend."

"I'm glad, Lucy. Because I need your help again."

"I thought you would," Lucy said. She stood and put the canteen's lanyard over her head, then picked up the cider jug.

"You're not a pack mule to be carrying such a load, after all. Shall we go back?"

"Oh!" said Pauline. "Yes. Yes, I suppose we should." The gum was bitter in her cheek but she could not simply spit it out. The subject must be broached in the right way. She stood, hoisted her pack, and followed Lucy through the wood.

They walked slowly across the meadow. The heat was stifling and Pauline was glad Lucy had come to help carry the water. She would have to break off a leafy branch to serve as a parasol before she went back to the boat. Lucy had her muffin cap, but Pauline was bareheaded and her ears would burn to a crisp.

"Pauline," Lucy said when they came in sight of the boat, "do you feel quite all right?"

Pauline stopped. "Whatever do you mean?" she asked.

Lucy hesitated. "I . . . I heard you talking in the wood," she said. "And at Smuts, when you said you were talking to Lil's cat . . . well, she seemed to be sleeping. What I mean to say is, I remember when I was orphaned. I used to climb up to Uncle Hock's hayloft and talk to Nancy, my doll. I wonder if something is troubling you?"

Pauline held up her hand against the sun.

"Why, what would be troubling me?" she asked, walking again towards the boat.

"I wonder what Lil might have told you," Lucy said.

"Lil? What has Lil to do with it?"

"Well, she is Vlad Orloff's sister."

They had come to the boat. Pauline set her pack in the prow and Lucy put the water under the oarsman's seat, where it might stay cool. Blaise and Mr. Furstival dozed in the shade of the larches.

"Lil can't help being his sister," Pauline said. "It's not her fault."

"So she *did* tell you," said Lucy, sounding relieved.

"Tell me? . . ."

"About your mother and Vlad Orloff. Luigi told me, you see, and I was afraid I should have to tell you. Luigi simply refused, which is just as well, I suppose, as he very likely would have died of stammering. Of course, it changes nothing between us."

So that was it! thought Pauline. Lucy had learned that Orloff had once courted Esmeralda. She was afraid Pauline might know and be upset.

"Oh, I admit I was bothered at first," she said. "The songs all spoke of how much she loved Papa. But I'm not so delicate as you seem to think me, Lucy. I've seen something of life, though I am a year younger than you."

Lucy gazed at Pauline.

"You're certainly taking it well," she said. "I should have been crushed to learn such a man was my father. And I don't mind telling you, I wept when I found we weren't blood sisters. But you're right — we must be strong. Besides, you'll always be the sister of my heart, Pauline. It has nothing to do with blood."

"What do you mean?" Pauline asked.

"What?" said Lucy.

Now Pauline felt she and Lucy had been talking about two very different things. Lucy had not been "crushed" to learn Lord Cant was her father. She had been surprised, certainly, but in the end it meant they were sisters. What did she mean by "sisters of the heart"?

"I don't follow you," Pauline said, wiping her brow with the sleeve of her chemise. "It's true we're only half-sisters, strictly speaking, but the blood of the house of Cant runs in us both. Surely you know how babies are made, Lucy?"

"What!"

"Don't you remember? Papa explained it. A man and a woman lie together . . . like Papa with that chambermaid . . . and . . . well, that's how *you* were born, Lucy!" she said.

"Yes, but Lord Cant isn't *your* father, if Orloff's claim is true."

"What?" asked Pauline.

"Not your natural father, that is. But you'll always — Pauline? Are you all right?"

Pauline sat down dizzily on the prow of the boat. She was not all right. She saw now that the misunderstanding was hers.

"Are you telling me," she asked, "that my father is . . . is someone else?"

She read the answer on Lucy's stricken face.

"Oh, Pauline!" Lucy cried. "I thought you *knew!*"

Pauline clutched the gunwale. "Who is it, then?"

Lucy took her hand. "But . . . surely you must know? —"

Pauline stared at her. "You can't mean Orloff!"

"I thought Lil had told you!"

"*No!*" cried Pauline. But now she remembered Lil's words to the constable. *She belongs to my brother Dick.* "I . . . I admit she hinted as much. But, Lucy, it's only hearsay! Lil believed Mother was tongue toed, but she admitted she was never even close enough to see Mother's eyes. If she was a plain-toed woman, Papa *could* be my father!"

Lucy looked away. "Did Lord Cant tell you she was plain toed?" she asked.

Pauline hesitated. "I suppose he never did. I . . . I simply assumed."

"Oh, I wish Luigi had told you!" Lucy said. "He saw a portrait of Esmeralda at Château Simone-Thierry. She was The Huntress, so her feet were naked. She *was* tongue toed, Pauline."

"And I'm as plain toed as a tinker!" Pauline wailed.

"It doesn't matter!" said Lucy. "I was adopted, and Mother and Father loved me as their own true child! Lord Cant will always be your father."

"But my sire is a villain and a gum peddler! And a *murderer*! He killed your parents!"

"Pauline, don't —"

"Oh, I'm the spawn of Vladimir Orloff!" Pauline cried. Her shoulders shook with sobs. "My father is a rake . . . and . . . and a killer. . . . I'm nothing but a plain-toed tinker's brat!"

"Don't say that! Esmeralda was a noble lady!"

Pauline shook her head. She could not speak.

"Pauline, you look *dreadful*," said Lucy. "Drink some water before you faint!"

Lucy uncorked the canteen and held it to Pauline's lips, but the gum, when Pauline drank, went down her throat and choked her. She coughed and coughed, spewing water, but the gum was firmly lodged. Lucy helpfully pounded her back but still the gum would not come up. Finally Pauline took another drink and the bitter cud slid down her throat.

The truth must be faced. She was Orloff's child.

"Why didn't Luigi *tell* me?" she sobbed. Lucy stroked her hair.

"Luigi is a good man," she said. "But you know how grown-ups are, Pauline. They'll never tell you anything awful, not even the well-meaning ones. They're afraid you'll be hurt."

"Weren't you afraid I'd be hurt?" asked Pauline.

"I was," said the sister of her heart. "That's why I had to tell you."

Chapter 18

In the shadow of Fort Gustaf clustered the town of Riddance, the last port of call on the River Leech. It was a ramshackle settlement, full of lean cats and lawless Cantlings. On its docks the carpets and cuckoo clocks of the Barony were loaded on to wagons for export, and the ships' empty holds were filled with goods from the outlands. From here silks and cottons, cocoanuts and chewing gum sailed upriver to delight or divide the people of Cant.

The market was hard by the fort and bustled with hawkers and pickpockets, matrons and tarts. Great warehouses and stables lined one side of the square and long mule teams pulled carts from the dockside, bound for distant lands. Here Mr. Furstival hoped to find transport out of the Barony. He insisted on seeing the fugitives safely to the Vale of Kandu.

"I believe we've all earned a good meal," said the Boondocker, taking out his purse to pay his crew their wages. "While you children are marketing, I'll make inquiries about our passage to Kandu. Let us meet by yonder fishmonger at the next bell."

"Thank you, sir," Lucy said.

"I want a roasted potato," declared Blaise, pointing to a stall.

"That sounds lovely. Will you have one, Pooter?" asked Lucy.

Pauline had no appetite. She had missed the chance to confess her gum craving to Lucy and had chewed the last of the Twite's, all the time cursing her weakness. With each tablet she felt herself more certainly the child of Orloff, whose gum purse, cold and hollow, rested in the bodice of her kirtle. Her belly revolted at the smells of the market, where vendors hawked meats and syrupy sweets. The straps of her knapsack hurt her shoulders.

"Potatoes grow in the dirt," she said. "No, thank you."

"But everything grows in the dirt," objected Blaise.

"Everything does *not*," said Pauline. "Respectable food grows *out of* the dirt. You two run along. I'm sure I can fend for myself."

Lucy cast a curious glance at Pauline but allowed the underfootman to pull her towards the potato stall. When they had turned their backs Pauline eyed the crowd. Mothers walked with marketing baskets while their children explored the dockside. Dockworkers chatted and vendors cried their wares. Finally she saw a richly dressed gentleman coming from a warehouse, his long, pointed slippers cleaving a path through the marketing hordes. She picked up her kirtle's skirt and hurried after him.

"Excuse me, good sir!" she cried. "A word with you, if I may."

The man glanced at her without slowing his pace. An ostrich feather bobbed in his hat.

"I've no money to spare for guttersnipes," he said.

"If you please, sir, I don't want money. See, I have it already!"

She held out her wages, the coins glittering in her palm. It must have seemed a trifling sum to such a man, whose velvet cape bespoke great wealth, but he stopped and glanced at the little pile of silver, as even a well-fed dog will sniff an uneaten morsel.

"What do you want?" he curtly asked.

"Please, sir, I'm traveling with my mistress, Lady Broadbeam of Lower Bogside. Do you know the name?"

"I am not familiar with it."

"I daresay it's one of the chief names of Lower Bogside. But no matter. My Lady is in want of chewing gum and has sent me to fetch it. But I find that Riddance has gone over to the rebel side and there's no gum to be found. Might you allow my Lady to buy a few pieces from you?"

The man eyed her narrowly.

"What makes you believe I have gum?" he asked.

"Why, you struck me as a person of the better sort."

A dockman walked past, his lading hook fitted over his shoulder. He tugged his forelock to the velvet-caped gentleman, who waited until he was out of earshot before answering Pauline.

"You're quite well spoken for a lady's maid," he observed.

"Thank you, sir. I —"

"And yet you did not make your courtesy when you met me."

"I . . . I beg your pardon, sir!" said Pauline, awkwardly curtseying.

"I grant it. Now be off before I take my stick to you."

"But, please, I want only a few pieces!" Pauline begged. Timidly she held out her coins.

"Begone, I say!" the man hissed. He struck Pauline's hand with his walking stick and the silver fell ringing to the cobblestones. Before she could protest or cry out, he had gone. Pauline at once fell to her knees and collected the fallen coins, for already the gutter children were racing towards the sound.

Her hand throbbed where the man had struck her, but far worse was the flush of shame on her cheeks. It had come to this! The Adored & Honorable Pauline had been whipped like a cur, and now crawled for silver on the gob-stained cobbles of Riddance. Never had a child of the house of Cant known such indignity — but she was no child of Adolphus, alas! Her true sire had risen from the gutters, and there she had fallen again. She pocketed the coins, grateful only that Lucy had not witnessed the scene.

Nearby a carter kicked a begging dog, and the animal ran past her with its tail between its legs. Pauline sniffed back tears and walked to Mr. Furstival, who was talking with a sausage vendor. A dozen blackened links smoked on his gridiron over a fire of broken crates. The vendor was missing one eye. He petted a three-legged cat.

"Haven't you eaten, Pooter?" asked Furstival. Pauline shook her head.

"I'll have a sausage, please," she said, with little enthusiasm, to the vendor.

"Crust or stick?" the man asked, pushing the cat off his lap.

"What?"

"Do ye want your weenie on a crust or a stick?"

A number of bread crusts, buzzing with flies, lay heaped on a trencher by the gridiron.

"A stick, please," said Pauline.

"Tuppence," belched the merchant. He picked up a barrel stave and, using a jackknife, peeled off a long splinter of wood, with which he speared the sausage. "Mustard?" he asked.

"If you please," mumbled Pauline.

The man opened a crock and slathered the sausage with brown, grainy mustard.

"Is this your daughter?" he asked.

"Aye, little Pooter," said the Boondocker. "She and the boys are traveling with me, as the missus is big with another one and can't look after them proper. As I said, the lads can earn their fare. They brought us down the Leech like seasoned tars."

"And you're looking for passage to Kandu, you say?" asked the vendor. He handed the sausage to Pauline, who gave him a shilling. "Looking to bring some gum back over the frontier, are ye?"

"Nothing of the sort," said Furstival. "I'm traveling on honest business."

"Well, good luck to you, mister. You need a guardsman from the fort to escort you to the border nowadays — that is, if you can find a carter who'll take you. For a while it was haymaking time for the smugglers, but all that changed when Mr. Gutz showed up."

"*Grmph!*" coughed Pauline. Arden Gutz! What was the Causist leader doing in Riddance?

"Your weenie go down the wrong pipe, lass?" asked the sausage man.

Pauline shook her head. She had blown mustard out of her nose and the vinegar fumes burned her eyes.

"Mr. *Gutz?*" she gasped. "Who is that?"

"Why, don't ye know? He's the big chief of the Barony, I reckon. Anyway, he's the top man of the Cause, and that's the side that's winning. The house of Cant is fallen, they say. Who would've believed it?"

Pauline wiped mustard from her lip. "The house of Cant is *not* fallen!" she insisted.

"*Shh!*" advised the sausage man. A number of bystanders had turned to stare at Pauline. "You're a Loyalist, are ye? Well, I advise you to keep your gob shut in Riddance, little girl. Me, I don't give a bean one way or other. I sell sausages and flip all else. But you'll not make friends in Riddance with them kind of slogans. When Gutz rode into town the other day they fairly threw their cloaks under his feet, they did. This here's a Causist town."

"You owe me the change of my shilling!" hissed Pauline.

"But what of Fort Gustaf?" said Primo Furstival. At this hour the fort's gates stood open and a lone guardsman kept watch, but from its ramparts the defenders of Cant had, in times past, reigned down destruction on invading armies. Rightly had Arden Gutz believed that the conquest of this stronghold would cement his power. "Do you mean to tell me the guard allowed Gutz to enter Riddance unmolested?" the Boondocker asked.

"Ah, you're from away in Trans-Poltroon and don't know these things," the sausage man said. "The guard don't bother no one but Loyalists, nowadays. Fatty went over to the Cause last week."

"Fatty?"

"The Commandant. Sir Geneva Trollopson is the name, but everyone calls him Fatty. Only man I ever met who could eat a half dozen of my weenies and not throw up. I sell a potent sausage. Would ye like another, lass?"

"Thank you, no," Pauline faintly said. The man in the ostrich feather hat stood with the sentry at Fort Gustaf, and both men were looking her way. "I can't believe an officer of the guard would go over to the Cause!" she added. The sausage did not sit well on her stomach.

"Gutz sent an envoy ahead of himself," said the vendor. "Seems the rebels got a look at his late Lordship's purse and found they couldn't say no to the gum trade, not if they wanted to feed their army. We figured Fatty'd toss the man into the Leech, for Gutz had sent an outlander to do his talking for him."

"An outlander!" exclaimed Furstival.

"The Reverend Mr. Pius Frodd, he calls himself," said the sausage man. "He must have brought a sweet offer from the Causists, 'cause the next day we learnt Fatty had switched sides. There's loyalty for you!"

"I feel I must be ill," said Pauline, wiping sweat from her brow.

"It is sickening, ain't it?" said the vendor. "These noble folks would sell their own mum for a handful of silver. And using an outlander as a go-between! That's what make me want to puke."

Pauline wished he had not said "puke." His sausage had been nothing but snouts, tails, and sawdust and the mustard was hot as a coal fire. The pig parts bubbled in her gut. Uneasily she watched the sentry lead the ostrich feather through the gates of the fort.

"The Commandant may regret his choice," Furstival said. "Gaspard Simone-Thierry has raised an army, with Vladimir Orloff as its commander. A ruthless man. He'll show no mercy to traitors if the Loyalists win out."

"You're well behind the times in Boondock!" the sausage man sneered. "Turn around and look behind you, man! I shouldn't think Fatty has anything to fear from Vladimir Orloff!"

Pauline followed his pointing finger. Not far from the gates of Fort Gustaf a man sat with his arms in stocks. He wore a dirty loincloth, and gray hair hung down over his face. The middle slot of the stocks was empty, for the prisoner's neck was pierced by an arrow and would not go into it. Orloff had been captured by the rebels.

"Behold the best hope of the house of Cant!" laughed the sausage man. He poked Pauline's ribs. "I hate to tell you, my little Loyalist, but it don't look like your side's winning!"

Pauline did not answer him. The prisoner's belly sagged. Moles covered his flesh and his shins bore the marks of guttersnipes' boots. He looked pitiably old, his skin like parchment too often folded, and the sun had burnt red the flesh of his neck, back, and arms.

"Pooter, no!" begged Primo Furstival, but Pauline scarcely heard him. She walked across the square, breaking free of the Boondocker's grip when he tried to hold her. Furstival called out to Blaise and Lucy, who ran from the potato stall. They gathered behind Pauline as, with burning cheeks, she read the notice of charges against the prisoner:

Vladimir Orloff, Esq.,

Being found *guilty*
of TREASON,
INSURRECTION,
PERJURY,
EXTORTION,
RIOT,
PECULATION,
and FRAUD,
shall by order of the Lenient & Merciful
Arden Gutz, August Provisional Regent
to Lady Wickwright, on the 29th June
be decapitated until *dead*.

Orloff looked up. The pavement at his feet was littered with potato peelings and rotted vegetables, it being a time-honored custom to hurl such refuse — along with insults and spittle — at prisoners in the stocks. Flies swarmed over this feast or settled on Orloff's face to drink his sweat. He squinted at Pauline and licked his parched lips.

"Miss Cant," he rasped. "Go away from here. The rebels have taken the fort."

Pauline stepped closer. She gazed at the prisoner's long, plain toes.

"For your own sake, go!" he said. Lucy took Pauline's arm.

"Pooter, come away!" she said. She was not wearing her glasses but Orloff knew her voice and he scowled darkly at her. Tendrils of damp hair stuck to his brow.

"Listen to the girl!" he urged Pauline. "Arden Gutz is within Fort Gustaf. Fly, unless you wish to share my fate. Fly!"

"Come, Pooter," said Lucy. "People are staring!"

"That is splendid advice, Jams!" said Furstival, glancing anxiously towards the fort. "Come away now, Pooter!"

Pauline tore her arm from Lucy's grasp and stepped nearer the prisoner. The charges leveled against him were doubtless just — treason, fraud, and the rest — and yet she found them wanting. She felt the cold weight of his gum purse on her chest, hidden within her chemise.

"Is it true you loved my mother?" she asked.

A drop of sweat fell from the Commissioner's face.

"Who told you such a thing?" he said.

"I met your sister on the way."

"You've met Lil, have you?" Orloff asked. "One would have thought the poteen had killed her by now. I've not spoken to my sister these many years. I'm sure I told her no such thing."

"Mr. Lemonjello heard it from your lips!" said Lucy.

Orloff glanced at her with cold contempt.

"Adolphus would grieve to know the company you keep, Miss Cant," he said. "Spies and pretenders and boys with swords. You'll end in a paupers' field if you don't quit such fools. For your mother's sake, if nothing else, forsake them! You may still wear the baronial cap if Gaspard prevails."

In answer Pauline reached up and pulled her spearhead ringing from its scabbard. A gasp rose from those standing around. At the fort's gates a huddle of guardsmen appeared, an ostrich feather bobbing in their midst. Pauline pressed her steel to the prisoner's throat.

"Answer me!" she demanded. "Did you love my mother?"

Orloff closed his eyes and grimaced.

"And what if I loved her?" he asked. "Mayn't a poor man know love, once in his life, though a fat prince must steal away his treasure? I did no crime by loving Esmeralda."

"You've done plenty others, by the look of it," said Blaise, who had been reading the charges. "Riots and pesteration, and worse!"

"Far worse!" said Lucy. "Murder, for one!"

"That is a lie!" Orloff cried. "There is no blood on my hands!"

"We're drawing considerable attention," said Mr. Furstival. "I suggest —"

"Are you my father?" demanded Pauline. Her hand trembled, and the Supreme Commander strained to hold his throat clear of the spearhead. A clamor arose at the gates of Fort Gustaf.

"I am," said Orloff. "I am in fact, though shamefully not in deed."

Pauline put the point of the spearhead under his chin, so that he had to look up at her from his low seat.

"And why should I not kill you for what you did to Lucy?" she asked.

"I committed no murder! Believe me, Pauline!"

"My parents are dead," said Lucy, "and Casio, who was only a child! I know it was you who came to the shop. I saw you riding after them up the road to the castle. How can you deny it?"

Lucy had lost her family on the day of the guildsmen's fair, when from the merchants of Tenesmus her parents were chosen to present the Baron a masterpiece of their craft. The Wickwrights were last seen alive as they took to the castle their great work, the Candle of Cant. Their bodies were later found among the rocks at the castle's feet.

"I never meant them to die!" said Orloff. He looked at Pauline. "I left my men on the road and told them not to let the chandlers pass. They claimed the man resisted them. Whether that was true or no, when I arrived the deed was done. Oh, put away that penknife, child! You may come back in two days and watch them take my head!"

"Yes, a point well taken!" said Furstival, glancing towards the gates. "Come along, children!"

Pauline sheathed the spearhead. She saw no remorse in Orloff's eyes, but neither did she detect a lie. The strain of looking up had made fresh blood seep into the rag around his neck.

"What did you intend to do with them, if not kill them?" she asked.

"Delay them, nothing more! If they arrived late to the castle I could use Lord Cant's anger to have them put in the dungeon, where he would soon forget them. They did not know whose child they reared and I meant to keep them in ignorance — and silent. In that way you would have no rival for the barony."

Almost Pauline believed him. His story fitted with the facts.

"Don't listen to him, Miss Cant," said Blaise. "If he was willing to leave Lucy in the woods as a little baby, I don't fancy he would stick at killing her folks later on. He's cold-blooded through and through."

Orloff glared at him.

"My blood once burned," he said. "It burned in love, and burned hotter with rage when I saw Esmeralda married to a fool who cared only for her dowry — a man who toyed with a maid and then locked her away to bring his unwanted babe into the world. Yes!" he cried. "I insisted that the child be left in the wood! It was my last gift to Esmeralda — that her first-born should have no rival." He gazed at Pauline. "I saw you grow in her likeness, child. You were . . . you are . . . the very image of Esmeralda. What I have done, I did for you!"

Dimly Pauline heard the commotion at the gates of Fort Gustaf. Every vile thing Orloff had done to Lucy, all his schemes and wickedness, he had done for her? The sausage roiled in her gut. Mr. Furstival beseeched her to run, but Pauline instead bent at the waist and threw up. The gum purse fell from her chemise and sprang open on the cobbles, its mouth gaping in the muck.

"Take hold, Blaise!" said Mr. Furstival. He and the under-footman grabbed Pauline's arms and raced with her across the square, Lucy hard on their heels. Guardsmen ran yelling from the gates. Pauline, flying backwards over the cobbles, saw Orloff lift his head as though to cry out, but the arrow made it impossible. The market dogs gathered to lap the vomit at his feet.

"They're a gang of Loyalists, I'm sure of it!" yelled the man in the ostrich-feather hat, running after the guards. "The little one as much as confessed to it!"

"Halt! All of you!" a soldier commanded.

"Hurry, Jams!" yelled Blaise over his shoulder. Pauline woke from her trance. A dozen guardsmen had emerged from Fort Gustaf and were gaining rapidly on Lucy, who brought up the rear. Blind without her glasses, she ran into a plump matron and fell, her knapsack sliding up over her head. Pauline struggled to get free of her rescuers' grasp.

"Stop!" she cried. "Jams has fallen!"

Blaise slowed to look around but Primo Furstival kept running, and for a moment Pauline dangled between them like laundry hung out to dry. Then Blaise lost his grip and she dropped to the cobbles.

The guardsmen had drawn their swords, and the crowd parted before them. Lucy leapt up and ran, shouting "Sorry!" to the matron she had tackled, but while her head was thus turned a cat ran into her path. She sent the unlucky beast flying and plunged headlong into a game of dice. The gamblers flung themselves out of her way, cursing and scattering coins, and before Lucy could stand again the swiftest guardsman had seized her ankle.

"Jams!" screamed Pauline. She scrambled up and would have run to Lucy's aid had not Primo Furstival thrown his arm around her. "Let me go!" she pleaded.

"It's no use!" he said. "Master Blaise! We stand no chance against them!"

Already Lucy was engulfed by the soldiers. Two swordsmen

now broke off and ran after Blaise, who had not even a broken-off spearhead with which to fight them. Reluctantly the under-footman turned and raced after Primo Furstival, who flung Pauline over his shoulder and ran through the open door of a warehouse.

Inside was a vast, gloomy space, lit only by slivers of sunlight falling from cracks in the walls. Dust motes hung in the air. The Boondocker, breathing heavily, carried Pauline down an aisle between walls of stacked barrels. Pauline looked for Blaise but her eyes had started with tears and she could make out nothing in the gloom. Their pursuers stopped at the threshold.

"There's but one door and they can't hide forever," growled one. "Keep your sword at the ready and I'll flush 'em out."

Pauline wiped her eyes. She stood a better chance of saving Lucy from outside Fort Gustaf than as a fellow prisoner, so now was not the time for tears. She squirmed on Primo Fursti-val's shoulder and the Boondocker put her down.

"Tiptoes!" he mouthed silently. Pauline nodded. The guards-man's scabbard slapped noisily against his thigh and it was easy to evade him in the maze of the warehouse. Furstival jumped when he bumped into Blaise creeping around a wall of crates.

"You can't play cat-and-mouse forever," the guardsman called. "Give up now and save yourself all this sneaking. That's my advice."

Blaise held a finger to his lips and beckoned them to follow. They went single file, Pauline keeping watch behind. The under-footman led them past heaped-up barrels and crates to the river end of the warehouse. Pauline held Furstival's back for fear of losing him in the darkness.

One corner of the warehouse had been walled off, and a dim, watery light came from the room. Blaise led them inside. Here the building extended out over the river. Pauline knew at once where she was, for similar rooms squatted over the moat at Castle Cant. Above a hole in the floor a wide plank had been set up with a half-moon cut out of one side, an arrangement that neatly combined chamber pot and sewer in one.

"The thing to remember," Blaise whispered, "is that the river's always moving."

Pauline was glad she had already been ill. The last visitor's business may have floated away on the Leech, but she guessed there were similar rooms upstream in the dockside taverns of Ramsford. What a long way she had come from the lofty towers of Castle Cant!

"Can you swim, Miss Pooter?" asked Furstival.

"Well enough," she admitted.

"I'll go first and you can toss down the packs," said Blaise, shrugging off his knapsack. "We'll paddle to shore and then head upriver. We don't want to go near the docks!"

Wasting no time he grasped the crude seat, dangled there a second, and then splashed into the river.

"Who goes there?" cried the guardsman.

Furstival tossed down the under-footman's knapsack and Pauline's after it. Blaise collected them and paddled away. The guardsman's sandals could be heard slapping through the warehouse.

"I've changed my mind," Pauline whispered. "I *don't* swim well. You go first and save me if I drown."

"Have no fear!" said Furstival. "Boondockers float like corks!"

He took a deep breath and dropped into the water. When he had gone, Pauline — who swam like an otter — hurriedly pulled up her kirtle and knotted it. She might be a tinker's child, but she had been reared as a noblewoman and she was not going to bare her legs with a man present.

"I hear you!" cried the guardsman. "Surrender, or taste steel!"

His footsteps pounded nearer. Pauline had begged some hairpins from Lil and with shaking hands she pinned up her braid. The plank crawled with warehousemen's cooties, no doubt, but then she was already infested, having picked up the pests at the inn at Ramsford. Perhaps some of hers would drown in the Leech.

She grasped the plank and dangled over the water. The Leech flowed green and sickly in the shadow of the warehouse, scabbed here and there with yellow foam. If Pauline meant to be a lady again she would have to rise up from the very cesspool of Cant.

"Halt, you gum-chewing wench!"

The guardsman threw himself headlong across the floor. He caught Pauline's wrist in a meaty hand but his palm was sweaty and she slipped through his fingers. Looking up, she saw his face framed in the hole, and she defiantly stuck out her tongue before plunging into the river.

Chapter 19

The Invalid

𝒯he Galloping Goose hid at the end of the alley next to a
rag-and-bone shop, whose stock of cracked bellows, bottomless
teakettles, and rusty tongs spilled out its doorway and littered
the way. Luigi Lemonjello found a path through the clutter and
ducked under the low doorway of the inn. A fat man in a vest
and trousers played Patience at a table near the unswept fireplace.

"What do you want?" he said, looking up.

"Are you the p-proprietor?" asked Lemonjello, taken aback
by his rude manner.

"I wouldn't be a customer in this hole. What do you want?"

"Er, I hoped to purchase a p-pint of ale."

"Six pence," the innkeeper said. He stood and shouted down
a corridor. "Brat! Leave off what you're doing and come in
here. Customer!"

A boy of five or six years, barefoot and with a yellow crust of snot on his nose, ran into the room and awaited his orders. The man waddled behind a counter and found a blackjack. He wiped its lip on his apron and handed it to the lad.

"Run down to the Mallard for a pint," he said. "Hop to it!"

He kicked the boy's backside for good measure and returned to his cards. Lemonjello, seeing no other place to sit, perched on a stool opposite him. The cards were thumbworn and grimy and arranged in haphazard files. The innkeeper frowned at the game.

"You can play the black knave on your queen," Lemonjello pointed out.

"I saw it!" the man growled.

Moments later the boy returned with a brimming pint. He must have been a champion runner, for he had not spilled a drop. The astronomer had bought many half-pints that day from innkeepers who would not answer questions until he gave up a few coins, but he had tasted none of them. Now, after a long, tiring search under a hot sun, he sipped the ale with relish.

"You wanting a room, mister?" the innkeeper asked. He shuffled the cards in his hand, which was cheating according to how Lemonjello had learned the game. He wiped his mouth.

"Actually, no," he said. "I'm looking for friends."

The innkeeper scowled.

"Well, you won't find one here. If you want to pass the time, go down to the Mallard."

"You don't understand," said Lemonjello. "I had arranged to m-meet friends here in Riddance. Two boys, accompanied by their young sister. Unfortunately, they failed to tell me at what inn they would be staying."

"Ah, I see. Nothing o' that sort here."

"The girl's name is Pooter."

The man shook his head.

"I never heard of *anyone* name o' Pooter! What kind of a name is that?"

"Er, she is of t-tinkerish heritage. The boys are Jams and Blaise."

The innkeeper looked up from his cards.

"Blaise, you say?" he asked.

"Yes!" said Lemonjello. "Have you seen him?"

"No, but it's funny. Quite a coincidence, actually. There's a young chap name o' Blaise in the back room. But it ain't who you're a-looking for. He's traveling with his dad and his little sis."

Lemonjello pushed back his stool and stood up.

"Are they here now?" he asked.

"Aye, as far as I know. Came yesterday and ain't been out since. But see here! —"

His words fell on the deaf ears of his kings, queens, and knaves. Lemonjello rushed down the corridor and knocked on a door at the end. A young woman opened it, her hair lopsided and the marks of a pillow on her face.

"Is there a Blaise here?" asked Lemonjello. The woman shook her head.

"Other side," she said, shutting the door.

The opposite door opened a hand's width in response to his knock. The man within was dressed as a merchant and gazed suspiciously at Lemonjello. He held a foot in front of the door.

"Blaise?" asked Lemonjello.

"I'm afraid I don't follow you. Please to go away."

"I'm t-told there is a Blaise in this room."

"You're evidently a crazy man, or have talked to one," the man said. "The fireplace is in the common room. Good day to you!" He tried to close the door but Lemonjello threw himself against it.

"Blaise!" he called.

"Sir, there is a sick child in this room!" the man protested.

"Mr. Lemonjello?" came a voice from within. Lemonjello squeezed his face through the opening, knocking awry his glasses, and glimpsed the under-footman hidden in a corner. "It's all right, Mr. Furstival!" Blaise said, coming forward. "He's our friend."

Furstival held open the door and Blaise embraced the astronomer. He explained to the Boondocker how Lemonjello had saved Pauline out of Jack Stonefeather's gaol, whereupon Primo Furstival grasped the astronomer's hand.

"It's an honor to meet you," he said in a low voice. "And you're a man of science! We are badly in need of a diagnosis."

"But where are Lucy and Pauline?" Lemonjello asked.

Furstival glanced at Blaise, who answered. "Miss Cant is here. We think the fever's broken. Come see."

An old sheet hung from a beam on one side of the room. Lemonjello followed Blaise around it. Pauline von Cant lay small and sickly in the middle of a broken-down bed. Blaise took a rag from a basin at the bedside, wrung it, and bathed the invalid's face.

"She was hot as blazes all night," he said. "We thought she might've took ill from being in the river, but it came on too sudden for that. She was half out of her head, and drank a bucket of water. But the worst of the fever's over."

Lemonjello sat on the bed and touched Pauline's face. While he took her pulse the under-footman, with occasional interjections from Mr. Furstival, told of all that had happened since the fugitives left Ramsford. The astronomer groaned when he learned of Lucy's capture. Why had the man with the ostrich-feather hat reported them to the guard? he wondered, but neither Blaise nor the Boondocker could tell him. Frowning, he opened Pauline's jaw and looked at her tongue.

"If it weren't impossible," he said, "I should almost believe she was a g-gum chewer deprived of her cud. I saw just such symptoms when I was held in the dungeon."

As though she had heard these words, Pauline slowly opened her eyes. She blinked, coughed weakly, and gazed at the astronomer.

"Luigi," she said faintly, "I must be dreaming. We left you with the marionettes."

"She's been talking out of her head," whispered Furstival.

"That — that — that is a recurring condition with Miss Cant," said Lemonjello. "If she made perfect sense I should be worried. As she's talking nonsense, we may consider her recovery well begun. How do you feel, Pauline?"

The astronomer had never been at ease using Pauline's name. But now she looked so pitiable in her sickbed, so like a common Cantling girl, that he used it thoughtlessly, as he might have talked to his parrot when the bird took ill.

"I feel *dreadful*," Pauline said. She pushed herself up and Blaise arranged the pillow behind her head. "Lucy's been captured and it's all my fault."

"Nonsense," he said. "You children are beset on every side by awful men and you have acted admirably. Admirably. I blame myself for trying to part you. When I found Lucy's note I knew you must be planning to cross the frontier. We set out at once t-to find you."

"We?" Pauline asked. "Is Swanson here, too?"

"Yes. And —"

"Poor Swanson! He must find the clothes appalling."

"He has expressed that sentiment."

"The food is frightful, too. Oh, Luigi!" Pauline said. "What are we to do? Arden Gutz is here, and he's got Lucy. He'll take her back and lock her in a tower of the castle and she'll *die* before her hair gets long enough for us to climb up it and rescue her! You saw how short it was!"

"Our situation is dire," admitted the astronomer. "We might let Gutz take her back to the castle. We have allies within its walls. We know its ways. But Lucy would be in danger on the road and it would put us that much farther from ending this dreadful war. No, we must act now, if p-possible. The frontier is at hand. We must get you both out of the Barony."

Pauline sat up.

"To Kandu? But you wouldn't let us!"

"P-please to lie down, Pauline. You must conserve your strength." Again Lemonjello touched her brow. What a fire burns there! he thought. "I believed it was my duty to protect you, and so I hope to do," he said. "But I can't help you by standing in your way. If you must leave the Barony, I shall see you safely to the b-border. I feel easier with Orloff under arrest."

"We were looking for transport when Lucy was caught," said Primo Furstival. "It won't be easy, I'm afraid. Everyone is on the lookout for smugglers."

"Transport, at least, will not p-present a problem," said Lemonjello. "Mrs. Lungwich is determined to take them in her wagon."

"Lil is here?" cried Pauline.

"She insisted on coming. She said her wagon had smuggled that much poteen, it could surely sneak two high spirits out of the B-barony. She is fond of you, Pauline. But the question remains, how are we to rescue Lucy?"

Pauline flicked away a bedbug that crawled on her chemise.

"What day is it?" she asked.

"The day after yesterday," said Mr. Furstival. "That is, you've slept only a day, Miss Pooter. It's Thursday, to be exact, the twenty-seventh day of June."

"We haven't much time," Pauline mused. "The execution is to take place on Saturday. That is our chance. Arden Gutz will not want to miss having his revenge on Vlad Orloff. He'll come out to watch the execution, so the gates will be open."

"But surely the square will be swimming with guardsmen," Furstival said.

"Crawling, I should say."

"Precisely. How will we get past them?"

Someone knocked at the door. Furstival looked up.

"Yes?" he called.

"Is that fellow with the spectacles in there?" said the innkeeper.

Furstival looked at Lemonjello, who nodded.

"Yes!" said the Boondocker.

"If you mean to sleep another man in there it's a shilling more," the innkeeper said.

"No, no, I shall be leaving p-presently," said Lemonjello.

"Well, are you going to finish your ale? 'Cause if you ain't, I am!"

"Blaise," said the astronomer, "would you be so k-kind as to fetch my beverage?"

"Aye, sir!"

He left the room and Lemonjello turned back to Pauline. She had started up when the innkeeper knocked. Her face was pallid. She fell back against the pillow and closed her eyes, her breathing quick and shallow. Lemonjello touched her arm.

"How rude-mannered I've b-been," he said, getting up. "I must let you rest."

Pauline clutched his hand.

"Luigi, wait," she said. "Lucy told me about Vlad Orloff — about him and my mother."

The astronomer glanced at Primo Furstival, and the Boon-docker, nodding, left the room. Lemonjello sat again on the bed and looked at Pauline. Her eyes glistened.

"I'm sorry, Pauline," he said. "I hadn't the heart to tell you."

"You didn't want me to be hurt."

"No. You'd b-been through so much."

"I understand, Luigi. I do. But I've done a beastly thing!" Pauline sniffled. "You see, when I was lost I found Orloff's gum in his saddlebag. I've always had a terrible sweet tooth, be-cause I was spoilt so. And so I chewed it, though I should have known better, and I've been sneaking about and chewing since."

She let out a sad little cough — *gooh! gooh!* — and tears fell from her eyes.

"O, Luigi, truly I am his child!" she wept. "I've been selfish and greedy and now I've got Lucy captured. I . . . I so badly craved gum, you see, that I tried to beg some from a man in the market. I raised suspicions. Now they've caught her because of *me*, after she'd twice escaped Orloff! But I've sworn off it, Luigi. I shan't let my sweet tooth rule me. I don't want to end like him!"

Lemonjello wiped the tears from her cheeks.

"I can't imagine you'll end like Vlad Orloff," he said.

"You don't think it's too late for me to turn back?"

"You m-made a thoughtless mistake. Anyone might have done so."

"You haven't yet heard the worst. Oh, I'm awful!"

"But what have you d-done?" asked Lemonjello.

Again tears welled in Pauline's eyes.

"When Lucy told me about Orloff and my mother, I lied to her!" she cried.

"What did you say?" asked the startled astronomer.

"Nothing!" wailed Pauline.

"But – but – but! –"

"I'd made up my mind to confess. I felt such a weakling, going about and chewing cud like a great stupid cow. Then Lucy told me about Mother and . . . and Vlad Orloff. I was so ashamed! I had a great wad of gum in my mouth, and yet I didn't tell her!"

"I hardly c-call that lying," consoled Lemonjello.

"But it is!" Pauline insisted. She touched her eyes with the sleeve of her chemise. "If you've done something wrong and you don't tell a grown-up, why, that's common sense. But if something is weighing on your heart and you don't tell your best and dearest friend — *gooh!* — that's simply beastly!"

Lemonjello squeezed her hand. "I'm sure Lucy will understand," he said.

"We must save her, Luigi!"

"We shall," said Lemonjello. "But first you must rest. I'll come b-back tomorrow and we'll lay our plans." He looked at his hand that held hers. "Oh, Pauline. I behaved rather badly, myself. That is, I learnt about . . . ah . . . that business of Orloff and Lady Esmeralda, and I didn't say a word to you. That was wrong of me, to say nothing of stupid. I trust you'll forgive me."

Pauline sniffled.

"I forgive you, Luigi. But let us promise not to keep secrets again."

"Yes, let's."

Pauline sat up and put her little finger into her mouth, then held it out to the astronomer. Lemonjello had almost forgotten this rite of childhood. He soberly wetted his finger and pressed it against Pauline's.

"It's done," she said.

Lemonjello kissed her brow and stood up.

"I'll come early, with Lil and Swanson," he said. "Sleep well."

The astronomer spoke to Blaise and Mr. Furstival in the parlor, and when he had finished his pint he walked back to Lil's wagon. How many spit-promises had he made as a lad? he wondered. He could not say, but to the best of his knowledge he had kept them all. How sad, he thought, that when we grow up we insist on contracts, seals, and signatures, and forget what is simple and solemn and right.

Chapter 20

The Fabulous Mr. Maurice

*I*f you wanted to have your way with grown-ups, Lucy had learned, you first had to give grown-ups *their* way. At Castle Cant she had been known as a meek and obedient maidservant, and this reputation had allowed her to engage in all manner of mischief.

So she bore patiently with Miss Poke's lessons. She waited. Arden Gutz's consort had spent almost all of yesterday teaching her to walk. She must learn to walk like a lady, Miss Poke said, because she was to walk with Arden Gutz to the execution. She must be at his side when he walked out from the fort to seal his triumph over Vladimir Orloff.

One could not walk like a lady in turnshoes, so Miss Poke gave Lucy a pair of her own shoes, their toes stuffed with tissue paper. She called them "high heels." They might have been stilts as far as Lucy was concerned. Her hands were raw from pitching off them headlong to the floor. She was staring glumly at these instruments of torture when the guard knocked on her door.

"Time for your lessons, Miss Wickwright!" he called.

"Very well," she sighed.

She waited while the guard ("your Ladyship's escort," according to Miss Poke) unlocked the cell ("your Ladyship's boudoir"). Then, with a groan, she picked up the outlandish shoes and followed him to the fort's ballroom. Why a fort wanted a ballroom Lucy could not quite grasp — unless the troops became lonesome away from their sweethearts, and took consolation by sharing a waltz.

Arden Gutz had not shown his face since Lucy's capture, leaving her entirely to Miss Poke's care. That was typical of him. She cared nothing for the man — and certainly she had never been "spurned in love" by him, as Pauline teased — but he might have had the decency to pay a call. Her spying, after all, had made possible his silly rebellion.

In the ballroom she took off her turnshoes and strapped the outlandish heels to her feet. Miss Poke arrived moments later, clacking smartly across the parquet and beaming her perfect, cheerless smile. Lucy's tutor wore a great deal of face paint, and her lips were a startling crimson, like a child's after it has sucked a lolly too big for its mouth.

"Good afternoon, Miss Poke," Lucy recited.

"Lucy, you won't believe this. You won't *believe* it!" Miss Poke said. She fell on to a chair next to Lucy.

"Believe what, Miss Poke?"

"The news. I can hardly believe it myself. It's fabulous!"

"What is it, Miss Poke?"

Arden Gutz's consort touched her arm.

"Promise not to scream, O.K.?"

"I promise."

"Are you ready? A gentleman showed up at the fort this morning to apply for a visa. He's from *Paris*, Lucy. Paris, *France*. And do you know what he does?"

"No, ma'am."

"He's a *fashion designer*, Lucy! From Paris!"

"That's wonderful, Miss Poke."

"Lucy," her tutor said breathlessly, "he's agreed to dress you for the execution!"

Lucy did not know what a fashion designer was, but she had been dressing herself as long as she could remember and she wanted no help from a man from Paris. She thought it silly that noble persons required servants to dress them. When she served Pauline she had sometimes spent whole mornings trudging back and forth from the wardrobes, waiting for her mistress to make up her mind. She hardly knew how to answer.

"O.K.," she ventured to say. Miss Poke often used this expression, which Lucy understood to mean "Yes," or "I agree," or "If you please," or nothing at all, depending on the speaker's whim. Her reply seemed to satisfy Miss Poke.

"Fabulous!" she said. "He's come to measure you. Would you like to meet him?"

"O.K."

Miss Poke leapt up.

"Mr. Maurice!" she called out. "Miss Wickwright is ready for you!"

The fashion designer's costume was like nothing Lucy had seen before, but his face was familiar. It belonged to Swanson. He had become a Parisian that morning in the rag-and-bone shop next to the Galloping Goose, where he had found the scarves, flounces, caftan, and cape that now fluttered around him. He bowed deeply to Lucy and pressed her hand to his lips.

"Miss Weakrat," he said. *"Enchanté!"*

Miss Poke clapped her hands.

"Isn't he *wonderful?*" she squealed.

"How do you do, Mr. Maurice?" asked Lucy.

"I am streeken, Miss Weakrat."

"Would you like a drink of water?"

"Streeken by such beauty as I haff never seen!" cried Swanson. "Miss Puck, you geef me zee honor of dressing thees enchanting girl? Can eet be? Eez thees happiness truly to be mine?"

Miss Poke could not contain herself. She threw herself on the dressmaker's neck.

"Oh, Mr. Maurice! Arden is going to *die!* Will you be able to work with the shoes?"

Swanson frowned at the "heels" Miss Poke had lent to Lucy. He took a measuring cord from within the folds of his costume.

"Eez nothing my gown cannot cover," he said. "Pleez to stand up, Miss Weakrat. Miss Puck, eef you will take zee note?"

"Gladly, Mr. Maurice!"

She jotted in a notebook as Swanson worked with the measuring cord. He stretched it from Lucy's wrist to her shoulder, from her hip to the floor, from nape to waist and from shoul-

der to shoulder. He declared her proportions to be mathemat-
ically sound. Then he handed an end of the cord to Lucy.

"Pleez to put around zee bust, Miss Weakrat."

Lucy looked down at her chest.

"Where is that?" she asked, blushing.

"Ah! . . . Eez no problem," said Swanson. "Up a leetle . . .
down a leetle . . . all zee same. Now to zee waist. Her La-
ddysheep haff a waist, no? Zee skinny part. Just so. And now
to zee heeps, pleez. Every girl haff heeps. Miss Puck, you haff
wreeten eet all down?"

"Yes, Mr. Maurice!"

Swanson had knelt to measure Lucy's "heeps." He stood
now and rolled up his cord.

"Organdy," he pronounced. "Vee shall dress her in organdy.
Also, organza."

"But — but, Mr. Maurice!" stammered Miss Poke. "Organdy *and* organza?"

"Organza!" insisted Swanson. "White organza! And zee organdy shall be yellow."

"Yellow!" cried Lucy.

"Yellow!" said Swanson. "I shall make you zee butterfly,
Miss Weakrat!"

"Oh, Mr. Maurice!" swooned Miss Poke. "It sounds *fabulous!*"

"I am zee genius," Swanson modestly replied. "Now, as to
zee cost . . ."

"You must buy whatever you need!" said Miss Poke. "Arden
will write a draught on the Exchequer, and we'll send a swords-
man with you to the milliner's shop. The shopkeeper won't give
you any trouble!"

"Splendid!" Swanson bowed to Lucy. "Zee butterfly, Miss Weakrat. You shall be like zee butterfly. On zee execution day, you break out of zee cocoon. In my creation you shall fly."

Lucy bit her lip. It was very hard not to smile.

"I understand, Mr. Maurice," she said.

She held out her hand. Swanson pressed it fervently to his lips and then Miss Poke led him out of the ballroom. Lucy waited until her tutor's back was turned, then hid away the note that Swanson had slipped into her hand.

Lemonjello had applied the burnt cork rather too freely, but Primo Furstival was glad of his disguise. His face was now known to the guard, who had begun patrols of Riddance after Lucy's "rescue" from her "kidnappers" (as Arden Gutz's proclamation put it). Tomorrow Vlad Orloff would face execution. Today he must be persuaded to give up his secrets.

Furstival waited until "Mr. Maurice" had been admitted to Fort Gustaf, and then he walked into the square. The sun beat on the cobbles. Many of the stall holders dozed in the shade of their awnings and the dockmen moved sluggishly, squinting against the glare off the river. The sentry at Fort Gustaf played at dominoes with a townsman.

Furstival tilted down his broad-brimmed hat and walked to the stocks, where flies droned lazily among the peelings and shells at Orloff's feet. The prisoner's back was sunburnt and his lips cracked; he blinked groggily when Furstival's shadow fell on his face.

"What do you want?" he rasped.

"You looked thirsty," said the Boondocker.

"I had forgotten until you came along."

"Allow me to give you a drink."

He kicked away the rotted vegetables and knelt beside the prisoner. Miss Pooter had given him Orloff's canteen as a token, and the old man drank greedily when he put it to his lips.

"Who are you?" he sputtered. Water dripped from his chin.

"I am Primo Furstival, chief traveling delegate of the Boondock Town Assembly."

"More!" Orloff gasped. Furstival held the prisoner's head so that he might drink more easily. The arrow through his neck made each sip a torment, yet so great was his thirst that he had soon drained the canteen.

A few passers-by glanced curiously at the scene, though it was not unknown for soft-hearted souls to take pity on prisoners. The stocks were rarely used even in rough-and-tumble Riddance, being reserved for the most hideous of crimes. In the middle of the nearly deserted square a stout hewn log stood on end in readiness for the execution.

"How came you by that canteen?" Orloff demanded.

"I think you must know."

"Where is she, then? Did she escape the guard?"

"Miss Cant has come to no harm," said Furstival, lowering his voice. "She is safe in Riddance. Lucy Wickwright was not so lucky."

"Wickwright!" said Orloff. "Curse the hour I heard that name!"

"Miss Cant owes her freedom to Lucy Wickwright," Primo Furstival reminded him.

"It is a strange freedom that skulks from village to village, thieving and sleeping under the stars," growled Orloff. "She owes her freedom to that guttersnipe? In another day Pauline would have been the Baroness of Cant. Now she is reviled like a common tinker!"

"She is out of the dungeon, at least, thanks to Lucy."

"Don't talk to me of dungeons, Boondocker!" Orloff hissed. "Tinkers live always in a dungeon, though they wander free as the wind. They are shackled by hunger, and prisoned by the cold, and kept down by ignorance. I did not rise in Lord Cant's service so that the child of my loins should enjoy a tinker's hollow freedom! Awk!"

He grimaced, his teeth clenched in pain. Furstival marveled that he could even speak with the arrow stuck through his neck. Every word must be an agony. The man who could endure such torment would be stopped by nothing short of the grave, Furstival mused — and, indeed, Orloff had let nothing turn him aside on his road from a tinker's camp to the most powerful office in Cant.

"Your concern for the child is admirable," said the Boondocker. He took off his hat and shaded Orloff's face with it. "For my part, I was loyal to the house of Cant from the start of this rebellion, which has dealt a dreadful blow to sightseeing. What concerns me now is the future. You must know the rebels intend to take over the gum trade."

"Of course," said Orloff. "Who controls the gum trade controls the Barony."

"And have you considered what will become of Miss Cant in a Barony ruled by Arden Gutz? Give him control of the gum trade and his power will be absolute."

"Then I beg you to take Pauline out of the Barony," said Orloff. "Better that she live in exile than in a land ruled by that popinjay, who scarcely merited the postmaster's berth I offered him. He is much like Lord Cant — full of words and conceit, and blind to his own weakness."

Primo Furstival wiped his brow with the sleeve of his tunic, which came away black with burnt cork. His disguise was melting in the sun. He glanced at the guardsman bent over his game of dominoes. Sooner or later he would wonder what the prisoner and his kind-souled friend were talking about.

"Miss Cant already intends to leave the Barony," he said. "Indeed she sent me here to ask for your help."

Orloff blew away a fly that had settled on his nose.

"Of what help can I be? I cannot help myself."

"You can tell Miss Cant where to find the gum plant."

The prisoner looked sharply at him. "What's this nonsense you speak?"

"Miss Cant has no intention of going meekly into exile," said Furstival. "If you imagine that, you do not know the child of your loins. She is as stubborn as you, Squire Orloff, and no fonder of Arden Gutz. She means to choke his rebellion by putting a final end to the gum trade."

"I don't believe it. You're a spy. Gutz has sent you to prise this knowledge from me."

"Did Gutz send this?" asked Furstival, showing him the canteen.

Orloff licked his lips.

"He may have. Perhaps Wickwright carried it when she was captured."

"Lucy Wickwright would carry nothing of yours, and you know it."

"Anyone might have stolen it."

"You saw Miss Cant carried your gum purse. Would not a thief have taken that, instead?"

"If Gutz finds the gum plant his triumph is certain!"

"If Gutz had sent me I would not wear this absurd disguise!" snapped Furstival. "For Miss Cant's sake, I beseech you! She wants a father's help. By destroying the gum plant she can put an end to the rebels' advantage. Then she may at least live in peace in Cant, though she does not rule it."

Orloff squinted at the Boondocker. "Where is she now?" he asked. "Who is with her?"

"I left her in the care of a friend. Indeed, I bring greetings from her guardian."

"Who in Cant sends greetings to me?"

"She is your sister, I'm told. Mrs. Lungwich. "

"Lil!" exclaimed Orloff.

"An honest woman, if not strictly law abiding," said Furstival. "Miss Cant wants smuggling out of the Barony, and Mrs. Lungwich has offered her services. She has made camp on the outskirts of Riddance."

Orloff looked away, and a deeper shadow seemed to cross his face than the one made by Furstival's hat. The Boondocker glanced anxiously at the gates and caught the guardsman staring back at him. Orloff's head dropped. He gazed at the buzzing flies.

"I was born in that wagon," he said, "but when I reached a man's age I turned my back on the tinkers. I despised their small ambition. Now everything that was good of me rides with Lil."

"Your sister sends greetings and a word," said Primo Furstival. Orloff looked up.

"What word?"

"She asked me to recall to you a proverb of the tinkers. 'There is no tree but has rotten wood enough to burn it.' She told me it was a famous saying of your grandmother."

"I remember it. Is that all?"

"One thing more. She asks, 'Must the acorn go with the oak to the fire?'"

Orloff looked away to the hewn log standing in the market square.

"I see the poteen has not dulled Lil's wit," he whispered.

The townsman slapped down a jubilant tile. The game of dominoes was finished.

"Will you help us?" Furstival begged.

A drop fell from Vlad Orloff's face, though whether it was sweat or a tear Mr. Furstival could not say. Furstival leaned close to catch the whispered reply of the Supreme Commander of the Loyalist Army.

"I will," he said.

Chapter 21

Execution Day

$\mathscr{I}$t was with no little pride that Swanson presented the Execution Dress. He had sewn through the night, burning lamp oil in a workshop beyond the horse paddock. Fort Gustaf was well stocked with sewing notions, he discovered. He was even provided a dressmaker's dummy. Evidently when the guardsmen were not taking a turn in the ballroom they kept alert by altering the hems of their frocks. He debuted his creation in the ballroom, where Miss Poke sat with her esteemed superior, the Reverend Mr. Frodd.

"Not a whole lot of foreigners come to Cant, Maurice," Frodd commented while Lucy, hidden by a folding screen, put on her costume. "What brings you to this part of the world?"

"I come for zee lass," Swanson said.

"The lass?" repeated Frodd. "Miss Wickwright?"

"Not Miss Weakrat, alzough she eez exquisite. Zee *lass* — bobbin lass, needle lass, pillow lass, and so on and so forth. Even at Paris wee hear of zee Cantling lass."

"They make fabulous lace," agreed Miss Poke. "Imagine how tedious it must be!"

"Will you help me, Mr. Maurice?" Lucy called from behind the screen.

"But of course, my sweet!" said Swanson. "Pleez to excuse me, Miss Puck."

Lucy needed help with the ties, which Swanson had put on the back. He snugly knotted them, and then hid Lucy's boy clothes within the folds of the flamboyant outfit, along with a few items she had brought concealed under her tunic. Everything else she had left behind in her pack.

"Wee are ready?" called Swanson.

"Oh, yes!" said Miss Poke.

Swanson pulled Lucy from behind the screen.

"Behold!" he cried. Miss Poke leapt from her chair.

"It's *fabulous!*" she screamed. "Just *fabulous!*"

"I don't get it," said Frodd. "Why does it have an 'X'?"

"Zee ecks is all zee rage in Paris," said Swanson.

The dress was dazzling. Swanson had found in the milliner's shop an organdy of such intense yellowness that it hurt the eye. His creation would have been startling even without the "X" of black silk braid that crossed what he was pleased to call Lucy's "bust." With its winglike sleeves the dress made her look like the prize specimen of a butterfly collection.

"It's different," Frodd admitted.

"Meester Gutz will be pleezed, you theenk?"

"Arden will *die!*" promised Miss Poke.

"Vee must hope so," said Swanson. "Shall vee go out?"

"*Fabulous!*"

Swanson offered Lucy his arm and escorted her to the yard, where the troops had lined up in files for a procession. Arden Gutz held a last-minute inspection, fixing the angle of a scabbard here and fussily dusting a helmet there. Swanson glanced at the horse paddock. He had crept away from his sewing in the night to pull the bolt from its gate, trusting that the docile, well-fed beasts had no desire to escape.

"Arden!" cried Miss Poke. "Here is your Baroness!"

Gutz turned around. Since the onset of war the August Provisional Regent had dressed in soldier's garb, and on this triumphal day he wore a long crimson cape over a white tunic girt with silver. A sword hung in a jeweled scabbard at his hip, and his eyes flashed with the confidence of a man who has risen from nothing to great heights. He cut such a figure that Lucy felt somehow cheated. On impulse she whispered to Swanson:

"What a consort he might have made, if he weren't so mean!"

The dressmaker frowned, puzzled.

"Consort, Miss Weakrat?"

"*Regent*," Lucy said, flushing. "I meant to say regent."

She stumbled across the rocky yard, still uneasy on high heels. A gust blew over the walls and ruffled the capes and tunics of the guardsmen standing with Arden Gutz, who held up a hand to shield his eyes from her costume.

"Lucy," he said, blinking. "May I ask why there is an 'X' on your dress?"

"It's the fashion in P-paris, sir."

"Zee fairy latest thing!"

"I see. Well, you certainly look . . . ah . . . very colorful."

He did not seem pleased. In their last meeting at the castle Lucy had kicked Arden in a sensitive organ, and days had passed before he walked upright again. But Lemonjello in his note had urged her to act the part of a chastened Baroness, so she humbly curtseyed to his flattery. The victorious regent offered his arm, and Lucy dutifully took it. Together they walked to the head of the procession.

"Open the gates!" Gutz commanded.

"Pull, you weasels!" ordered a sergeant.

Straining underlings opened the gates of Fort Gustaf and four trumpeters marched out, swallowtail pennants fluttering from their horns. They blew a deafening fanfare as Gutz led Lucy into the square.

"Hail Lucy, Lady Wickwright, and the Honorable Regent, Arden Gutz!" bellowed the sergeant.

"Hooray!" shouted the people of Riddance.

A great multitude thronged the square, and the cheers nearly blew Lucy from her heels. Ladies waved kerchiefs and men jostled for a sight of the maidservant whom Lord Cant had claimed on his deathbed. Children wept, their eyes stung by her costume. Arden Gutz waved his plumed hat and led Lucy to a dais erected in view of the prisoner. She waved timidly to the adoring crowd.

"They are pleased," Gutz observed, leaning over to her. He scanned the throng coldly, as though calculating the benefit to himself of its devotion. "You'll make a more popular sovereign than Adolphus, after Miss Poke has finished with you."

Lucy scarcely heard his words. She had witnessed scenes like this countless times, but always Pauline had been the object of the crowd's idolatry. Lucy might follow only a step behind her mistress, and yet remain invisible. Now she grasped how noble persons became so proud and headstrong! Such floods of adulation, whether deserved or not, could only buoy the heart.

Sir Geneva Trollopson and his officers were already seated, along with Mayor Boot and the chief burghers of Riddance. They stood and bowed to Lucy, who, as instructed by Miss Poke, inclined her head slightly to each admirer. Arden Gutz escorted her to a grand chair at the center of the viewing platform, and then sat on an even grander one beside it. Miss Poke and Mr. Frodd sat on Gutz's right, while a place of honor had been reserved for "Mr. Maurice" to Lucy's left.

By immemorial custom the condemned man had knelt since dawn in the square, watched over by a black-hooded executioner on whose hairy shoulder rested the Instrument of Justice (a large, double-edged axe). Fences of barrels linked by ropes kept the common folk from blocking the view from the dais. Of all people, Lucy had reason to approve this grim pageant, for Vlad Orloff — wittingly or not — had made her an orphan in the world. He surely deserved his fate.

But when she gazed out from the dais she could summon only pity for the man. After days in the stocks he could barely hold himself upright, and he flinched from the peach stones and other missiles hurled by boys in the crowd. To Lucy's ears the cheering spectators sounded like a pack of ravening wolves.

When she last watched an execution, Arden Gutz had knelt by the Stone of Justice, and Vlad Orloff had been at the Baron's right hand. Now, as in a mirror, the roles were reversed. In the older man Lucy saw a reflection of the younger — not as he now was, but as he one day might be. Would that we all had such a looking-glass, she thought, when we waved the vain plumage of our youth! "Behold the future," the mirror would say, "and weep."

Pauline von Cant sat uneasily on Guinevere. She liked to be astride a horse, not perched on a sidesaddle like a dainty court lady. But Guinevere had stubbornly refused to be straddled — mulishly refused, to be precise — so Pauline would have to make the best of it. She had rehearsed the fancy riders' trick in the open lands beyond Riddance, with Lemonjello standing in for Lucy. The astronomer was bruised and tender today, but Pauline had thoroughly mastered it.

She had a broad view of the square from an alley next to the corn factor's depot. Her mount whinnied at the trumpets' blast, but Pauline soothed her with a lump of sugar and gazed anxiously down the high street. The fanfare was Lemonjello's cue, and for a dreadful moment she thought he had missed it. Then she saw him ride out on Lil's cart mule, a cape from the rag-and-bone shop fluttering behind him. Even from this distance Pauline could see his corked eyebrows furrowed in resolve.

"Hey! You make a better door than a window!" someone yelled. Pauline looked around. A dockman was perched on a rain barrel at the alley's mouth and Guinevere blocked his view.

"Sorry!" said Pauline.

She reined the mule into the alley and waved her cap overhead. Lil had been watching from the stocks and at this signal she jumped down and pushed through the crowd. The soldiers remaining in Fort Gustaf had climbed to the battlements to witness the spectacle, and a lone sentry kept watch at the gates. Lil forced a path to him, her progress marked by the curses of those whose toes she trampled. Lemonjello slowed his mule to a walk. Timing was everything now.

When she reached the sentry Lil uncorked a jug of poteen. She took a snort with great relish, and then elbowed the young man and offered him the jug. The guardsman, not looking at her, only shook his head. Pauline sucked her teeth. Oh, please don't let him have scruples! she thought.

Lemonjello had nearly reached the gates. Again Lil prodded the guardsman. He sternly shook his head — *No!* — but then the trumpeters lifted their horns and blew a chord that brought huzzahs from the crowd. Every eye followed Arden Gutz as he strode to the edge of the dais. The sentry looked right and left — even up to the ramparts — and then snatched the jug from Lil and greedily sucked at its mouth. The instant he threw back his head Lemonjello spurred his mule. Under cover of the trumpets' fanfare he galloped through the gates of Fort Gustaf.

Lucy squinted in the sunlight. By longstanding custom the sentence of death was always averted at the last minute, when a chicken (or some other succulent fowl) was placed under the axe as a ransom for the prisoner. A number of coops roosted among the vendors' stalls, but no one had brought forth a bird.

Her fingers moved anxiously over the braids that twined like a handle over her chest. *I shall contrive to make a diversion,* the astronomer's note had said, but what that might be, Lucy could only guess. Would wet laundry rain from the sky? She saw Pauline waving her cap at the mouth of the alley, and moments later Lil leapt down from her perch on the stocks. The trumpets rang, and Arden Gutz walked to the edge of the dais. He lifted his arms to command the crowd's attention.

"Vladimir Orloff!" he cried. "You have earned the condemnation of the Cantling people and their heroic little Baroness, Lady Wickwright. As regent to her Ladyship it is my happy duty to execute your sentence!"

Lucy scowled at the phrase "little Baroness." It reminded her of those silly pageants the children of the orphanage used to perform for Lord Cant. They would strut about as miniature knights and ladies — "Little Lady Pureloins" and "Wee Sir Simpleheart" were typical names — while Miss Poke hissed their lines from behind a curtain. When it was done, the Baron, having slept from the beginning, would start up and congratulate Mr. Frodd on penning such a gripping drama.

Arden Gutz lifted a hand to quiet the crowd's cheers.

"Your hour of justice is at hand," he told the prisoner, "and your crimes will no more trouble this Barony, whose people — sorely oppressed by the tyranny of Nobles — cry out for that just retribution, prescribed by ordinance and tradition, which ever, though oft delayed, falls upon the heads of scofflaws, brutes, and tyrants." Here Gutz paused, as though to let the crowd savor this morsel of oratory. "Yet we are merciful," he went on. "If you nurture any remorse for your deeds, you may speak now and unburden your heart."

Orloff looked up. The arrow in his neck cast a shadow on his breast.

"Remorse is all that is left to me, and I shall carry it to my grave," he rasped. "But I will unburden myself of a confession, and a warning. Lucy Wickwright!" he cried. "I sought to bring honor to Miss Cant, and if I have erred I did so to win her rightful place. Yet I confess you have bested me. You have won her heart."

The crowd murmured at this declaration, and Lucy gazed in wonder at Vlad Orloff. Almost she could believe the beating sun had melted his cold pride — or perhaps he knew at last some feeling beyond ambition for the child he had sired. Arden Gutz angrily stamped the dais.

"Do not let this criminal deceive you!" he yelled. "Pauline von Cant is a pretender, a spoilt and coddled puppet of the Loyalist oppressors. She will no longer trouble the peace of Cant!"

Someone snorted loudly in the mouth of an alley.

"My warning, Master Gutz, is for you," Orloff went on. "Seek not to win the love of outlanders, for they love nothing but money. When they can no longer profit from you they will kick you aside like a moth-eaten purse!"

"Silence!" commanded Gutz. "Executioner! Do your duty!"

Again Lucy looked for the chicken. Everything else stood ready — the prisoner, the eager spectators, the axeman under his hood — yet nowhere did she see the bird. A pair of guardsmen dragged Orloff to the block, and with a start Lucy realized that her regent meant actually to kill his rival.

A hush fell in the square, followed by shouts of protest as the crowd reached the same conclusion. Cantlings adored a spectacle, and they liked to see bad deeds punished, but they were not a bloodthirsty folk. Arden Gutz ignored their cries.

"What say you now, Commissioner Orloff?" he mocked. "Perhaps you regret offering a post in Trans-Poltroon to an Oxford man? The days of your arrogance are over, Commissioner! You are dealing with a bachelor of the arts! Kill him! Kill him!" he screamed.

Lucy leapt up as a dreadful rumbling sounded from the gates of Fort Gustaf. Townsfolk fled in a stumbling panic, for behind them charged the loosed and maddened horses of the corral, their hooves churning a storm of dust. On a struggling cart mule at the rear, swinging a bullwhip and hallooing like a madman, rode Luigi Lemonjello.

Pauline had to snort. "No longer trouble the peace of Cant," would she? Arden Gutz obviously did not know her. She had troubled the peace of Cant when she came howling from Esmeralda's womb, and from that time until now she had thrown enough tantrums and tossed enough teacups to trouble the peace of whole kingdoms, never mind one small barony. Peace would come to Cant in due time, but only after she and Lucy had dealt with the likes of Arden Gutz.

When the horses thundered from Fort Gustaf she spurred Guinevere out of the alley.

"Hyah!" she cried.

In her left hand Pauline held an iron hook that Lemonjello had tethered to the saddle, and as she rode up on the fence of barrels she whipped the mule's flank with it. Guinevere had never known such abuse. She jumped the fence in sheer outrage and, when she landed, her shoes struck sparks from the cobblestones. A woman with a child on her arm leapt from the mule's path.

"Steady!" Pauline shouted, spurring the animal towards the dais. The people of Riddance ran for their lives ahead of the stampeding horses of the fort.

When Gutz saw Pauline he left off berating Fatty Trollopson and lunged for Lucy, who waited at the edge the platform. But Swanson could not have sewn a better target. Pauline slid the hook under the braided "X" on his dress and Lucy flew up from the dais, a butterfly on organdy wings.

"Seize that ungrateful wretch!" Gutz screamed at Trollopson.

Somehow Lucy landed on the mule's back. Pauline pulled hard on the reins, needing only to turn around to make good their escape. Guinevere was willing — indeed, her head obeyed the command — but her hooves found no purchase on the cobbles. She slid drunkenly over the smooth stones and then, whinnying madly, crashed into the dais.

The devastation was profound. The platform did not sway and list and fall politely over. It collapsed with a roar. Dignitaries screamed like unoiled hinges, and ladies showed their linens. Pauline was thrown like a circus tumbler from the saddle and fell into the embrace of Fatty Trollopson. She leapt up unscathed but the Commandant shrieked when she stepped on his fingers. Arden Gutz flung a high heel at her as she ran from the wreckage.

"The pretender!" he shouted. "Guards! Unsheath your swords!"

Pauline raced after Guinevere. The mule had lurched to her feet and was trotting into the square. Lucy bounced at the end of the tether like an unloved doll on a string.

"Whoa!" Pauline shouted. "Whoa, Guinevere! Whoa! Blast it, Guinevere, STOP!"

Chaos reigned. Guardsmen screamed at bewildered civilians, and ragamuffin children ran wild, reveling in the unexpected pageant of anarchy. Pauline caught up with the mule and jerked its reins. She knelt and unhooked Lucy, who looked very small in a bright puddle of organdy.

"Lucy! Are you hurt?"

Lucy's eyes blinked open.

"Hullo," she said. "I bumped my head."

"Oh, Lucy, you're *always* bumping your head! Come, we must hurry!"

She helped her up. It was a wonder Lucy had any head left, Pauline thought. Back when she spied for the Cause, Lucy had got a great goose-egg in Vlad Orloff's office, and then she had taken a bruising tumble when they escaped Castle Cant. If the war went on much longer, Pauline would have to give up being a poetess and enlist as Lucy's bodyguard. What a lot of trouble she got into!

"Stop, wretch!" cried Arden Gutz.

He ran after them, his crimson cape fluttering behind, but the vain garment proved to be his undoing. Out of the turmoil leapt Swanson. With a swiftness that astonished Pauline he ran after the August Provisional Regent and seized the cape's billowing hem. Gutz's feet flew from under him and he dropped to the cobbles. The dressmaker had snatched a piece of lumber from the wreckage and, when Gutz offered to stand, Swanson brought the board down smartly on the Causist's plumed hat.

"Crimson is *so* wrong for daytime!" he scolded.

Lucy tried to reach Guinevere's stirrup but her foot kept tangling in organdy. One of the soldiers saw his chance, and as he ran towards the fugitives Lucy stumbled from the mule and clutched her brow.

"My head hurts awfully," she said. "Save yourself, Pauline. Go without me!"

"Oh, don't be a ninny!" Pauline said. She seized Lucy at the knees and threw her like a sack of corn over the mule's rump. She was struggling to get her own foot into the stirrup — she had climbed from a butter churn earlier — when Swanson fell at her feet.

"Allow *me*, Miss Cant!" he begged.

Pauline leapt from his back to the saddle. As she took hold of the reins, Swanson jumped up and swung his lumber at the approaching guardsman, who dropped without a whimper. But before she could spur the mule to a gallop Lucy plucked at Pauline's dress.

"Wait!" she begged.

"Oh, what is it *now*?"

"Pauline, there's no chicken!"

Had Lucy cracked her skull? Pauline wondered.

"How can you think of food at a time like this?"

"The chicken for the ransom!" said Lucy. "Gutz means to kill him!"

Pauline had been intent on her mission and had not noticed the missing bird. Gutz's cries of "Kill him!" she had put down to the ravings of a madman. But there knelt Orloff at the block, and no fowl in sight.

"How awful!" she murmured. It was not a feeling for justice that moved her, for if anyone deserved death it was Vladimir Orloff. She simply knew that the old man had loved, and lost, and seen his last hope come to ruin. Plain pity moved the heart of Pauline von Cant.

"We can't let him die!" said Lucy.

Pauline measured the situation. A dozen armed guards surrounded the prisoner, and the executioner's axe might cut Guinevere to pieces. Facing these determined men were two young girls — one fabulously overdressed — and a mule whose ears did not match. Altogether Pauline liked their chances.

"Hyah!" she cried.

The guardsmen, as she expected, threw themselves out of the way, for even a comical mule is frightening when coming at full gallop. She drew her spearhead from a sheath fixed to the saddle and cut the bonds that held the prisoner's wrists. She would have left him, then, but as she took up the reins again Orloff grabbed her arm.

"Don't leave me!" he begged.

Already the guardsmen had sprung up and drawn their swords. Pauline threw the dangling iron hook to Vlad Orloff.

"Hang on!" she yelled.

The old man kept his feet for a remarkably long time, racing after the mule like a child playing crack-the-whip. Lil, the old horse thief, had captured one of the loosed steeds of the fort and circled round to fetch Swanson, who leapt up behind her from atop a barrel. Lemonjello on the cart mule led his comrades past the gates of Fort Gustaf, and together they galloped down the dusty high street of Riddance.

There Orloff fell, and Guinevere dropped behind the others as she pulled him through the dust. At the edge of town Pauline prepared to cut the tether, but as she reached for the spearhead Orloff gave a strangled cry and she heard him no more. Pauline pressed on. She had done for him what she could, and more than he deserved.

Beyond a bend in the road Primo Furstival waved a white flag overhead, meaning their hideout was secure. Pauline urged on her mount. When she reached Lil's wagon, Blaise helped her lift Lucy down from the mule. The little Baroness had fainted, and a great goose-egg welled up on her head.

Chapter 22

The Black Arrow and the TRUE POZEEN

$\mathcal{T}$he squash of Riddance was pretty poor stuff, in Blaise Delagraisse's view, but the day was hot and at least it wet his tongue. Mr. Lemonjello seemed no more pleased with the ale. The other patrons of the Blazing Bedbug drank deeply, however, being immune to the local vintages. Like daytime tipplers everywhere they were full of opinions but sorely lacking in knowledge. The astronomer had got very little out of them about the fate of Vladimir Orloff, but he sipped his ale with a grimace and tried again.

"They say the prisoner was quite an important man among the Loyalists," he said.

"Aye, he was a big 'un," said the innkeeper. "The Supreme Commander of the Loyalist Army. You don't expect Pauline Cant risked her neck to save the chief bottle-washer, do ye?"

"He won't be commanding no army now, anyway," offered the innkeeper's maid-of-all-work. "My Charlie rode out with the others after them. You could see where that Orloff was dragged along, he said, but then there was a mess of blood where he let go. Charlie says there ain't no man could live through being dragged by that horse."

"It weren't a horse, but a mule," objected a man in a blacksmith's apron.

The maid shrugged. "Horse, mule — it's all the same. Dead's dead."

"But Orloff hasn't been seen?" Lemonjello persisted.

"If he's alive, he daren't show himself in Riddance," said the innkeeper.

"Poor little Lucy Wickwright!" an old woman sighed over her knitting. "She was a sweet thing in her yellow dress, though I would've left off that black braid. And who'll be our Baroness now she's dead?"

"Dead!" cried Blaise.

"Aye, dead!" the woman said. "Do you think Pauline Cant kidnapped her to serve her tea and biscuits? They say she led her a dog's life up in her castle, beating her every day and making her sleep in the ashes. It's awful what rich folks'll do to a poor little orphan girl."

"It's worse than you imagine," the blacksmith darkly muttered.

"What are you on about?" asked the innkeeper.

The blacksmith put down his ale.

"The way I hear the story," he said, "is that Lord Cant was

lying ill, and called for Miss Wickwright. He felt bad about what he'd done — adopting her out to poor folks when she was born, on account of him not being married to her ma."

"Her ma was a maid-of-all-work, I hear," said the maid-of-all-work.

"Well, she weren't Lord Cant's wedded wife, that's for certain," said the blacksmith. "Anyway, Lord Cant had a change of heart, they say, and was a-going to make Lucy his heiress. Well, little Pauline von Fancypants didn't like that one bit. No sir! She weren't about to let no maidservant take *her* place. So she had Mr. Orloff make up some poison chewing gum. She fed it to her pa and killed him before he could claim Lucy in front of witnesses."

"No!" the knitting woman cried.

"Her own pa?" said the innkeeper. The blacksmith nodded.

"How else do you suppose a Postal Commissioner got to be Supreme Commander of the Loyalist Army?" he asked. "They was in league together. He took care of killing off her pa, and she promised him that he'd be her regent when she got to be the Baroness. That was the deal."

This, with the squash, was more than Blaise could stomach.

"What a lot of nonsense!" he said. "Miss Cant wouldn't kill her own pa!"

"Wouldn't she?" countered the blacksmith. "Tell that to the guards she cut down!"

"Oh, bosh! Miss Cant wouldn't hurt a fly."

A man got up who had sat with his back to the others. Despite the great heat, he wore a cape, and Blaise saw too late that he had on a guardsman's tunic under it. He put an empty blackjack on the serving counter and looked down at the under-footman.

"You know a lot about Miss Cant, it seems," he said. "What's your name, boy?"

"Er, Freddie Mallard, sir," said Blaise. Broadsides tacked up in Riddance offered rewards for the capture of Blaise Delagraisse, Luigi Lemonjello, and all other "kidnappers, Loyalists, and conspirators against the common weal." The under-footman wore eyebrows of burnt cork.

"Never mind the lad," begged Lemonjello. "He's full of moonbeams."

"Is this your son?" the guard asked.

"Yes," said the astronomer. "Horton Mallard at your service. Please to excuse my boy, Captain. I've tried to teach him to keep quiet, but I can beat him till my arm's falling off and still he will blabber. He takes after his mother, I'm afraid."

"And is he a friend to Pauline von Cant?"

"A friend to Pauline Cant!" cried Lemonjello. "Why, that's a good one! Ho ho ho!"

"He talks like he knows all about her."

"Aye, talk! It's all he's good for, I'm afraid. Takes after his mother's family! No," he went on in a soberer voice, "I'll tell you how it is, Captain. The boy got hold of one of those pictures of Miss Cant, that they used to sell for a shilling. Well, it was about six months ago, when he went all spots in his face, and since then he's been hopeless. He fell in love with her picture, you see."

"Here! Are you all right?" asked the maid-of-all-work. Blaise had been sipping squash, and when he heard of his love for Pauline the beverage spurted out of his nose like jets from a fountain.

"Boys will be boys, I suppose," said the guardsman to Lemonjello. "I confess I used to carry a portrait of Lady Esmeralda, when I was a young lad." He waved the empty blackjack at the innkeeper. "Just a drop more, if you please. Where are you from, Mr. Mallard?"

"Tenesmus," said Lemonjello, who had worked out a story beforehand. "Every summer I come north and mend glasses for the shipmen. I'm a lens grinder, you see. I brought the boy this year so he could learn the ways."

"Another ale for you, Mr. Mallard?" asked the innkeeper.

"No, we must be off!" said the astronomer. "I thank you for your hospitality, sir. Your ale was like nothing I've tasted! And here's something for you, lass, on account of your trouble." He handed two pennies to the maid-of-all-work, who was mopping up the nose-blown squash.

"Thank you, sir," said the girl.

The blacksmith scowled as Blaise stood and followed Lemonjello out of the tavern. The astronomer heaved a sigh when the bell tinkled behind them, as though he had held his breath the whole time.

"That was n-not a very fruitful expedition," he said.

"Do you think Mr. Orloff might really be dead?" asked Blaise.

Lemonjello frowned.

"If that arrow through his neck could not k-kill him, then I fear there may still be mischief beating in Orloff's heart," he said. "But p-perhaps I misjudge him. He might easily have given us away before the execution, yet he did not."

"And he did tell Mr. Furstival the way to the gum plant," Blaise reminded him.

"So he did. But — but I still — Hush! What's that?"

He looked around. Two children rolled a hoop far away, but otherwise the high street was deserted. Lemonjello peered at the mouths of alleys and the shadowy doorways of shops.

"What is it, sir?" asked Blaise.

"I . . . I thought I heard the tavern's doorbell."

"I didn't hear anything."

Lemonjello chewed his lip for a moment, scanning the street, then took the under-footman's arm and continued walking.

"I d-didn't like that guardsman's questions," he whispered. "We should have been more cautious."

"But you threw him right off the scent, Mr. Lemonjello," said Blaise. "That was a fine piece of spy work, I thought! Why, you'll be topping Lucy before long. You didn't stammer once the whole time!"

Again the astronomer stopped.

"I . . . I didn't, did I?" he marveled.

"No, sir! You were Horton Mallard down to his toes. I thought it was ripping!"

Lemonjello smiled.

"Perhaps I haven't such a c-catch in my speech as I fancy, Master Blaise," he said. "Come! The others will be anxious to hear our report."

They hurried down the street and never saw the caped figure run out from an alley to a shop's doorway behind them. Their footprints were plain as a trail of crumbs on the dusty road out of Riddance.

Lil had made a poultice for Lucy's goose-egg and after two days the swelling was nearly gone. It was time to set out for Kandu. Lemonjello took Blaise into town to learn what he could of Orloff while Furstival and Swanson gathered provisions and filled canteens. To escape the heat, Pauline and Lucy had climbed up the slope behind their hiding place, where they might catch the wind blowing through the firs. Below them the River Leech wended its way out of Cant.

"I never saw anything so funny as that dress, Lucy," said Pauline. She had spent the past two days teasing Lucy about "the Organdy Ogre" (as she called it). "You looked like one of those targets the guardsmen shoot arrows at!"

"It *was* a prominent 'X'," Lucy admitted.

"If only Swanson had enough organdy and braid, you might have a whole alphabet to wear!" screamed Pauline. She rolled to her belly and beat the ground, weeping with laughter. How good it was to have Lucy back! Their grown-up friends were wonderful, and she could even begin to see the usefulness of Delagraisse, but Lucy was the ideal target for a joke. She never got cross!

"It really was a lovely dress," Lucy said. "Except for the braid. And the color."

"Yellow doesn't suit you," agreed Pauline, wiping her eyes.

"Swanson says I ought to wear green and silver," Lucy told her. "He says I should look grand in a silver clasp from the time of Gustaf the Fey."

"I'm sure you would," said Pauline, spitting out a husk. Lil had taught her the art of chewing seeds, and, as Lemonjello had promised, the craving for gum soon passed.

"Are you feeling quite better?" asked Lucy. "You've stopped chewing in your sleep, I noticed."

"I don't miss gum at all. Tinkers' cud is good enough for me." It was even better having Lucy back, thought Pauline, now that there were no more secrets between them.

"Green, or magenta," said Lucy a moment later.

"What?"

"Magenta would suit me as well."

"Did Swanson tell you that?"

"No. But I fancy it would suit me, all the same, with a silver clasp." Lucy looked up the river, where the towers of Fort Gustaf rose through the haze. "Pauline," she said hesitantly, "am I pretty?"

"What!" cried Pauline, sitting up.

"Oh, never mind," said Lucy.

"Lucy! Are you turning into a lady?"

"Don't be silly! But . . . well, it feels grand to wear a fancy dress, doesn't it?"

"You are!" insisted Pauline. "You're a little lady!"

"I'm nothing of the sort," Lucy said. "It's just that . . . everyone has always said you're beautiful and adorable, and I feel such a drab with my hair all gone and dressed like a boy. I . . . I fancied maybe I was at least tolerable to look at, in a pretty dress."

"That dress hurt the eye!" complained Pauline. Then she squeezed her former maid. "Oh, Lucy, you shall make a lovely

Baroness. Don't you know that people only flatter one because it's expected of them? Lady Brightling, for example, is supposed to be a great beauty, although frankly she resembles a horse. But her reputation precedes her — much like a cart before a horse — and so gentlemen flatter her. Now, you have the advantage of really *being* pretty, so here's what I shall do. I'll write a sonnet likening your face to the sun, and I'll send it with Lemonjello. By the time we get back to Cant your beauty will be legendary."

"You'll have to write it quickly," said Lucy, kissing her. "Here he comes."

Pauline looked up the road. She thought at first a cur had followed the spies out of town, but a second glance showed plainly it was a man. He walked far behind and at the edge of the road, as though ready at any moment to throw himself into the ditch.

"Someone has followed them, Lucy. Do you see?"

Lucy peered up the road. She wiped her glasses on her tunic.

"I don't see anything," she said. "Wait — there he is! Oh, we're found out!"

"Come, we must warn the others. Put on your shoes!"

Lucy hurriedly jammed her feet into the turnshoes. Pauline's feet, once blistered, had developed tough pads and she had come up the slope barefoot. She raced over the pine needles ahead of Lucy, her chemise flapping in the air. She had left her kirtle in the wagon. It was too hot for such niceties.

Swanson and Furstival had come back with the water and rested with Lil and Roto in the shade of the wagon. The dressmaker bolted up and covered his mouth when Pauline fell panting beside the hound.

"Miss Cant, where is your *dress?*" he shrieked.

"No time!" Pauline gasped. "Trouble!"

"It can't be so bad you have to go about in your underclothes!"

"What is the matter?" said Lemonjello, running up with Blaise. They had seen the girls hurtling down the slope and guessed that something was amiss.

"You've been followed," Lucy gasped. "We saw a man on the road."

"Are you certain?" the astronomer asked.

"Yes!" said Pauline. "He can't be far behind!"

"Into the wagon, both of you," said Lemonjello.

"Surely he'll search it!" said Pauline. "I suggest —"

"Up you go!" said the astronomer, seizing her waist and almost throwing her into the wagon. Was this the timid stargazer she had known at Castle Cant? wondered Pauline.

Lucy climbed up after her and pulled the curtain. Peeking out, Pauline saw a guardsman of Fort Gustaf rounding the hillock that hid the wagon from the road. He wore a leather scabbard, but it appeared to be empty.

"Ho! Captain!" cried Lemonjello. "Did I leave something behind in the tavern?"

"You left me curious, that's all," the guardsman said. He eyed suspiciously the party of wayfarers. "Who are these folks?"

"Ah, let me introduce you," said Lemonjello. "This is Mrs. McGillicuddy, whose cart I've hired. These fellows are Mr. Azimuth and Mr. Smoot — met them on the road. My son Freddie you know. But you have the advantage of us, captain. I didn't catch your name at The Bedbug."

"I didn't offer it," said the guardsman, "but it is Fletcher, if you want to know. And your name, if I'm not mistaken, is Luigi Lemonjello."

Lucy, peeking out the other side of the curtain from Pauline, drew in her breath.

"I beg your pardon?" said Lemonjello.

"It's no use pretending," said Fletcher. "I saw the girls running down the hill."

Pauline reached back to where her knapsack lay and slowly pulled out the spearhead.

"Mr. Fletcher, I assure you —," Lemonjello began.

"Enough!" shouted the guardsman. "If you wish to play games I shall rouse the fort against you. Pauline von Cant, come out of that wagon! I bring you a message!"

Pauline had heard enough. She threw back the curtain and in two bounds stood before Fletcher with the point of her spearhead pressed to his throat.

"Who sends a message to me?" she demanded.

Swanson squealed and covered his eyes. The guardsman did not flinch.

"May we not sit down?" he calmly asked. "You see I am unarmed."

"Sit, then!" Pauline said. "Blaise! Look down the road and see if he is followed."

"Yes, ma'am!" said the under-footman. He ran off. Fletcher

sat cross-legged in the grass but Pauline remained standing, her weapon at the ready. Lucy climbed down from the wagon and stood behind her.

"Don't be carving up no guardsman, Pooter," Lil advised. "Not unless you liked the inside of Jack Stonefeather's gaol."

"I've been in worse places," said Pauline. "I shall carve out his tongue before I let him give Lucy away!"

"Don't do it!" begged Swanson. "You can never get blood-stains out of linen!"

"The road is clear, Miss Pauline!" called Blaise from atop the hillock.

"Very well," said Pauline. She sat and thrust the spearhead into the ground. "Kindly explain yourself, Mr. Fletcher. Who sends a message to me? Is it Arden Gutz?"

"I do not run errands for that peacock," said the guardsman.

"May I come down now?" asked Blaise.

"Stand guard!" Pauline snapped. She glared at Fletcher. "Who is it, then? Speak, man! Who sent you?"

"The message is from Vladimir Orloff," the guardsman said.

Pauline, for once, was at a loss for words. Lucy knelt behind her.

"I don't believe you," said Lemonjello. "You heard the g-girl at the tavern. No man could live through such an ordeal."

"Maybe not. But you oughtn't to believe tavern tales, Mr. Lemonjello," said Fletcher. "I was the man that followed those mules."

"Go on," said Lemonjello.

"We rounded up the horses and Fatty sent out riders, but I went on foot to read the tale of the road," Fletcher said. "His trail was easy to follow where he let go the mule, for it was painted in blood. I found him resting against a fallen tree."

"He's lying," said Lucy, putting her hand on Pauline's shoulder. "I could see Orloff from the back of the mule. The road was smooth. He'd taken no hurt."

"And did you see him when he let go, your Ladyship?"

"No," admitted Lucy. "I'd turned away. I couldn't bear to look at him."

Fletcher nodded.

"He did not imagine you'd easily believe a stranger's tale," he said, reaching for his scabbard. Pauline snatched the spearhead from the ground but Fletcher showed no fear. He gazed at her calmly and slowly upended the scabbard. "Orloff has sent this token," he said, "that you might know I speak the truth."

An arrow slid into his hand. The point had snapped off and most of its length was black with blood. Its feathering had molted. Fletcher handed this gruesome token to Pauline, who held the shaft gingerly between her finger and thumb.

"The barbs had caught on the rope, and the shaft went clean through his neck when he let go," Fletcher said. "He was an awful sight, I can tell you. I stopped his wounds as best I could, but when I got up to fetch help he would not let me go. You would not credit the strength left in that arm! He forbade me to leave until I had promised to bear a message to Miss Cant."

The arrow's shaft was worn where it had lodged in Orloff's neck, for in the weeks that he carried it — weeks that saw his dreams vanquished and his child denied the barony — his flesh had slowly consumed the bitter dart. Pauline's hand closed around it, her fingers pale against its blackness.

"What is the message?" she asked.

"Vlad Orloff sends this word: Who rules the gum trade rules Cant, no matter who wears the baronial cap. As long as the gum plant stands, Lord Cant's daughter will be a Baroness only in name."

Pauline looked up from the arrow.

"Is there nothing more?" she asked.

"There is, Miss Cant. 'Tell her,' he said, 'that if I have seemed heartless it is because I gave my heart away. Would that I had it back, that I might give it to another.' He said that you would understand."

The arrow trembled in Pauline's hand.

"Poor Dickie!" whispered Lil.

Pauline looked down. In her left hand she clutched the broken spearhead, in her right the blackened dart. Lord Cant, the man she had loved and called Papa, had never had time to spare for his plain-toed child. Now came this message to pierce her. Was the heart always given in vain? she wondered.

She felt Lucy's hand on her shoulder. The sister of her heart.

"Is he dead, then?" Lucy asked.

"That I cannot tell you," said Fletcher. "I hastened into town to fetch the doctor, who brought his boy and a litter. I marked the place well, but when I came back Orloff was gone."

Pauline wiped her cheeks with the heel of her hand. She had let go the spearhead.

"Thank you, Mr. Fletcher," she said.

"I couldn't refuse the man. He was a pitiable sight."

"Why did you not report to the fort that you had found him?" asked Lemonjello.

The guardsman snorted.

"I swore my allegiance to the house of Cant, not to Arden Gutz," he said. "That peacock takes his orders from outlanders, they say — from that woman, Miss Poke, and the old man Frodd. Beggar me if I ever bend the knee to such a regent!"

"He is no regent to me!" swore Lucy. Pauline reached for her hand.

"Do others among the guard feel as you do?" asked Lemonjello.

"Aye, many," said Fletcher. "We joined the guard to defend our liege and kinfolk, not to keep clear the roads for gum traders. Especially not if it means giving outlanders control of the Barony."

"Does this mean you're not going to arrest us?" asked Swanson.

The guardsman rose and kicked the dust from his sandals.

"I have done what I came for," he said. "Good day to you, Miss Cant."

He turned smartly and would have left them. Pauline leapt up.

"Fletcher, wait!" she said.

The guardsman turned around. Pauline clutched the black arrow in her fist.

"Captain," she said, "did you not say you had sworn allegiance to the house of Cant?"

"Aye," he said. "I bent the knee before Lord Cant himself, when he came to inspect the fort."

"I must say you have a strange way of keeping your oath!" said Pauline.

The guardsman gaped at her. "I beg your pardon?" he said.

Pauline took Lucy's hand and pulled her to her feet.

"Rather you ought to ask her pardon!" she cried. "Here is the firstborn child of Lord Cant, Mr. Fletcher. Do you mean to shake off the dust of your feet before her, as though she were a common maid? Your liege stands before you. Fall to your knees and ask her will!"

"But — but — but I didn't think to —"

"On your knees!" Pauline said. She seized the spearhead and lunged at the guardsman, who fell and cowered at her feet, shielding his face with his hands.

"Really, Pauline, there's no need for this!" said Lucy.

"Speak, liegeman!" Pauline demanded. "Beg your Lady's pardon!"

"I — I — I'm sorry, Miss Wickwright!" stammered Fletcher. "Forgive me!"

Lil clapped her hands.

"That's standing up for your sis, Pooter!" she cried.

"But I feel silly!" said Lucy.

"My Lady," said Pauline, turning to face her. "I understand that the trade in gum in this Barony has been carried on under the government of the Postal Commission?"

"What are you talking about, Pauline? Let that poor man up."

"In a moment, my Lady," said Pauline. "I also understand that, owing to the defection of Vladimir Orloff, the office of the Postal Commissioner is presently unfilled. I herewith offer my services. As my first act of office I intend to outlaw the trade in gum and put an end to it. Will you accept this offer, my Lady?"

"You sound like you're in one of Miss Poke's pageants!" said Lucy.

"Ask me if I require anything of you to fulfill my mission," Pauline whispered.

Lucy rolled her eyes.

"Do you require anything of me," she recited, "to fulfill your mission?"

"Yes, my Lady!" Pauline said. She looked down at Fletcher. "I require an escort to the frontier. The road to Kandu is full of dangers, and I would not have my Lady kidnapped by that foul imposter who claims to be her regent. This guardsman should suffice, along with a few trustworthy comrades."

A wry smile spread across Lucy's face. Lemonjello winked at Primo Furstival, and Lil clapped her hands again, and poked Swanson's ribs.

"I think that calls for a snort of poteen!" she said.

A voice cried from atop the hillock.

"Miss Pauline!" said Blaise. "May I *please* come down now?"

With Fletcher as escort the party set out the next morning. Lil would cart the fugitives to the frontier and then turn back, bringing with her the guardsman, Swanson, and Lemonjello. The astronomer had accepted that his duty lay in Cant. He would ride with Lil as far as Muckleston, then turn south and attempt to rescue Lucy's uncle from the dungeon. He rode with Pauline and Lucy in the back of the wagon.

"Uncle Hock will be a great help to you," Lucy said, putting a pencil behind her ear. She tore out and gave him a page from Orloff's notebook. "I've told him that you may speak for me in all things. It doesn't matter whether you stammer, Luigi. Tell the people what Gutz is about and they will rally behind you."

"I shall do my best," said the astronomer.

"Lucy," said Pauline. "Is that a letter?"

Lucy gave her a puzzled look. "You know it is, Pauline. It's a note to Uncle Hock."

"I don't see a stamp on it," said Pauline.

"Don't be silly. Luigi is carrying it."

"That's no excuse, Lucy," Pauline sternly said. "Letters carried on the post roads must have postage paid. I shan't let the postal corridors fall into anarchy while *I'm* Commissioner."

Lucy heaved an enormous sigh, and Pauline fairly wiggled at the success of her mischief. Pauline softened a stick of wax and sealed the letter with a ha'penny stamp from Blaise's pack, then returned the note to Lemonjello.

"See that you deliver this with due haste," she instructed him. "You owe me one-half pence, Lucy."

"I'm afraid I left my wages in my knapsack at Fort Gustaf," said Lucy. "But I thought you wanted to be the poet laureate, Pauline, not the Postal Commissioner."

Pauline put away the wax and the seal.

"I can easily do both things at once," she said. "You forget that I have tinkers' blood, Lucy Wickwright. We can turn our hand to anything. Isn't that right, Lil?" she yelled.

"Whatever you say, Pooter!" Lil called back.

In the late afternoon they reached the Mettlesome Falls — one of the Seven Wonders of Cant and the utmost limit of the Barony. Here the Leech fell in a boiling cataract to the Puddle of Despond, which lay far below in the Vale of Kandu. The place was a famous lovers' leap, where countless Cantlings — forbidden by their parents to marry or under the spell of romantic poets — had plunged into oblivion. A tongue of rock by the torrent served as a viewpoint for sightseers and a diving spot for the lovelorn. Here the wayfarers said their goodbyes.

"Shall I give you a wee jug of poteen for the road, Mr. Furstival?" asked Lil. The Boondocker had grown dizzy looking at the Falls and now gazed instead at the Outland Road, which fell in perilous switchbacks to the valley floor.

"Thank you, no, Mrs. Lungwich," he said. "Plain water will suffice."

"As you wish," said Lil. She shook her head at the ways of nobs.

Swanson begged the girls to bring back word of the fashions in Kandu.

"You might just sketch any designs that catch your fancy," he suggested. "If you could bring back some fabric samples that would be fabulous. And pay special attention to shoes and handbags."

Lucy, without exactly promising to make sketches, told him she would keep her eyes open. Lemonjello gave Blaise most of the contents of his purse, and urged Pauline to keep her spearhead sharp. When he said farewell to Lucy he openly wept.

"Be brave, Luigi!" she said, throwing her arms around his neck.

"I don't know that I can," he answered, "but for your sake I shall pretend."

The Outland Road turned sharply at the viewpoint and passed between two stone pillars. Erected in the reign of Baron Roland, and surmounted by carved wolves' heads, the pillars marked the frontier of Cant. Lucy hoisted her pack and walked to them with Blaise and Primo Furstival, who would guide them in the Vale of Kandu. Even Lil, that much-traveled tinker, feared the shadow of these monoliths, and she drew Pauline aside at some distance from them.

"Here's a little somewhat to nibble as you walk," she said, giving her a bag of seeds.

Pauline put it in the pocket of her kirtle. She wished for a moment she might forget about the war and chewing gum and the Vale of Kandu. How much better it would be to travel about with Lil and learn the tinkers' ways! She would be always in the air, among the fragrant wild herbs and the quickening touch of the rain. The days would end with dances around a fire, and poems would grow out of her like wildflowers.

But that would mean leaving Lucy, and it was plain that Lucy — who lately had shown a troubling interest in dresses and nice manners — wanted looking after. She threw her arms around Lil and kissed her.

"How shall I find you again?" she asked. Lil wiped a tear from her cheek.

"Ah, Pooter, you're a rare beauty," she said, brushing back her hair. "That's your mother coming through. But you have tinkers' blood in you, too, and that is stubborn and strong and will lead you back to Cant. This land was ours long before the nobs came. Your roots are here, my darling, and they are old and deep."

She took a small flask from her pocket.

"Here is how you may find your aunt Lil," she said. "Wherever you be in Cant, you betake yourself to a tinkers' camp and sit by the fire, where the grandmothers are warming their bones.

Bring out this flask and offer a snort to one and all. They'll know the true poteen! And they will tell you where to find Lillian Lungwich."

Pauline hugged her a long time. Lil then climbed to the riding board, took up her whip, and steered the wagon on to the Outland Road. Pauline waved a last goodbye to Swanson and Lemonjello and then raced down the road to where Lucy waited with Blaise and Mr. Furstival. The Vale of Kandu — indeed, all the wide and unknown world — stretched out below their feet.

~End~